Florida Happens

Florida Happens

Tales of Mystery, Mayhem, and Suspense from The Sunshine State

EDITED BY

Greg Herren

THREE ROOMS PRESS

New York, NY

Florida Happens:
Tales of Mystery, Mayhem, and Suspense from The Sunshine State
Bouchercon 2018 Anthology
EDITED BY
Greg Herren

ISBN 978-1-941110-74-4 (trade paperback)
ISBN 978-1-941110-75-1 (ebook)
Library of Congress Control Number: 2018946732

ACKNOWLEDGEMENTS
All stories @2018 except
"The Burglar Who Strove to Go Straight," excerpted from
The Burgler Who Liked to Quote Kipling © 1979 by Lawrence Block
"Hangover" by John D. MacDonald © 1956 by the Hearst Corporation.

COVER AND INTERIOR BOOK DESIGN:
KG Design International
www.katgeorges.com

DISTRIBUTED BY:
PGW/Ingram
www.pgw.com

Three Rooms Press
New York, NY
www.threeroomspress.com
info@threeroomspress.com

TABLE OF CONTENTS

INTRODUCTION
BY TIM DORSEY

"The sun was going down behind the Big Burger when the alligator came flying in the drive-through window."

There is a novel that actually begins with that sentence. But it's a true story. Except it was a Wendy's. Some guy just decided to play a prank. And of course he just happened to have the reptile in the front seat with him.

Gee, in what state do you think that occurred?

As they say, Florida happens. And if you're a crime writer, you couldn't ask for a more target-rich environment. It started more or less back in the 1960s, when the godfather of Sunshine State mysteries, John D. MacDonald, launched his now iconic Travis McGee series from a boat slip at the Bahia Mar marina in Fort Lauderdale (and fittingly, one of his short stories is contained in this collection).

Then, in the 1980s, a journalist for the *Miami Herald* who was heavily inspired by MacDonald, one Carl Hiaasen, jumped in and broke the Florida sub-genre wide open. He was quickly followed by James W. Hall, Edna Buchanan, Les Standiford, Randy Wayne White, and the list keeps growing to this day.

The one thing they all have in common is a genuine sense of this place. There's just too much good material lying around to resist not picking it up. Open any newspaper, and a year or so later you might find bits of the same stories scattered in several authors' works (if you doubt, Google: "woman crashes car while shaving on drive to Key West").

At first it all prompted the question, "What's up with the Florida writers?" It was commonly assumed that the members of the Florida school were feeding off each other and had mutually developed an off-kilter style. Then came the reader comments online that were essentially variations of: "I thought they all had wild imaginations until I visited Florida and realized they're actually backing up from reality."

Hiaasen himself likes to use a phrase about the genuine (and genuinely weird) news items down here: Stories that are too true to be good. And therein lies the other edge of the sword of plentiful material: Choose wisely. Almost all the times I've been criticized for going too far over the top, it was something that really happened . . .

Hold that thought. A reader just sent me an e-mail: "Wildlife officials rescued an opossum that got drunk on bourbon after breaking into a Fort Walton Beach liquor store."

Google it.

Florida happens.

—Tim Dorsey

Florida Happens

THE BURGLAR WHO STROVE TO GO STRAIGHT

BY LAWRENCE BLOCK

Excerpted from The Burglar Who Liked to Quote Kipling *by Lawrence Block, originally published in 1979, when St. Petersburg was decidedly less scenic than it is now.*

Browsers came and went. I made a few sales from the bargain table, then moved a Heritage Club edition of Virgil's *Eclogues* (boxed, the box water-damaged, slight rubbing on spine, price $8.50). The woman who bought the Virgil was a little shopworn herself, with a blocky figure and a lot of curly orange hair. I'd seen her before, but this was the first time she'd bought anything, so things were looking up.

I watched her carry Virgil home, then settled in behind the counter with a Grosset & Dunlap reprint of *Soldiers Three.* I'd been working my way through my limited stock of Kipling lately. Some of the books were ones I'd read years ago, but I was reading *Soldiers Three* for the first time and really enjoying my acquaintance with Ortheris and Learoyd and Mulvaney when the little bells above my door tinkled to announce a visitor.

I looked up to see a man in a blue uniform lumbering across the floor toward me. He had a broad, open, honest face, but in my new trade one learned quickly not to judge a book by its cover. My visitor was Ray Kirschmann, the best cop money could buy, and money could buy him seven days a week.

"Hey, Bern," he said, and propped an elbow on the counter. "Read any good books lately?"

"Hello, Ray."

"Watcha readin'?" I showed him. "Garbage," he said. "A whole store full of books, you oughta read somethin' decent."

"What's decent?"

"Oh, Joseph Wambaugh, Ed McBain. Somebody who tells it straight."

"I'll keep it in mind."

"How's business?"

"Not too bad, Ray."

"You just sit here, buy books, sell books, and you make a livin'. Right?"

"It's the American way."

"Uh-huh. Quite a switch for you, isn't it?"

"Well, I like working days, Ray."

"A whole career change, I mean. Burglar to bookseller. You know what that sounds like? A title. You could write a book about it. *From Burglar to Bookseller.* Mind a question, Bernie?"

And what if I did? "No," I said.

"What the hell do you know about books?"

"Well, I was always a big reader."

"In the jug, you mean."

"Even on the outside, all the way back to childhood. You know what Emily Dickinson said: 'There is no frigate like a book.'"

"Frig it is right. You didn't just run around buyin' books and then open up a store."

"The store was already here. I was a customer over the years, and I knew the owner and he wanted to sell out and go to Florida."

"And right now he's soakin' up the rays."

"As a matter of fact, I heard he opened up another store in St. Petersburg. Couldn't take the inactivity."

"Well, good for him. How'd you happen to come up with the scratch to buy this place, Bernie?"

"I came into a few dollars."

"Uh-huh. A relative died, somethin' like that."

"Something like that."

"Right. What I figure, you dropped out of sight for a month or so during the winter. January, wasn't it?"

"And part of February."

"I figure you were down in Florida doin' what you do best, and you hit it pretty good and walked with a short ton of jewelry. I figure you wound up with a big piece of change and decided Mrs. Rhodenbarr's boy Bernard oughta fix hisself up with a decent front."

"That's what you figure, Ray?"

"Uh-huh."

I thought for a minute. "It wasn't Florida," I said.

"Nassau, then. St. Thomas. What the hell."

"Actually, it was California. Orange County."

"Same difference."

"And it wasn't jewels. It was a coin collection."

"You always went for them things."

"Well, they're a terrific investment."

"Not with you on the loose they aren't. You made out like a bandit on the coins, huh?"

"Let's say I came out ahead."

"And bought this place."

"That's right. Mr. Litzauer didn't want a fortune for it. He set a fair price for the inventory and threw in the fixtures and the good will."

"Barnegat Books. Where'd you get the name?"

"I kept it. I didn't want to have to spring for a new sign. Litzauer had a summer place at Barnegat Light on the Jersey shore. There's a lighthouse on the sign."

"I didn't notice. You could call it Burglar Books. 'These books are a steal'—there's your slogan. Get it?"

"I'm sure I will sooner or later."

"Hey, are you gettin' steamed? I didn't mean nothin' by it. It's a nice front, Bern. It really is."

"It's not a front. It's what I do."

"Huh?"

"It's what I do for a living, Ray, and it's all I do for a living. I'm in the book business."

"Sure you are."

"I'm serious about this."

"Serious. Right."

"I am."

"Uh-huh. Listen, the reason I dropped in, I was thinkin' about you just the other day. What it was, my wife was gettin' on my back. You ever been married?"

"No."

"You're so busy gettin' settled, maybe marriage is the next step. Nothin' like it for settlin' a man. What she wanted, here it's October already and she's expectin' a long winter. You never met my wife, did you?"

"I talked to her on the phone once."

"'The leaves are turnin' early, Ray. That means a cold winter.' That's what she tells me. If the trees don't turn until late, then that means a cold winter."

"She likes it cold?"

"What she likes is if it's cold and she's warm. What she's drivin' at is a fur coat."

"Oh."

"She goes about five-six, wears a size sixteen dress. Sometimes she diets down to a twelve, sometimes she packs in the pasta and gets up to an eighteen. Fur coats, I don't figure they got to fit like gloves anyway, right?"

"I don't know much about them."

"What she wants is mink. No wild furs or endangered species because she's a fanatic on the subject. Minks, see, they grow the little bastards on these ranches, so there's none of that sufferin' in traps, and the animal's not endangered or any of that stuff. All that they do is they gas 'em and skin 'em out."

"How nice for the minks. It must be like going to the dentist."

"Far as the color, I'd say she's not gonna be too fussy. Just so it's one of your up-to-date colors. Your platinum, your champagne. Not the old dark-brown shades."

I nodded, conjuring up an image of Mrs. Kirschmann draped in fur. I didn't know what she looked like, so I allowed myself to picture a sort of stout Edith Bunker.

"Oh," I said suddenly. "There's a reason you're telling me this."

"Well, I was thinkin', Bern."

"I'm out of the business, Ray."

"What I was thinkin', you might run into a coat in the course of things, know what I mean? I was thinkin' that you and me, we go back a ways, we been through a lot, the two of us, and—"

"I'm not a burglar anymore, Ray."

"I wasn't countin' on a freebie, Bernie. Just a bargain."

"I don't steal anymore, Ray."

"I hear you talkin', Bern."

"I'm not as young as I used to be. Nobody ever is but these days I'm starting to feel it. When you're young nothing scares you. When you get older everything does. I don't ever want to go inside again, Ray. I don't like prisons."

"These days they're country clubs."

"Then they changed a whole hell of a lot in the past few years, because I swear I never cared for them myself. You meet a better class of people on the D train."

"Guy like you, you could get a nice job in the prison library."

"They still lock you in at night."

"So you're straight, right?"

"That's right."

"I been here how long? All that time you haven't had a single person walk in the store."

"Maybe the uniform keeps 'em away, Ray."

"Maybe business ain't what it might be. You been in the business how long, Bern? Six months?"

"Closer to seven."

"Bet you don't even make the rent."

"I do all right." I marked my place in *Soldiers Three*, closed the book, put it on the shelf behind the counter. "I made a forty-dollar profit from one customer earlier this afternoon and I swear it was easier than stealing."

"Is that a fact. You're a guy who made twenty grand in an hour and a half when things fell right."

"And went to jail when they didn't."

"Forty bucks. I can see where that'd really have you turning handsprings."

"There's a difference between honest money and the other kind."

"Yeah, and the difference comes to somethin' like $19,960. This here, Bern, this is nickels and dimes. Let's be honest. You can't live on this."

"I never stole that much, Ray. I never lived that high. I got a small apartment on the Upper West Side, I stay out of night clubs, I do my own wash in the machines in the basement. The store's steady. You want to give me a hand with this?"

He helped me drag the bargain table in from the sidewalk. He said, "Look at this. A cop and a burglar both doin' physical work. Somebody should take a picture. What do you get for these? Forty cents, three for a buck? And that's keepin' you in shirts and socks, huh?"

"I'm a careful shopper."

"Look, Bern, if there's some reason you don't wanna help me out on this coat thing—"

"Cops," I said.

"What about cops?"

"A guy rehabilitates himself and you refuse to believe it. You talk yourselves hoarse telling me to go straight—"

"When the hell did I ever tell you to go straight? You're a first-class burglar. Why would I tell you to change?"

He let go of it while I filled a shopping bag with hardcover mysteries and began shutting down for the night. He told me about his partner, a clean-cut and soft-spoken young fellow with a fondness for horses and a wee amphetamine habit.

"All he does is lose and bitch about it," Ray complained, "until this past week when he starts pickin' the ponies with x-ray vision. Now all he does is win, and I swear I liked him better when he was losin'."

"His luck can't last forever, Ray."

"That's what I been tellin' myself. What's that, steel gates across the windows? You don't take chances, do you?"

I drew the gates shut, locked them. "Well, they were already here," I said stiffly. "Seems silly not to use them."

"No sense makin' it easy for another burglar, huh? No honor among thieves, isn't that what they say? What happens if you forget the key, huh, Bern?"

He didn't get an answer, nor do I suppose he expected one. He chuckled instead and laid a heavy hand on my shoulder. "I guess you'd just call a locksmith," he said. "You couldn't pick the lock, not bein' a burglar anymore. All you are is a guy who sells books."

THE BEST LAID PLANS
BY HOLLY WEST

June 1948

BEV MARSHALL WAITS ANXIOUSLY BEHIND the wheel of the Buick, watching for the rest of the crew to emerge from the house. It seems they've been gone at least an hour, but her watch shows it's only 10:45 p.m. Less than ten minutes since they went in. The boys work fast, but not that fast.

There are four of them in the crew. Joe Scullion is their boss and Bev's boyfriend. Alex McGovern is the brawn, and Sean Cregan is a master lock picker. Bev's their driver. They earn their living burgling wealthy neighborhoods all over the Eastern Seaboard, coming home to Philly with thousands in cash and valuables. Five years working together and not a single arrest, not that the coppers haven't tried.

It's been a good run, but after tonight, Bev will be done with all of them.

She thinks she sees movement out of the corner of her eye and snaps her head toward it. Is it them? She squints into the darkness, her hand resting lightly on the key in the ignition. Everything is still and she concedes it must've been her imagination. Wrecked by nerves, she quashes the urge to chew a fingernail and slips her hand into her purse in search of cigarettes. Her fingers brush the thick envelope containing every cent she has—nearly five thousand dollars. Along with whatever money she's able to get for tonight's haul, it's enough to keep her going for a year, maybe more if she lives modestly.

She lights a cigarette and pulls the smoke deeply into her lungs, thinking about Richie O'Neill. She'll miss him when this is done. He runs a hockshop on Vine Street and fences most of the loot they steal. Over the years he's become her trusted friend, so when he let it slip recently that Joe had his eye out for a new driver, she believed him. Turns out Joe had fallen hard for some dame he'd met in Atlantic City and he wants to marry her, maybe have some kids.

Richie's words cut her deeply. She'd been waiting for Joe to pop the question nearly ten years and he always put her off, saying their love didn't need the government's stamp of approval.

"Maybe this is a sign from God," Richie said, trying to console her. "Maybe he's telling you it's time to give up this life and find a nice guy to settle down with."

Bev has to admit Richie's a nice guy. He's a criminal, sure, but he's a good, solid man all the same. A heart condition spared him from the war and, never married, he lives at home with his ailing mother and wheelchair-bound sister.

Bev knows he has a thing for her and if things were different—if *she* were different—maybe she'd give him a chance. But she stopped believing in God the day they wheeled her mother's dead body out of the house when she was fifteen. Beyond that, she loves Joe Scullion. Can't help herself, never could. He's well-groomed, six-foot-three, smart as a whip, and handsome like a movie star. Richie, bless his soul, is none of these things.

But that was before the punch. She glimpses the red mark on her cheek in the rear-view mirror, left over from the shiner Joe gave her two weeks ago after a copper pulled her over for speeding. His diamond pinkie ring broke the skin and it's slow to heal.

Richie doesn't know about the punch—she told him she walked into a door and, dumb lug that he is, he believed her.

She grew up watching men knock her mother around. The physical damage was bad enough—endless cuts, scrapes, and bruises. Once, a broken arm. The emotional damage was even worse. Her mother built the walls slowly, brick by brick, solid and impenetrable, until there was nothing left of her but empty bottles of booze and a vacant stare.

Bev won't let any man get away with hitting her. She'd put up a fight to keep Joe if it hadn't been for that punch. Instead, she began to plan her revenge.

She returns her attention to her surroundings. This weekend, Joe chose a hoity-toity neighborhood in Winston-Salem, North Carolina. The homes here are opulent, each seemingly larger than the next, and according to the real estate section of the local paper, not one is worth less than a hundred grand. On Saturday nights, neighborhoods like this are as quiet as cemeteries. Most of the residents are out, off to parties at exclusive country clubs or attending $100-a-plate philanthropic dinners at swanky downtown hotels. They have no idea they're simultaneously making charitable contributions to Joe Scullion and his crew.

The minutes tick by and she lights another cigarette. It makes her stomach cramp and her bowels clench, but she smokes it down anyway. What's taking so long? It's nearing eleven-thirty when Alex, followed by Joe and Sean, emerge from the shadows, their gaits made awkward by the heavy canvas duffels they carry. She crushes the cigarette out, starts the car, and steadies her foot over the gas pedal. Her timing must be perfect.

Alex opens the trunk and the car's rear drops a little when he loads the first bag, then the second. Joe and Sean catch up and set their bags next to him, five in all. Joe comes around to the front and Bev fights to keep her breathing even as he tries the passenger side door. He raps on the window with his knuckle after he finds it locked.

Not yet. Wait for Alex to finish loading the bags.

"Open up," Joe says, his voice muffled by the glass.

She reaches over as though to lift the lock. A moment later, the trunk slams shut. It's her cue. She rights herself behind the wheel, shifts into drive, and steps on the gas. The front tire scrapes the curb as the car lunges forward and she speeds away.

* * *

THE TWO-DAY TRIP TO MIAMI is uneventful, but as Bev turns the corner onto Ocean Drive, she has a feeling that's about to change. The air here is energized, humming. Palms line the street, swaying in the balmy breeze. Sunlight reflects off every surface. Latin music hangs in the air and she can already feel an ice cold *Cuba Libre* on her lips.

It was Richie who'd sent her south, though he wasn't happy when she called to tell him she'd stranded the crew in North Carolina and made off with the goods. "Damn it, Bev, I told you Joe wasn't worth it. Why'd you do it?"

"You know why, Rich. I couldn't let the cheating bastard get away with it. Now, you gonna help me or what?"

He sighed. "Where are you?"

"At a pay phone in Charlotte."

"Any idea where Joe might go?"

"How should I know?" She was getting impatient. "Listen, Rich, I don't have time for this. I gotta get the hell out of this state."

He was quiet for a moment, then said, "Give me your number. Stay put and I'll call you back in ten minutes."

It took more than fifteen minutes, but he finally got back to her with the number of a fence named Roger in Miami. "Thanks a lot, Rich," she said, after she wrote the information on the inside flap of a match book. "I owe ya one."

"You take care of yourself, Bev."

She promised she would.

Now, in the heart of Miami's famous South Beach, beautiful hotels rise majestically, cloaked in glitz and glamour like Hollywood starlets. She passes the National Hotel and recalls reading in a gossip magazine that Lana Turner and her millionaire boyfriend stayed there recently. But her destination is the Shalimar Motel, a place recommended by Richie, which turns out to be a long row of white cottages, strung together with common walls. At a distance, it almost passes for charming, but Bev has seen too many of these cheap roadside accommodations to be fooled. The place is a dump.

She pulls into the lot, noting the lone Ford sedan parked at the opposite end. She cuts the engine and gets out. The sun has yet to set and the air is warm and heavy, but not oppressively so. She pauses to straighten the seam of her stocking then checks her wristwatch. 7:36 p.m. Looking up, she sees a man standing at the window of room sixteen, a lewd grin on his face.

Ignoring him, she gets her purse from the passenger seat and heads for the motel's office. The Lysol-scented room is paneled top-to-bottom in honey-colored pinewood and the windows are festooned in tropical-themed fabric. A rack behind the desk displays hooks for sixteen keys, each identified by a numbered plastic ring. Number sixteen is missing.

Bev taps the bell and waits. A few moments pass, and she hits the bell again, harder this time. "Be right there," a female voice calls from an adjacent room in back.

The woman who enters is tall and slim, probably younger than Bev by a few years. She wears no makeup and she's pretty in an innocent way that suggests she's never been further than ten miles from home. "Sorry about that," she says. "I was tending to my boy. I'm Lena, welcome to the Shalimar." She scrutinizes Bev's face. "Don't mind me saying, but that looks mighty painful."

Bev touches her cheek. She thought the bruise had sufficiently healed so that no one would notice, especially after she'd applied a thick layer of pancake. "It's fine," she says. "I'd like a room for the night."

Lena reaches under the desk and pulls out a ledger. She opens it to the latest page, turns it around, and pushes it toward Bev. "Your name and address here, please."

"Just the town okay?"

"It'll do."

Bev removes the pen from the holder affixed to the desk and writes, *Theresa Simmons, Richmond, Virginia.*

Lena takes the book back and glances at the entry. "That'll be $3, Miss Simmons."

Bev removes a five-dollar bill from her purse and hands it over. As Lena makes a notation in the ledger, Bev notices she isn't wearing a wedding ring, in spite of mentioning her son earlier. Perhaps she isn't so innocent after all. "You own this place?" she asks, suddenly curious.

"I inherited it from my parents a few years ago."

"All by yourself? Seems like a big job."

She shrugs. "Been doing it since I was a teenager. And I've got my boy to help. He's seven. Anyway, we don't get as much traffic as we used to." She turns toward the rack of numbers and selects one. "Room ten okay? You'll have some privacy there."

"Yes."

Lena gives her the key. "I'll call my boy to help you with your bags."

"That won't be necessary. I've just got an overnight case."

"All right, then. You let me know if you need anything."

* * *

Bev backs the Buick into the spot in front of room ten. The room key sticks in the lock when she tries to turn it, but a little jiggling is all it needs. The door swings open and she takes a quick survey; the room looks like the office, only the fabric curtains are red and green plaid to match the bed's coverlet. Christmas in June. She uses the dingy bathroom, unceremoniously breaking the paper strip across the toilet that reads, "Disinfected for your comfort."

She sits on the bed and roots through her purse, searching for the matchbook. She'd already called Roger, the fence, when she stopped in Georgia the previous night, to check if he was square and to give him some advanced notice. Satisfied he was on the up-and-up, she promised she'd contact him as soon as she arrived in Florida.

A woman's raspy voice answers and Bev hears the phone clunk when she drops it to go get Roger. There are footsteps, then, "Hello?"

"It's Bev. I'm in Miami, at the Shalimar Motel. Ready to make a deal?"

"Like I said, I can't make any promises until we see what you've got. Which room are you in?"

"Ten."

"We'll be there by midnight."

She waits until well after dark before going back out to open the car's trunk. By this time, room sixteen's curtains are closed and the Ford is gone. She takes one more look around to make sure no one is watching then heaves the first bag out with an unladylike grunt. It bangs against the rim of the trunk and slips out of her hands onto the ground. *Damn it.* She's sure something inside has broken. She drags it into the room, hoping there aren't too many casualties.

She's struggling with the last bag when a car turns into the parking lot, its headlights momentarily blinding her. It's the Ford. There's no time to close the trunk before a short, puffy man gets out and ambles over. He flashes the same disgusting grin as before and says, "Hey darlin', let me help you with that."

Bev knows his type: traveling salesman, always on the lookout for an opportunity to play around. Not a wolf so much as a possum. Before they met Alex and Sean, she and Joe made a good living running cons on these guys. She'd accept an invitation to their rooms, coyly implying they were about to get lucky. Joe stood by, pounding on the door just as their pants fell to their pasty white knees, holding them at gunpoint while she cleared the room of cash and valuables. How many suckers had they sent home with "lost" wedding rings? Too many to count.

"I can manage it myself, thank you," Bev says.

"Aw no, honey, you'll hurt yourself."

He takes hold of the bag's straps, staggering when he realizes its full weight. "What do you have in here, rocks?"

Bev moves to block the door to her room. "Thanks for your help. You can leave it right here."

"Nonsense, sweetheart. Step aside so I can bring it in."

"That's quite all right, Mr.—"

He sets the bag down and removes his hat. "Harlan Jennings. You got any plans tonight, darlin'? How 'bout you let me take you out for a little supper?"

"I appreciate your offer, Mr. Jennings, but I'm afraid I can't join you."

Jennings grabs her forearm. "Come on now, little lady, you can spare a quick half hour. I did you a favor, remember?"

"You need any assistance there, Miss Simmons?" It's Lena, calling out to them from the office doorway. The light above the door illuminates a shotgun in her hands.

Jennings releases Bev's arm. "No trouble here, I assure you," he says. "I'm just helping this little lady."

"Doesn't look like she wants your help," Lena says.

Jennings mumbles something about no good deed going unpunished before walking toward his room. Lena and Bev exchange understanding smiles before Lena goes back into the office.

Bev lugs the bag into her room and locks the door behind her. Five canvas duffels lie on the crunchy brown carpet and she's almost afraid to look inside them. But whatever these bags contain, they represent her future and it's time to face it. She unzips the first one.

There's the usual assortment of treasures: sterling silver flatware sets, furs, tangles of expensive jewelry, coin collections, gold-plated candlesticks, fine china, crystal. A few pieces are chipped or broken, but most are intact. She lays the items on the floor, separating them into piles. Bag two contains a sterling desk set, a humidor filled with expensive cigars, three watches—one of them encrusted with diamonds. Items from a man's study.

She opens the third bag, putting her hand in slowly in case of broken glass. She touches fur—not the soft pelt of a mink or fox, but something wiry. She screams and pulls her hand out, her heart pumping hard enough to pop out of her chest. She waits a beat, certain whatever it is will scurry out, but nothing happens. She pulls out a stiff gray raccoon, its menacing glass eyes shining, claws permanently stiff, clutching at nothing. *Damn that Sean Cregan.* He has a fascination with taxidermy and probably stole this monstrosity to display as a trophy.

There's a knock on the door and Bev freezes. "Miss Simmons? It's Lena."

She's relieved it isn't Mr. Jennings, but she isn't eager to open the door for Lena, either. *Doesn't anyone around here have anything better to do than stick their noses in other people's business?*

As it happens, Bev's business is strewn across the floor. She opens the door, careful to block the view into the room with her body. "Good evening, Lena."

"I just wanted to make sure you were all right, Miss Simmons."

"I'm fine, really. But thank you for intervening before." She shakes her head. "Men. Sometimes they won't take no for an answer."

Lena hesitates. "I don't want to make assumptions, but this here is a respectable establishment. I can't allow any funny business, you understand?"

"Of course. You've got nothing to worry about from me."

Lena gave an awkward nod. "Well. Good night then."

"Good night."

It bothers her, knowing Lena's watching. She wonders if she should call Roger back and arrange to meet somewhere else. But where? She's already got everything unloaded and she'll face the same challenges no matter where they meet. At least she knows what she's dealing with here.

There's nothing else unusual in the bags—thank God, her nerves have suffered enough—and when it's all done, she appraises the take. She figures the haul is worth at least two grand. They'd had better nights, but she doesn't care because this time she doesn't have to share it.

She flushes with excitement. A person can last a long time on seven thousand dollars, especially in someplace cheap, like Mexico. She pictures a little *hacienda* on the beach, maybe a handsome *caballero* by her side. Yes, Mexico would suit her nicely.

* * *

BEV IS IN THE BATHROOM re-applying her lipstick when the knock comes. Her watch says it's a quarter to eleven, they're early. Or has that lout Harlan Jennings come back to bother her?

She fluffs her hair and slips her feet back into her shoes before putting her ear to the door.

"Who is it?"

"Roger."

She takes a deep breath and opens the door without removing the chain lock. She wants to get a look at these guys before letting them in. The crew never carried guns when they were on a job—Joe wasn't after that kind of trouble. When they found weapons inside the houses they robbed, they hid them so nobody got hurt if a homeowner returned while they were there. Consequently, Bev doesn't own a gun. She's never even fired one. But she'd taken a switchblade from Joe's bedside table before they left for North Carolina and now she fingers its mother-of-pearl handle in her pocket.

The man at the door is wearing a black stocking cap and mask. "You're gonna to have to open the door a little wider if you want us to come in," he says. He's disguised his voice, but not well enough. Her heart gives a jolt as she realizes it's Alex, the muscle from Joe's crew.

Bruiser that he is, he rams his shoulder into the door, splintering the trim as the chain gives. Bev screams and fumbles for the knife, but Alex knocks her down before she can grip it. She falls into the pile of the family silver and folds herself into a ball on the floor, trying to protect her head and stomach as Alex kicks her.

A second masked man enters and tells Alex to stop it. He pulls the mask down under his chin and hovers over her. It's Joe. His voice is calm, even if his words are angry. "You stupid bitch. You thought you could get away with it." He grabs her by the wrist and pulls, twisting her arm painfully so that she has no choice but to get up. He throws her against the bed.

A third masked man, this one tall and gangly, is standing in the broken doorway. Bev knows it's Sean. He surveys the loot on the floor and says, "We gotta get this stuff outta here. Where are the bags?"

Alex throws the closet door open and finds it empty except for a couple of dresses. "Must be in the car," he says. He addresses Bev, who is struggling under Joe's weight. "Where are the keys?"

"Please, Joe," she coughs. "I can't breathe."

Joe backs off just enough so that she can speak more clearly. "Tell him where the keys are," he says.

Before she can reply, Sean spies her purse lying on the chair. He opens it and rummages until he finds the keys. "Here they are."

Bev thinks of the envelope filled with her money and prays he'll ignore it. No luck—he tosses the keys to Alex, freeing up his hand to pull it out. He lifts the flap and a broad smile spreads across his face. "Well, well. Take a look at this, fellas."

"Hot damn," Alex says. "How much is in there?"

Joe takes the envelope and slaps it against Bev's thigh. "Where'd you get this, huh? You steal this from me, too?"

"I earned that money myself, every penny of it," Bev says. She makes a grab for it but misses. "Take the loot if you want, but the money is mine."

Joe laughs. "Believe me, we're taking the loot. I'll consider this money compensation for the time and expense it took to come down here to get you. Get the bags and pack this stuff up, boys. We're getting the hell out of here."

Nobody notices Lena standing in the doorway until she cocks the shotgun. She's got it raised and ready to shoot Alex's head off. Relief rushes over Bev like a cold shower. With the boys distracted, she slips the knife out of her pocket and releases the blade.

She has a split-second to decide: how badly does she want to hurt Joe?

She jams the knife into his arm.

Joe cries out and falls back, clutching at the blade's handle. "You goddammed bitch," he screams. "I'll kill you!"

Alex's eyes dart between Lena and Joe. "What'd she do, boss?"

Bev crawls away from Joe, intending to join Lena by the door. But Sean lunges at Lena and she takes the gun off Alex to bat Sean's head with its barrel. Alex uses the reprieve to hunker down and run toward her, pushing her into a table set in front of the window. She loses her grip on the gun and Sean grabs it and trains it on her.

Joe is sweating now, clearly in pain. The knife is still in his arm. "Tie her up," he says.

"Let her go," Bev says as Alex moves toward her. "This is between you and me."

"We turn her loose and the first thing she does is call the cops." Joe says. "Tie her up."

Sean forces Lena into a chair while Alex holds Bev's arms behind her. Joe grunts with pain as he takes hold of the knife and pulls it out of his arm. He lays it to the side and breathes heavily, trying to get his bearings.

Lena's eyes are brimming with fright. "Just do as they say," Bev tells her. "It'll be all right."

The barrage of uniformed men with guns that storm in takes everyone by surprise. There are only five of them, but in the chaos the small room feels full to bursting. Bev doesn't know whether to be terrified or relieved.

One of them shouts, "Nobody move. Put your hands up."

The crew, including Bev, does as they're told and stand stock still. A short, puffy man enters the room, his badge held up for everyone to see.

It's Harlan Jennings, and this time, he isn't grinning.

* * *

Bev sits alone at a table in a gray-walled interview room. It's hot in here and the dirty ashtray beside her makes her crave a cigarette. They took her purse—her cigarettes and the envelope full of money with it—when they brought her in. She's been here for an hour, but it feels like much longer. Exhausted, she scoots the chair back and rests her head in her arms. A nap is out of the question, but at least she can rest her eyes.

Funny that in ten years of running cons and pulling jobs with Joe, this is the first time she's seen the inside of a police station. She has Joe to thank for that. From start to finish, his planning had always been meticulous.

Trusting Richie was the fatal flaw in her own plan. She thought his feelings for her meant he'd put loyalty and friendship above money, but he'd apparently contacted Joe as soon as he hung up the phone with her. How else would the crew know where to find her?

The door opens and she sits up to see who it is. "Sorry to keep you waiting," Harlan Jennings says. He lowers himself into the metal chair across from her. "You want anything? Cigarette? Coffee?"

"A cigarette, please."

He gives her one and holds out a lit match so she can light it. "You haven't called an attorney yet," he says, pausing to light a cigarette for himself. "I'm glad to hear it. Lawyers just muck things up. The truth is we've got enough evidence to put you all away for a very long time. But you've got a fine future ahead of you if you put your mind to it. I don't want to see you go to jail."

You and me both, Bev thinks.

"I'm here to see if we can come to some kind of understanding," he continues. "See if we can make a deal."

Recalling his piggish behavior earlier, Bev thinks she knows precisely what kind of deal he wants to make. She stiffens and folds her arms in front of her.

Jennings chuckles. "Nothing like that, Bev. May I call you that? Believe it or not, I'm a happily married man. No, what I want from you is information. Your pal Richie O'Neill was kind enough to provide us with quite a few details, but now we need you to fill us in on the rest."

"Richie ratted us all out?" Bev is taken aback. She knew Richie told Joe where she was, but had he dropped a dime on the entire crew?

"Don't judge him too harshly. We gave him the same choice we're giving you—turn state's evidence or face a trial which would almost certainly result in a conviction and jail time. In the end it wasn't a tough decision for him—he's a mama's boy. What would happen to old Mrs. O'Neill if her son went to jail? Not to mention his poor little sister." Jennings pauses and takes a long drag on his cigarette. "If it makes you feel any better, Richie was concerned about what would happen to you if he cooperated with us. We told him we couldn't make any promises. Now, what happens is up to you."

It was true Richie encouraged her to get out of the life. Begged her, even. And he hadn't been happy when she called to tell him she'd pulled a fast one on Joe. Still, a rat was a rat, and he could've warned her that the Feds where on their tail. It's his fault she's in this mess.

She'll deal with him later.

She reaches up and grazes her cheek with her fingers. It's no longer tender to the touch, but the scab Joe's ring had caused felt rough. It'll probably leave a scar.

Bev had known Joe Scullion for ten years and less than a month ago, she never planned to leave him, let alone rat him out. But that was before the punch. If there was one thing lower than a rat, it was a man who beat up on his woman.

Sometimes, plans change.

She grinds her cigarette out in the ashtray and asks Jennings, "What do you want to know?"

THERE'S AN ALLIGATOR IN MY PURSE

BY PAUL D. MARKS

The Teaser

"SHE MAKES A BEAUTIFUL CORPSE, doesn't she?"

"You just kill me."

"No, I just *killed* her."

"You know what they say, live fast, die young and leave a good lookin' corpse."

"Or at least a dead one," I said, with a wink.

I'm a pro. I like to do a competent job. I like to have my marks look presentable, both for themselves and for my clients. It's good for word of mouth and getting killed is hard enough, on both the mark and their family, so at least they should leave a suitable lasting impression.

I also take a lot of pictures. Much easier in these digital days. Back in the day, it was hard to take pictures of dead bodies to your local photo store to get developed—some of them even called the cops. And I like to add a little art to my work. Give the client a little something extra for their money, so I try to shoot from interesting angles, in low key light, like in an old film noir. I find it works on two levels. It gives me satisfaction and, of course, it gives my clients some kind of closure.

Let me fill you in on some of what led us here. Someone has to tell the story and it might as well be me. I'm probably the only one who can see the big picture. True, I wasn't there for everything, but I was there for enough of it and I heard about the rest from first person sources. How much of it you should trust, well, that's another story. You don't know me and I don't know you, but I like to think I'm a pretty reliable source. So, this is the tale as best I know it.

But before I start, I'd like to talk about my adopted state of Florida. I was becoming too well known in my native California and had to relocate. Florida gets a bad rap because it has a bad rep because what's normal for Florida isn't necessarily normal for anywhere else. But in reality we're just like any other state, only more so. So, here I am in St. Augustine F-L-A, the Sunshine State, which some people call the Gunshine State. Partly because it looks like a gun and partly because of all the guns standing their ground. So there I was, and you know what they say, one door closes and another door opens. After my California door closed, Door Number Two opened and Ashley Smith stepped through.

* * *

Backstory

Ashley Smith needed a job done. I was the right man for the job. A symbiotic relationship that serves everyone's purpose—capitalism in action, payment for services rendered. My services had been recommended to her. So we met at the Egret Café: "No Regrets at the Egret". The Egret, a St. Augustine institution, inhabited a Spanish Colonial style building near the water. I sat at a table on the windward side, the breeze blowing my Fabio-long hair—like something out of a romance novel, if murder is the price of romance.

I ordered gator tails and waited. I figured they were something she would spark to. Tough guy eating gator tails instead of chicken wings, even though they taste almost the same.

And then she walked in, standing in the archway, silhouetted by the sun, the golden light making a halo of her hair. I knew it was her right away—more romance novel stuff.

Considering my research on her, she was dressing down, trying to be one of the folks. But the $500 strategically torn jeans gave her away. And maybe that rock on her finger was a giveaway, too. She had the innocent, gamine-like face of Audrey Hepburn, if Audrey Hepburn was on the stroll in South Beach—yeah, I catch the old movies late at night.

"Ed?"

I nodded. Okay, it's not as cool a name as Fabio, but what do you expect? I wasn't really in a romance novel.

"How come guys who do what you do are always named Ed?" She spoke with a slight Southern lilt, which meant one of two things. Either she was from the northern part of the state, or she was originally from another state altogether.

"It's a calling."

"And they always look like you."

"What do I look like?"

"A cross between Vin Diesel, if he had long black hair, and a diesel engine."

She sat across from me. Looked me up and down, staring. I'd say she was undressing me with her eyes, but more likely she was trying to see if I was wearing a wire, or maybe she just dug my smiley-faced Florida Valencia orange T-shirt. I hoped my six-pack showed through. Aw forget it, the only six-pack I have these days comes from the local liquor store.

"You come highly recommended."

"I take pride in my work. What can I do for you?" No time for small talk in this biz.

"I have a little job I need done."

None of these jobs are "little." And I'm sure the people on the receiving end don't think of them as *little.* Discretion being the better part of valor, I kept my trap shut. And if this really was a romance novel, well, by now we'd be on some secluded corner of the beach, the wind ruffling our hair, our clothes streaming in the breeze, passing amorous glances and ready for some *bed and breakfast.*

"Before we get down to business, tell me a little about yourself," she said, after ordering the Egret's famous stone crabs.

"What, I have to interview with you?"

"Well, it is sort of a job interview, isn't it? So, how long have you been doing this?"

"Seven years, maybe eight."

"Do you enjoy your work?"

"It beats working a nine to five job. Every gig is different and I like the challenge. Plus, it's a living."

"You mean a killing."

"Yeah, that too."

"What's your greatest strength?" She said it without any sense of irony.

"I have an extremely strong work ethic. I go until I get the job done." I toyed with my gator tail.

"Good. Greatest weakness?"

"My love of money." I'm sure that worked in my favor. She smiled broadly. "I have no emotional attachment to anyone. Just 'show me the money' and I'm yours."

"Why did you leave your last job?" Her demeanor was dead serious. All business.

"Well, once the job is done there's really no point hanging around, is there?" I gave her my best knowing grin.

"I see what you mean." She scrolled through her phone. I wished I could see what she was looking at. "What skills do you bring to the job?"

"Guns, bottles, fists, knives, clubs—all the same to me. All the same to you?"

"Huh?"

"I was just quoting from an old late-night movie I like, *Cat Ballou.*"

"Haven't heard of it."

"Maybe I should just leave my CV with you."

"Do you have one?" She looked at me now instead of the phone.

"Why don't you just tell me exactly what it is you need done?"

She hemmed and hawed. "It's a long story."

"A sordid tale, I'm sure. But, believe me, I've heard it all." I smiled—a smile that said, *I've heard it all, I've seen it all...I've done it all, lady.*

"Well, I married my husband James Hartley III." She grabbed one of my gator tails—without asking. "He was a bit older than me."

"You mean he was a geezer." She glared at me—a glare caused by guilt, no doubt.

"And he was quite *comfortable.*" Now she gave me a conspirator's smile. One that said, *You know what I mean.*

"You mean loaded."

"Yes, loaded. And he died not too long after we were married—a few days."

"So I'd think you'd be sitting pretty."

"So did I." A tear escaped her eye. "Unfortunately, he hadn't gotten around to divorcing his first wife."

"You would have done better at the track at Hialeah." There was a part of me that felt a good deal of *schadenfreude* at her misfortune. Yeah, even people like me know big foreign words like that. "So, let me guess. If First Wife is out of the picture, the estate lands in your lap."

"It would be tragic, but yes."

"Tragic."

"So that's why I need you, Mr. . . . "

"Let's just leave it at Ed."

"Mr. Ed. . . . " Even though she said it, I don't think she got it. "So this is what I need from you. My husband's first wife, who is now quite wealthy, needs to go on a very long vacation. . . ."

"A forever vacation." I tried for my most evil grin. "Club Med for the dead—Club Dead."

"Yeah." She nodded. "And now for the big question: salary expectations?"

"I work on a sliding scale and since you seem like you can afford it. . . . "

"Yeah, I get it. 10K. I'll double it after I get the insurance money. Even more when the estate is settled in my favor."

"That's great." I was trying for enthusiasm. People like interviewees to be enthused about the prospect of working for them.

"And it needs to look like an accident," she said.

"O-kay, an accident." Everyone thinks making things look convincingly like accidents is as easy as Florida key lime pie. "And then the money goes to you."

She grinned like the Cheshire Cat, a grin that hung in the air. Just one of those folks—who wants their rival for a fortune offed.

"Okay, but I still need a down payment. Did you bring it?"

"Just watch out for Desi," she said, slipping me an envelope.

Who the hell was Desi? And that's how I came into the picture.

* * *

Flashback—The Climax

IT WAS A DARK AND stormy night. Well, it was—they do happen, you know. Winds howling. Rain slashing. Roads flooded. Just another romance novel cliché. Or just another Sunshine State cliché. I wasn't there for this one, but this is how Ashley Smith, who kept her own name, said it went down.

James Hartley III—and, according to Ashley Smith, you have to say that name with the proper intonation even in Florida, well, maybe with a lilting Southern accent—was having the time of his life. He and his second wife, Ashley Smith, were, how shall I put this delicately, engaging in a bit of afternoon delight. He squealed in carnal bliss. His breath came fast and short. Sweat beaded on his face. He grinned large . . . until he flushed, gulped for air. Even then he didn't want to stop. And she definitely didn't want to stop. He was in steamy, Florida ecstasy. His arms flailed. And then he stopped. Dead. Just dead. James Hartley III's heart blew up right there in the bed. Deader than a Florida palmetto bug after you've bathed it in a bath of boric acid. Ashley Smith grabbed her cell from the nightstand.

"911. What's the nature of your emergen—"

"My husband's dead."

Two police cars beat the paramedics there. They confirmed that James Hartley III was, uh, dead.

"Deader than a lobster in butter sauce," one of the cops told the arriving paramedics.

Yup, Ashley Smith *blanked* her husband to death—on purpose, knowing he had a weak heart. I hope he died happy and I guess it was a better way to go than the man who was stabbed to death by his wife, who then skinned him and cooked him up (possibly with fava beans and a nice Chianti, though I would have preferred Jack Black myself), and fed him to her children. Yeah, as opposed to that guy, James Hartley III died happy.

* * *

Flashback—Conflict

THE DAY AFTER JAMES HARTLEY III died happy, Ashley Smith found herself in one of the most prestigious buildings in the city. It wasn't the tallest and far from the newest, but it was very well appointed. Expensive furniture and original artwork of the avant-garde Eurotrash school. Something every nouveau riche dilettante like her could appreciate. She was dressed in a fashionable LBD, Little Black Dress, with a crimson scarf for just a hint of color. After all, this mourning thing could go too far.

"Firstly, the coroner's office has labeled Mr. Hartley's death as from natural causes," Craig Bertram, James Hartley III's estate attorney, said. Everything about him said swanky—does anyone use that word anymore?—lawyer smarm.

A look of relief swept over Ashley Smith's face.

"And secondly?" Anticipation leapt from her voice. This was the moment she'd been waiting for.

"Secondly, Mr. Hartley III left a very sizeable estate." Bertram toyed with his bow tie. Anyone who wears a bow tie is smug and that makes them suspect in my world. "And thirdly . . . "

"Thirdly? What thirdly?" Ashley Smith's soon-to-be-rich heart beat in time with her Rose Gold Patek Philippe Twenty~4 watch, which cost more than some people's houses.

"Unfortunately, it all goes to his first wife, Veronica Betancourt Hartley."

Ashley Smith tried to maintain a stoic face.

"You see, Mr. Hartley III never got around to changing his will, so the entire estate goes to Ms. Betancourt Hartley."

"What, but I'm his wife."

"Well, it seems there's some complications."

"Complications?"

"Apparently, Mr. Hartley and Ms. Betancourt Hartley were never divorced."

"I thought she just kept his name. What're you saying?"

"She never actually signed the papers. So your marriage to him is invalid and—"

"How can you be sure?"

"I'm sure." Bertram held up a sheaf of papers. "According to Florida law—"

"Screw Florida law." She jerked out of her chair. "What about the insurance money?"

"That's yours. All seven hundred thousand."

"Seven hundred thousand." She said it as if you couldn't buy a cup of coffee with it. Well, maybe at Starbucks you couldn't. "I thought he had more."

"He was coming in later this week to up the amount. So you should have waited to kill him just a little longer. You know what they say, patience is a virtue." Bertram smiled a smile that defined beatific.

Her face twisted into a rictus of hate, camouflaged by a sweet Southern smile.

She said, "But surely his intention was to take care of me."

"Intentions don't count in the law."

"And the house?"

"Everything. Everything goes to Ms. Betancourt Hartley."

"She's my best friend. Maybe she'll be feeling generous and want to split it."

"I don't know, but since you broke up her marriage, I'm thinking not." There was that smile again.

* * *

Rising Action

AFTER SOME SUPER SOUL SEARCHING research, less soul searching than research, Ashley Smith decided on a course of action. She wasn't about to let it all go without a fight. She needed someone to make it right, while she was kept in the clear, just the innocent, grieving current *wife.* Someone to do the deed while she was in a public place so it would be clear that she couldn't be the perp. Someone who would work for a reasonable fee, with references and a good rep. She found that someone at her gym, who gave her my name, because the gym, filled with sweaty, sleazy characters, is the place to go when you're looking for a hitman.

And that's how we came to meet at the Egret Café. She was a good looking woman. Seemed quick and smart. I might have asked her out when the job was over, but I didn't want to be on the receiving end of one of my colleagues when she got tired of me.

* * *

All the World's a Stage

SOMEHOW IT ALL ENDED UP here, at Castillo de San Marcos, the old fort, in the oldest city in the USA. I figured using that as a background would give the pictures a bit of high drama. It was a gorgeous day for Florida, the humidity only at 180. We had chosen a great location. We wanted everything to be just right. We got it all here, great light, vivid color palette. And the perfect corpse. Veronica Betancourt Hartley's body lay on the ground, baking under a scorching Florida sun. Makeup perfect, if a bit melted, hair perfectly coiffed and spread out like some demented Rorschach test. Dress disheveled, her arms and legs splayed. Even so, she really did make a lovely corpse. A tiny rivulet of blood ran down her cheek under the glaring sun. It had taken ten minutes to get that right.

Snap-snap. Proof-of-death pictures for Ashley Smith.

Veronica Betancourt Hartley looked up. "How's my makeup? I feel like we're both melting like the Wicked Witch of the West. Does water really make witches melt?"

Sergeant Frannie Oakley said, "You're makeup's fine, hon."

"Are you sure?" Veronica Betancourt Hartley reached down to a vanity mirror that had spilled from her purse. Held it to her face. "I think I could use a little more color."

"She could use a little more blood," Sgt. Oakley said.

"Put your head back on the rock," the director of this little saga, Sergeant Juan Wayne, said.

"Can I lay with my right cheek showing? I think it's my better side."

"Not this time. Maybe next time."

Veronica Betancourt Hartley didn't laugh. She stared up at him. "I'm sorry, Sergeant, I'm just not feeling it. I need to feel the part. Can you give me some direction? What's my motivation?"

"One acting class in high school, now she needs motivation," Sgt. Oakley muttered.

"Your motivation," Sgt. Wayne said, "is staying alive."

"Staying alive by pretending to be dead." Veronica Betancourt Hartley chuckled.

"Yeah. Do you feel it now?"

"I do, but I still think I need a little more blush. Oh, and I'd like to get some extra pictures for my composites. And a copy of the video you're shooting for my reel."

"She wants it for her reel . . . ," Wayne said. "Nothing here is real."

"Maybe we should make it real—y'know, replace the blanks in the pistol?" Oakley whispered to Wayne.

"What the hell is that?" Wayne caught a glimpse of something in Veronica Betancourt Hartley's purse. "Are you carrying a concealed weapon?"

"No, the only concealed *weapon* I have is Desi."

"Desi?"

"The alligator in my purse."

Sgt. Wayne almost looked surprised, then again this was Florida. "May I see it? And why would there be an alligator in your purse?"

She opened the purse. A ten inch alligator lifted its head to the light. Snapped its jaw. "He goes everywhere I go, the way some people carry small dogs. He's my therapy animal."

"Your service animal?"

"Yes, my service animal." She rubbed Desi's belly with her finger. The gator smiled a toothy smile.

"He must be a big hit on airplanes," Sgt. Oakley said, rolling her eyes.

"People don't seem to like him, I don't understand why. He's very sweet. And he understands everything I say." Veronica Betancourt Hartley stroked Desi's snout. Was he really smiling back at her?

"Well, this is Florida, after all," Sgt. Wayne grinned, looking at Desi.

See what I mean about normal . . . for Florida anyway.

"And a very nice alligator I must say," Sgt. Wayne said. "A few years ago your purse would have been made out of alligator, today there's one inside of it."

* * *

Complication

I MET WITH ASHLEY SMITH again, this time at the Conchtiki Diner. It was time for my payday. It's always hard at moments like this, talking money. So we eased into it with some small talk first . . . about oranges. Yeah, oranges, since I came from California. Just go with the flow.

"Florida oranges are juicer," she said.

"California's are better for eating."

"Well, I'd rather sip my juice. And, Florida oranges are bigger." She gave me a wry little smile.

"You know what they say, size doesn't matter."

"You would say that." She peeled an orange. This joint set oranges on the table the way others gave you a bowl of chips. "Florida oranges are sweeter."

"And thinner skinned."

"What're you saying?" The smile washed off her face, the way one of the waves a few yards off might wash away lovers' names written in the sand.

"Nothing." Now I turned on the wry smile, at least that's what I was going for.

"Besides," she said. "California has earthquakes. How good is that for oranges?"

"Florida has hurricanes and humidity."

"California has heat," she said.

Speaking of heat, I'd seen a Sig 9mm in her purse. I was afraid if I said the wrong thing about oranges, she might just pull it to show me how wrong I was.

"Yeah, but it's a dry heat," I said. And why was I feeling so cold on such a sultry day?

Between the heat and the conversation, I thought I might be losing my mind. I wanted to get to the subject at hand, get the money and get the hell out of there. And even though we'd done the deed, so to speak, staging the murder, taking pix and video, we hadn't made it public, so I gave her one more chance to bow out, which I'd done a couple times before. Once in a Publix parking lot and once on the phone. We always do that for legal reasons. They never do.

"You have the rest of my money?"

She was non-committal. "Did you do it?"

"Are you sure you really want it done?"

"Ten-thousand percent sure."

"That's good, 'cause . . . " I slipped several photos across the table. I could have shown them to her on my phone, but a glossy photo says so much more, don't you think? What used to be called Kodak Moments.

Ashley Smith's face lit up. She slid an envelope into my hands.

"You'll get it all now, the house, the money."

"Everything. I'm really gonna get it."

And she was.

* * *

2nd Climax—On a Good Night You Get More Than One

Ashley Smith went out and bought herself a Tesla Model X P100D to celebrate. She flew to New Orleans for a meal at 3.14159265359, the most expensive and pretentious restaurant in the city, to celebrate. She thought about buying a new, younger husband—to celebrate. Eventually she went home to celebrate in private. But I'm guessing she didn't have much chance to do that as the doorbell rang not more than half an hour after she arrived. She looked resplendent in Dolce & Gabbana when she answered the door.

"Ashley Smith?" Sgt. Juan Wayne said.

"Yes."

He introduced himself and Sgt. Frannie Oakley. Ashley Smith missed the connection on their names. Three other members of the department were with them. They held cameras and were filming everything like some big—little—Hollywood production. Ashley Smith put on her best Meryl Streep for the cameras. In fact, everyone put on their best faces for the cameras, cheating their best sides to the lenses.

"We're sorry to inform you that Veronica Betancourt Hartley is dead," Sgt. Wayne said.

"Veronica, my husband's ex?" Her face registered the proper amount of S&S, surprise and sorrow. Then crocodile tears, or should I say alligator tears.

“I’m afraid so.”

“No, not Veronica. She’s my best friend.” She mugged for the cameras. I think she was showing her bonafides from the William Shatner School of Acting. “I’m truly sorry to hear that and I don’t mean to seem, uh, cold, but why are you coming to me? I’m not a relative or . . .”

“I’m also afraid to inform you that you’re under arrest, turn around and put your hands behind your back.”

“What? What for?”

“Solicitation of murder.”

“I didn’t do anything. I just wanted to be on TV. We were all just doing this to get our own reality TV show.”

Everybody’s a star these days. Everybody living their own reality show.

* * *

Falling Action

Ashley Smith got her chance to be on TV, but not the way she had hoped. The courtroom was dressed like a Hollywood set, complete with a deluxe Neiman Marcus gavel and Lady Justice with her scales—there I go sounding like some Hollywood set decorator. Ashley Smith was dressed like a demure librarian from an old-time movie, hair up in a bun. I was one of the first called to testify.

“State your name and occupation, please,” the prosecutor said.

“Sergeant Ed Duff of the St. Augustine Police Department. I’m an undercover detective.” As if you haven’t figured that out by now. Ashley Smith hadn’t. Her face fell.

“And what is your specialty in the department?”

“I’m a professional fake hitman.”

The prosecutor asked and I laid it out: the story of how I met Ashley Smith and Veronica Betancourt Hartley. Ashley Smith’s plan. Everything. It was pretty cut and dried, but not as sweet as a Florida orange.

“How’s business?”

“Better than you’d think—or wish.”

After several witnesses, including the most honorable Craig Bertram, in a spiffy Colonel Sanders bow tie, and Veronica Betancourt Hartley, Ashley Smith was called to testify on her own behalf. In her best proper English she said, "I didn't do it. I would never hurt my husband. And why on earth would I hurt his ex?"

"Because with her gone you were set to inherit everything." The prosecutor leaned toward her in the witness stand.

"But Veronica and I got on fine."

At that point the prosecutor introduced the various audio and video recordings of Ashley Smith and I talking that had surreptitiously been recorded, including me giving her every chance to get out of the deal. She continued to deny that she was serious, reiterating that all she wanted was to get a show on reality TV.

"It was all a game. We just wanted to be on reality television. We just wanted to be TV stars, Jim, Veronica and me."

I actually believed that, since everyone in this case seemed to be acting all the time. Everyone except James Hartley III. Unless he was acting dead.

"James Hartley III is dead. I'd say that's a lot of reality," the prosecutor said. "And Veronica Betancourt Hartley might have been had she not had the good fortune of your hiring an undercover cop instead of a real hitman."

"It was all a game to get on TV."

It might have been a game to Ashley Smith, but nobody else was playing. She might have been venal, but she wasn't dumb. Certainly not dumb like the Florida guy who called the cops to say his cocaine was stolen from his car. Still, Ashley Smith was convicted and sent to prison, where she'll get more reality than she bargained for. Oh, yeah, cocaine man got convicted too.

* * *

Denouement

I WAS ENJOYING MY TIME in Florida. Somerset Maugham called the French Riviera a "sunny place for shady people." Florida has adopted that motto as its own. And I wouldn't want anything to change. The shady people in the Gunshine State—er—Sunshine State keep me employed and well supplied in guns and oranges. There's a lot of folks who want to off their friends, relatives, lovers, husbands and wives. And I guess I have the right look 'cause I'm always the one sent in as Your Favorite Hitman. There's awards for everything these days, I could get Hitman of the Year. Hell, maybe I should take some acting classes and head to Hollywood, C-A or F-L-A.

And as lawyer Bertram said, patience is a virtue and good things come to those who wait. Veronica Betancourt Hartley had that virtue in spades. She played the game, she waited and she got it all. And then she got slammed by a car while crossing the street. And she did make a beautiful corpse, this time for real. I had to wonder who ended up with James Hartley III's estate. Maybe Desi, who was now doing time at his own private swamp, a full staff to cater to his every need and a lifetime supply of artisanal, free-range road kill. I had to wonder if he ever bit the hand that fed him? But, hey, forget about it, this is F-L-A.

MR. BONES

BY HILARY DAVIDSON

I'D BE THE FIRST TO admit that Mr. Bones wasn't going to win any prizes for Pet of the Year. He was a pugnacious alley cat with mouse breath and an anger management problem, but I loved him. So when I got home from a three-day dermatology conference in New York and discovered he was missing, I was devastated.

"Tell me exactly what happened," I pleaded with my boyfriend.

"Nothing happened. Your cat just hasn't come home," Andrew said.

We were standing in the kitchen, and I couldn't help but turn and look at the door to the backyard. Mr. Bones' three bowls were there—dry food, wet food, and water—and they were all full.

"He didn't eat anything today?" I asked. "Was he sick?"

"Come on, Monica. There's always something wrong with that cat."

"What time did he go out this morning?"

"I don't know. It was early. He woke me with his screaming to get outside."

"Are you okay?" I asked him.

"What do you mean?"

"Your hand is bandaged up."

"Oh, that's nothing," he said. "I was cutting an avocado. Should've known not to try that without you around." He gave me a sweet smile, which made him look even more like Tom Hiddleston than usual. "I picked up takeout from Moe's for dinner. I know you love their Southwest salad with tofu."

Andrew and I had been living together for almost six months, and it was going well. But I was too wound up about Mr. Bones to think about eating. "Thanks, but I need to look for Mr. Bones. He's probably sulking right now."

I stepped outside onto the patio behind the house. "Honey, I'm home!" I called out. Something rustled in the warm stillness of the night, but my cat didn't come running. If he heard me, he would have, because he was more like a dog in that way. I called for him and waited.

Andrew rapped on the storm door. "Come on, Monica. He'll be back when he's ready."

Reluctantly, I stepped inside. Mr. Bones was stubborn, and while I wanted him to remain indoors all the time, that wasn't on his agenda. Sometimes he stayed out late. In this case, since I'd been away for three days, he was undoubtedly angry. Mr. Bones didn't care for Andrew, and I had the feeling that his disappearance was calculated in that sharp feline brain of his as punishment for my abandonment of him.

Aware that Mr. Bones might be perched nearby, amber eyes slitted in anger, I went out to the yard every fifteen minutes to check for him. He'd stayed out overnight a couple of times, but it was uncharacteristic of him. When I finally went to bed that night, it was with a heavy heart.

* * *

WHEN I WOKE UP AT dawn, I half-expected Mr. Bones to have plopped his big, furry body on my pillow in the middle of the night and be tapping my head, something he liked to do when I was unconscious and he wanted attention. But of course he wasn't there, and he wasn't in the yard, either. I thought about setting his food and water bowls outside, in case he was hungry, but I knew that was a terrible idea. Our West Palm Beach neighborhood was elegantly manicured, but that didn't stop a range of critters from opossums to foxes from trotting through.

Before I left for work, I made Andrew promise to call me as soon as Mr. Bones showed up. He had a marketing gig that allowed him to work from home, which meant he'd be there whenever Mr. Bones did finally show his furry black face.

"You have to stop worrying, Monica," he insisted. "He's probably tomcatting around."

"He's neutered. He's not romancing some lady cat."

Andrew shrugged. "Okay, fine, but you know what I mean. He loves being outside. He's probably terrorizing mice right this moment."

Stupidly, I was hoping for news by the time I drove to my office, but there was nothing. At my dermatology practice, I had a full schedule of patients coming in, looking for Botox and fillers. They kept me busy, but it was boring work, and I was actually happy when a guy showed up with an ambitious-looking mole that needed to be biopsied. At noon, I called Andrew to check in, but he hadn't seen Mr. Bones. I tried to eat a salad, but my eyes kept roaming in the direction of a photo of me and Mr. Bones on our first Christmas together six years earlier. He'd been a mangy, matted bundle of fur when I first met him, shivering on my doorstep one rainy morning during hurricane season. But all I saw that day was a bundle of black fur stretched over big bones and a pair of pleading amber eyes. I brought him a saucer of milk, and that was followed by many more. I expected him to vanish, but he took up residence on my doorstep, mewing and nuzzling me whenever I went by. Finally, just before Christmas that year, I took him to a vet. The cat was an adult of six or seven, and he wasn't microchipped.

We can put him in a shelter, the vet had told me. *But he needs shots and pills and the costs add up. No one's going to adopt a cat with medical bills.*

So I took him home. He was still just fur and bones, and I called him Mr. Bones as a joke, but the name stuck. He was a big, dignified feline with strong opinions, a hot temper, and a stubborn streak. He wasn't aloof at all; in fact, he was almost doglike in the way he whined when I went out the door and the way he reclaimed me when I returned. He wasn't above playing tricks to get attention—he'd been known to pull clothing off hangers to express his feelings—but he liked to stay by my side. When Andrew moved in with me, Mr. Bones had taken his measure and hissed a warning.

By the middle of the afternoon, I couldn't take it anymore. *Are you sure Mr. Bones isn't in the yard?* I texted Andrew.

Positive, he wrote back. *He's not there.*

Desperate, I called the veterinarian. "Mr. Bones is missing," I blurted into the phone. "Is there any way to find him with the microchip?"

"Sorry, but no," she answered. "That works with a scanner, so if someone finds a lost cat, we can get the pet back home. But it's not like a tracking device."

"What should I do? He's been gone since early yesterday morning."

"Have you talked to your neighbors?" she asked. "A cat like Mr. Bones likes to prowl, but he's got a route he likes, places he's familiar with. Does anyone else feed him?"

"I'm not sure," I told her. "But I'll find out."

That evening, I went up and down the street, talking to anyone I could find. Several people claimed to have seen Mr. Bones, but not over the past several days. *What a good-looking cat,* one woman said when I pulled up some photos on my phone. But not everyone had a warm reaction.

"You let your cat roam free?" one gray-haired woman asked me. She lived on my block, six houses down, but I couldn't remember ever speaking to her before. The way she stared at me made me feel like she was nursing some secret grudge for something I'd done when I moved into the neighborhoods years earlier.

"Mr. Bones insists on it," I admitted. "He will actually run out the door when I open it if he feels cooped up."

"Did you know that cats are the primary murderers of songbirds? Do you have any idea how many we lose because of pet cats who hunt for sport?"

"Mr. Bones has a little bell on his collar. He definitely doesn't catch any birds, though it doesn't keep him from collecting mice."

"Any hunting by a housecat is murder."

Before I could answer that, my phone buzzed. "What are you still doing out?" Andrew demanded when I answered. "It's almost nine o'clock and we haven't had dinner. You need to come home."

Part of me knew that he was right, but I was reluctant to let go. "Thanks for your time," I muttered to the cat-hating woman; she hadn't mentioned her name. Then I retreated home. Andrew was in a mood when I got back.

"This is kind of crazy, Monica," he told me. "It's just a cat. He'll come home. Or maybe he won't."

"It sounds like you don't care either way."

"I'm just saying you can't go crazy about this."

"You've never liked Mr. Bones," I said. "You're probably happy he's gone."

"That's ridiculous. I like cats, normally. I'm just saying you can't go nuts because of this. We can always get another one."

My jaw fell open. "Another one?"

"Pets are replaceable," Andrew said. "People aren't."

I stormed out of the room and headed for the den. I found a photo of Mr. Bones lying in the sun next to our deck and made a missing poster. I printed a dozen copies and headed for the front door.

"What are you doing?" Andrew called.

"Putting up missing notices."

"It's dark out, Monica," he pleaded. "There's no point right now."

He had a point about that, so I left the pages on the table in the hallway. I got up at dawn the next morning and tacked them to every tree and pole on our street and the surrounding ones. Mr. Bones had wandered into my life six years earlier. If he'd wandered into someone else's, I'd find out.

I was a mess at the office that day. My nerves were shaky and I needed my nurse to help with even the simplest Botox injection. "You don't seem well," she told me late in the morning. "Do you want me to cancel the rest of your appointments today?"

"No," I answered immediately, but I changed my mind just as quickly. I wanted to be busy, to take my mind off Mr. Bones. But a dermatologist who was a bundle of nerves was a lawsuit waiting to happen.

On the drive home, as I turned onto my street, I noticed some of the posters I'd put up were gone. Then I saw a gray-haired woman tearing one off a tree.

I slammed on the brakes. I didn't know her name, but I recognized her. It was the same woman who'd lectured me about how cats were a threat to songbirds.

I opened my window. "What are you doing?" I called.

She turned and glared at me. "I don't want this on my property."

"And what about all the other notices you tore down? Those weren't on your property."

"A gust of wind must've blown them away."

She gave me a wicked little smile and walked away. I turned into my driveway, but I was anything but calm.

"What are you doing home?" Andrew asked me when I let myself in.

"I couldn't concentrate." I swallowed hard. "I think that woman down the street did something to Mr. Bones."

Andrew gave me an incredulous look, but his voice was calm. "She did?"

"I think so," I said. "And I'm going to prove it."

* * *

ANDREW SEEMED TO BELIEVE THAT he could cajole me into forgetting what had happened. He made a restaurant reservation at CityPlace for that Saturday night, but I only picked at my food. He suggested getting tickets to a concert at the Kravis Center, but I had no interest. I put more posters up, but no one called about Mr. Bones. Because I couldn't think of anything else to do, I started watching my elderly neighbor very closely. Over the next three weeks, I figured out her schedule. On a Wednesday night when I was sure she wouldn't be home until late, I changed into an all-black ensemble. I even had a black scarf to hide my blond hair.

"What are you doing?" Andrew asked when he saw me. "You look like a ninja."

"It's Miss Tabitha's mah-jongg night," I said. "I'm finally going to get into her house."

Andrew blanched at that. "You're going to break in?"

"Not exactly. She keeps a spare key in that peacock statue next to her door. Her maid uses it to let herself in on Tuesdays and Fridays."

"What's in that bag?"

"This?" I hoisted a small black nylon backpack on my shoulder. It was stuffed with medical supplies and samples I'd grabbed from my office. I wasn't entirely sure what I would do with them if I found out Miss Tabitha Orriss had harmed Mr. Bones. Botox was a powerful drug even in small doses, and I knew how to paralyze a person's vocal cords with it if I needed to. There was no muscle in the human body that wouldn't freeze up instantly when it came into contact with botulism toxin.

Andrew grabbed my shoulders. "Monica, listen to yourself. You've lost your mind over a cat. What do you think, that old lady taxidermied him or something? What would you do if she had?"

I don't know why his words hit me so hard at that moment, but I crumbled. For the first time since Mr. Bones vanished, I cried. "I miss him so much," I gulped. "But it's not just that. I can't stand not knowing what happened to him."

Andrew led me to the bed and sat down next to me. "Look, I'm really sorry, Monica. I should've told you this before. I guess I didn't because I knew you'd be upset, but I never realized you'd be this miserable."

"Tell me what?"

"I let your cat go."

"Go?" I repeated. "Go where?"

"He was a nasty piece of work," Andrew said. "He scratched me after you left for your conference. It wasn't the first time he'd attacked me, but I decided it would be the last."

"What did you do to him?"

"I took him for a drive and left him in a nice spot. He's a scrappy cat, Monica. A fighter. He's undoubtedly got a new home by now."

"You released him…where?" I was so horrified that I was having trouble thinking clearly. Andrew had deliberately taken Mr. Bones away? What kind of monster would do that?

"It was a really nice place. Lots of food around for him."

I got to my feet. "Take me there. Right now."

He looked at his watch. "It's late. It'll be dark soon."

"That doesn't matter. Let's go. We'll take your car."

I was prepared for a long drive—Mr. Bones would've found his way home from twenty miles away, I had no doubt—but I was surprised when he pulled onto the I-95. We headed south in silence. After more than half an hour on the highway, I spoke. "Did you really hate Mr. Bones that much?"

"Yes," Andrew said. "He was the worst. It's not that I don't like cats. Actually, I think we should get a kitten. That would be cute, don't you think?"

"Kittens," I murmured absently. "Who doesn't love them?"

"I mean, if we raised it from kittenhood, it would be my cat, too. Not a creepy thing that used my clothes as a litterbox and bit me."

It was like the floodgates opened. The rest of the drive was a litany of Andrew's complaints about Mr. Bones. I'd known my cat was a something of a thug, but I'd never realized my boyfriend was the kind of man who'd hold a grudge against a pet.

I knew exactly where we were heading by the time we approached Boca Raton. Andrew steered west, and I knew we were going to the Everglades. By the time I saw a sign for the Francis S. Taylor Wildlife Management Area, I was ready to start crying again.

"This," I gulped. "This is where you brought Mr. Bones."

"It's a great place. I mean, it's dark now, but there are lots of birds and wildlife..."

"You dropped him off here, at the entrance?"

"A little further in."

"Then keep driving," I told him.

A few minutes later, he stopped. The car windows were rolled up, but I could smell the marsh. In the bright moonlight, I could make out trees and sawgrass. "Why here?" I asked him.

"Because I read about people dropping off pets in the Everglades," Andrew said. "That happens a lot. There's so much in this ecosystem, they can survive."

"When you say *pets,* you mean Burmese pythons and other creatures big enough to eat humans. Not cats."

He looked around. "I'm sure it's..."

As he spoke I jabbed a needle into his neck. He made a wet, choking sound, and his eyes cut to look at me even though his head couldn't turn.

"You brought Mr. Bones here because you wanted to kill him, but you were too much of a coward to do it." I jabbed another needle into his shoulder, and one into his thigh. I put one needle after another into him, freezing him into a human sculpture with botulism toxin. I could have stopped him from breathing, but I wasn't going to. That would've been too quick. I wanted him to experience terror.

"The thing is, I know you're still lying," I added. "Because Mr. Bones never would've gotten into a car with you. I guess I'll never know exactly what happened but, as awful as your story is, I know it was worse than what you're admitting."

I unlatched his seatbelt and reached over to unlock his door. It wasn't easy to push him out of the car, even though he couldn't move a muscle to fight back. He was a dead weight. Finally, I got him out and kicked him off the roadway, so that he was partially submerged in the marsh.

"Remember when you said that pets are replaceable but people aren't?" I asked. "You were wrong on both counts."

The marsh water wasn't deep, but Andrew has landed in in face-first. Once I was sure of that, I put the car into reverse for fifty yards, turned it around, and headed out of the Everglades.

Back on the highway, I could feel a tear rolling down my cheek. *Pets are replaceable,* Andrew had claimed. But that wasn't true, because there would never be another cat like Mr. Bones. Still, I liked the idea of kittens. Not just one, but a pair, to keep each other company. First thing the next morning, I'd go to an animal shelter, I decided. I didn't think I'd be ready to bring a man home for a long time to come, but there was no way I was going to forego feline companionship.

COLD BEER NO FLIES
BY GREG HERREN

Dane Brewer stepped out of his air-conditioned trailer, wiped sweat off his forehead, and locked the door. It was early June and already unbearably hot, the humidity so thick it was hard to breathe. He was too far inland from the bay to get much of the cooling sea breeze but not so far away he couldn't smell it. The fishy, wet sea smell he was sick to death of hung in the salty air. It was omnipresent, inescapable. He trudged along the reddish-orange dirt path through towering pine trees wreathed in Spanish moss. The path was strewn with pine cones the size of his head and enormous dead pine needles the color of rust that crunched beneath his shoes. His face was dripping with sweat. He came into the clearing along the state road where a glorified Quonset hut with a tin roof stood. It used to be a bait and tackle until its resurrection as a cheap bar. It was called My Place. It sounded cozy—the kind of place people would stop by every afternoon for a cold one after clocking out from work, before heading home.

The portable reader board parked where the parking lot met the state road read *Cold Beer No Flies.*

Simple, matter of fact, no pretense. No Hurricanes in fancy glasses like the touristy places littering the towns along the Gulf Coast. Just simple drinks served in plain glasses, ice-cold beer in bottles or cans stocked in refrigerated cases at simple prices hard-working people could afford. Tuscadega's business was fish, and its canning plant stank of dead fish and guts and cold blood for miles. Tuscadega sat on the inside coast of a large shallow bay. The bay's narrow mouth was crowned by a bridge barely visible from town. A long two-lane bridge across the bay led to the gold mine of white sand beaches and green water along the Gulf Coast of Florida. Tourists didn't flock to Tuscadega, but Tuscadega didn't want them, either. Dreamers kept saying when land along the gulf got too expensive the bay shores would be developed, but it hadn't and Dane doubted it ever would.

Tuscadega was just a tired old town and always would be, best he could figure it. A dead end that the best and the brightest fled as soon as they were able.

He was going to follow them one day, once he could afford it.

Towns like Tuscadega weren't kind to people like Dane.

Dane unlocked the back door of the bar, turned off the alarm, and flicked on the lights. He clipped his keys to a belt loop of his khaki shorts. He put in his ear buds, selected his Johnny Cash playlist, and mariachi horns rang in his ears.

He got to work. My Place opened at five.

He moved from table to table, taking stools down. Some tables weren't level and wobbled a bit. The overwhelming scent of pine cleaner didn't quite mask the stench of stale beer and week-old cigarette smoke. Once all the stools were down, he made sure every table had a clean black plastic ashtray in the center. He sang along with Johnny Cash. He learned how to play guitar listening to Johnny Cash's music when he was a kid, picking out the chords to "Sunday Morning Coming Down" over and over until he had them right, singing in his high-pitched kid's voice. He'd loved that guitar until his father had smashed it to pieces in a drunken rage.

He'd never touched another guitar.

He sprayed cleaner along the bar counter and ran a towel over its length. There was always dust, no matter how many times he wiped down the damned bar. It was everywhere, an endless battle that aged his mother before her time. Sometimes he wondered if it was his father's drinking that got her to leave, or the dust. She complained about both. One day when he came home from school she was gone, no note, no goodbye, no nothing. Some of her clothes were gone, a couple of things precious to her, and her car. Gone like she never existed in the first place, never to come back, never to call, never a Christmas or birthday card. She just walked away and never looked back.

One day he'd do the same.

There was a rumble of thunder as he started stocking the glass front refrigerator cases with cans and bottles of beer from the stockroom. "Ballad of a Teenage Queen" started playing as rain started drumming on the tin roof. It took about three songs before he was done, and moved on to filling the ice. The muscles in his shoulders and back strained as he lugged buckets of ice from the storeroom behind the bar and dumped them into the bins. He checked the kegs. Both were at least half full. He glanced at his watch. He had fifteen minutes until My Place opened for business.

Dane turned on the sound system, and hit this week's designated playlist. The boss paid a deejay from one of those bars in Fort Walton Beach popular with the spring break crowd to come up with a playlist for the bar every week, and Dane hated every last one of them. He went behind the bar and lit a cigarette.

The bar didn't get busy until about nine thirty or ten. There was a small rush from guys stopping in for a beer on their way home after work, but the real busy time was those last two and a half hours before closing. It wasn't a bad job. Sam McCarthy was a good boss, and Sam trusted him to open the place five nights a week. It wasn't a bad gig for a twenty-year-old. He made minimum wage plus tips—and the tips more than made up for the low hourly wage. Working at My Place beat working at McDonald's, where he worked before he turned eighteen and Sam gave him this job. It was better than working at Walmart, like so many of the jerks he'd gone to high school did, and he'd be damned if he was going to work at the cannery, coming home smelling like fish every damned day and never getting that smell out of his clothes or the house, like his father.

Fuck his father.

He'd be twenty-one soon. If everything worked out the way it should, he'd be able to get out. He'd started looking at apartment listings in Pensacola online. Once he moved over there, he'd get his GED, maybe take some classes at Pensacola State, get his degree. Sam said accountants never had to worry about getting work, and he'd always been good with numbers. He could get a job at a club in Pensacola—it was never a bad idea to have some extra cash, just in case things went bad.

Wasn't that how his mother managed it? Scrimping and saving and taking in people's laundry and sewing and putting aside every cent until she had enough to go?

That might be the best lesson he'd ever learned from her.

Maybe he could even work at one of the gay bars in Pensacola.

He'd never been inside one—the gay bars were strict with ID, and he'd never bothered to get a fake one. His experiences with other guys were limited to meeting guys on apps or online—local men with wives and kids, guys who weren't gay and would kick the shit out of you for even saying the word.

Like in high school.

The biggest bullies were the ones who had the most to hide.

Like Billy Werner.

Nah, that wasn't fair, was it? Billy had never been a bully. Billy had been his friend . . . at least until—

He put the cigarette down in a black plastic ashtray and wiped sweat from his face with a bar rag. No matter how many times he explained to Sam it was cheaper to keep the air going overnight,

Sam just couldn't wrap his mind around it. Considering how Sam pinched every penny he touched, Dane thought it weird Sam never figured out how to lower the power bill at the bar—or that someone in his business office didn't figure it out. The clock behind the counter turned to five o'clock, so he unlocked the front door, turned on the OPEN light.

A couple of leathery-faced older guys came in after about ten minutes, ordered bottles of Budweiser, took them to a table back in the far corner, back near the open patch of concrete drunk couples sometimes used as a dance floor on weekends. None of his regulars came in, probably because of the rain. Rainy nights were always slow. He made himself a cup of coffee with the Keurig machine he'd talked Sam into buying.

Closing time seemed hours away.

He was making a couple of screwdrivers for a pair of women still wearing their Walmart smocks and nametags around seven when Finn Bailey walked through the front door. He was wearing his police uniform and looked tired. Finn was in his late thirties, kept his body fit and trim with regular workouts. His wife was the teller at the bank where Dane had his checking account, and was always friendly and nice to him. He was the cop who'd come to the high school the day his bullies kicked the crap out of him in the locker room, busted his lip and cracked a tooth and a couple of ribs.

His last day at Bayside High School. He hadn't gone back.

Finn had the decency to come to his house and apologize to him about there being no charges filed. He also had the decency to look like he felt guilty about it. Finn checked in on him from time to time, made sure he was doing okay, tried to talk him into going back to school.

Guilt was a wasted emotion, Dane realized, unless you can use it.

"Get you a beer, Finn?" he asked as Finn put his cap down on the bar, climbed up on one of the bar stools. He was going gray, Dane noticed, cobwebs of lines radiating from the corners of his eyes and mouth.

Finn wiped sweat from his forehead with a cocktail napkin, leaving little paper crumbs across his forehead. "On duty, can I get a Coke instead?" His voice sounded as tired as he looked.

Dane dunked a plastic cup in the ice bin and filled it with the hose, put it on a cocktail napkin, waved his hand when Finn pulled out his wallet. House rule: never charge a cop in uniform. Dane felt a trickle of sweat under his arms. *Calm down,* he reminded himself. *He can't know. He's just a dumb hick cop in a dumb hick town. Besides, he feels guilty about you. Always has.*

"Did you hear Kaylee Werner went and got herself killed this morning?" Finn slurped down the Coke, gasping for air when he finished, muffling a burp.

"Did she?" He kept his voice even, flat.

"She was in your class, wasn't she?"

"Yeah, I think so. I didn't mix much with the cheerleaders and them. So, what happened to her? Finally pep herself to death?"

Finn put the cup down, popped a piece of ice in his mouth. "Left the gas on, I guess. When she woke up this morning and lit her cigarette, kaBLAM." Finn crunched the ice with his teeth. It sounded like bones cracking. "Smoking is hazardous to your health, I guess."

Dane shook a cigarette out of his pack. "That's what they say."

"The weird thing is Billy didn't come home last night." Finn tilted his head to one side, a knowing smirk on his lips. "You know anything about that?"

Dane inhaled. "Why don't you ask him?"

"I stopped by the Firestone and talked to him. He said—" he paused, looked from side to side, and took a deep breath. "He said you knew where he was. He come in last night?"

"He was here. Until closing."

"You served him?" He raised his eyebrows, looked surprised.

Dane flicked ash. "He's not a minor. And what happened in high school was a long time ago. Billy's been coming in here for a while. His money's as good as anyone else's."

"And you're okay with that?"

Dane crushed the cigarette out. "I'm okay with that. Like I said, high school was a long time ago, Finn. Besides, like the district attorney said, I had it coming, didn't I? Someone like me?"

Finn had the decency to flinch. "I never believed that, or said it, either, you know that, Dane."

"I know. Any other questions?"

Finn slid down off the barstool. "He said he didn't go home last night, and you'd vouch for that."

"He was too drunk to drive home, yeah." Dane shrugged. "I let him sleep it off on my couch. That a problem?"

"He was on your couch all night long?"

"He was there when I went to bed. He was there when I got up this morning at seven to go to the gym." Dane shrugged. "I didn't hear his truck start. I'm a light sleeper."

Finn just looked at him for a moment, then shook his head. "You're sure?"

Dane held up his right hand. "Swear to God."

"I hope you know what you're doing."

"I appreciate your concern."

"Thanks for the Coke. If you think of anything—" Finn turned to go.

"I'll be sure to let you know."

Dane watched him walk out of the bar. He lit another cigarette, and this time his hand shook.

Billy Werner had come in the night before, around nine o'clock, a purplish bruise on his forehead. He'd been wearing a white ribbed tank top and a tight pair of jeans worn through in places: the knees, the cuffs, just under the curve of his left ass cheek. He'd always been sexy, even in the seventh grade all those years ago when Dane used to sneak looks at him in the shower. His dad was a minister, and part of his ministry was *your body is your temple to God,* so all of his kids exercised, lifted weights, jogged. Billy had abs you could slice your finger on when he was thirteen, a bubble butt, veins that bulged over the lean muscles of his arms. He also had an acne problem, so despite the strong jaw with a dimple in the center and the bright blue eyes, the lightly tanned skin and the body, Billy never had much luck with girls. Being the son of a minister who also owned a used car lot didn't help much either. He was a nice kid, not too bright, but when Dane was alone in his bed at night he'd think about the way Billy looked in the showers, in the locker room, in his underwear, until he ached down there and had to do something about it. He'd always watched Billy, marveling at the graceful way he moved, how he walked on the balls of his feet so he kind of bounced with every step.

And Billy wasn't the ringleader. He wasn't sure Billy even hit him.

He was just . . . there.

"What'd you do to your forehead?" Dane asked, opening a bottle of Bud Light, Billy's usual. Billy had taken to coming in to My Place a couple of times a week. It had been a little awkward that first time, sure. How do you serve one of the guys who gay-bashed you back in high school without it being a little weird? But Billy had never bullied him, Billy had never called him *fag*, Billy had just gone along with the other guys . . .

He'd just been there.

It was easier to believe that, wasn't it?

Billy had always . . . always been nice to him.

And it had just been a little kiss.

"Hit it on an open cabinet door." Billy took a drink and grinned sheepishly. "You know me, clumsy as ever."

"Kaylee didn't hit you with a frying pan?" He was joking, but only a little bit. He didn't put much past Billy's wife.

Kaylee Werner had a temper, always had, even back in high school. She had a mean streak, would get a glint in her eye that spelled danger for whomever had provoked it.

Dane always believed it was Kaylee behind it all.

He and Billy had been friends since they were kids.

It was just one little kiss . . . he thought she'd seen it that night on the beach, but couldn't be sure. She'd called hello, and they'd sprung away from each other. She didn't say anything, just smiled, eyes glittering, as she took Billy by the hand and led him away, gave him a little wave as they disappeared behind a sand dune.

He wasn't sure until some of the guys on the football team—and Billy—cornered him that day in the locker room.

He thought they were going to kill him.

But Billy—Billy just looked sick when they threw him up against the lockers so hard it knocked his breath out, his head slamming against the metal. As they started kicking and punching and he slid down to the ground, Billy just stood there.

He hadn't said anything, didn't throw a punch.

But he was there. He hadn't tried to stop them, either.

He hadn't gone back to school after the janitor found him there in the locker room, called an ambulance, repeated his story through bruised lips and broken teeth again and again, and for what?

No charges filed. They didn't even get suspended.

No, he'd dropped out and went to work at McDonald's. He'd see them here and there, Billy and Kaylee, spoiled princess in her yellow Mustang with her prize driving around town. He missed Billy, missed his old friend, and remembered that night on the beach in the moonlight when their lips had touched for just a moment. . . .

Kaylee got pregnant their senior year, and they got married at City Hall right before graduation. Her parents disowned her, and Billy was stuck married to an angry, bitter woman who hated her life and blamed him for everything. And Billy got a job as a mechanic working at the Firestone, changing oil or fixing tires.

The town was too small for Dane not to know everything that was going on with them. Everyone knew everyone and everyone knew everyone's business.

So, it wasn't an accident that first night when Billy turned up at My Place. He knew that as sure as he knew Billy's beer was $3.75.

It took several visits for Billy to start telling Dane his woes.

It took several more before Dane stopped enjoying hearing about Billy's pain, and started feeling sorry for him.

And it wasn't long for him to feel his old attraction to Billy again. It hadn't ever gone away. Despite everything.

And thinking maybe, just maybe, Billy felt the same way, maybe he always had. He'd only pulled away from the kiss all those years ago when they heard Kaylee calling. He'd closed his eyes and kissed back, hadn't he? Dane wasn't remembering that wrong.

"No." Billy laughed but looked away, wouldn't meet his eyes. Which meant she *had* gotten violent again.

It wasn't the first time. She'd hit him before, thrown things at him, and there was a scar on his side where she'd come at him with a knife in one of her rages. "Why don't you leave her?" Dane had asked when Billy had pulled up his shirt to show him that scar, noticing the lightly tanned skin, the still-defined abdominal muscles, how deep the line from his hip bone heading into his groin was before it disappeared into the jeans. Billy shook his head. "She's on the outs with her parents, but they want her to leave me," Billy said mournfully. "She'll get everything if I walk out on her. Her dad will see to it. And who'd believe me?" His face flushed. "I mean, what kind of man lets a woman hit him?"

What kind of man lets a woman hit him.

Dane poured out a shot for Billy, slid it across the bar to him. "You need this."

"No, man, I can't. I've got to be able to drive home."

"You can't go back there, man. She's going to kill you one of these times."

Billy looked at him for a long minute, then picked up the shot glass.

"You can stay at my place, tonight." Dane held up his hands. "You can sleep on the couch, or I can. Nothing more than that, man. Just a place to stay the night."

Billy downed the shot and turned the glass upside down, snapping it down on the bar. He looked Dane right in the eye and said, "That's not what I want and you know it."

It was raining the first night Billy was too drunk to drive back home. Kaylee was on a girls' weekend with some of her old friends, off to a beachfront condo in Panama City Beach with some of her buddies, who felt sorry for her in the dead-end she'd wound up in, too stubborn to admit she'd made a mistake and go back to her parents, "bitches," Billy had slurred over his fourth or fifth beer, "who're too good to set foot in our house. They make her crazy, you know, they always make her feel bad about herself and then I'm the one who has to pay for it." He'd taken Billy's keys from him around midnight, told Billy he could crash in the trailer that night.

Maybe he'd known then what would happen that night. Maybe he'd hoped, maybe he'd planned, maybe.

He'd never forget how Billy looked when he took his wet shirt off in the trailer, the way the overhead light made the beads of water on his smooth, muscular chest glisten like diamonds, the way he'd almost fallen over taking his jeans off, how hot his skin had felt to the touch when Dane caught him to keep him from falling.

Later, Billy said he'd been drunk, hadn't known what he was doing, was sorry and it could never happen again.

In a way, Dane thought as he got another beer from the cooler for Jed Mathews, *Kaylee was my fault. If we hadn't gotten drunk that night on the beach when we were camping, if we hadn't kissed and gotten caught, he wouldn't have been so scared, he might not have stayed with Kaylee to prove he wasn't like me. Wouldn't have slept with her to prove he wasn't like me.*

But he was like me.

And there was the insurance. Kaylee made sure the insurance on the house was paid every month. They had a gas stove and an old gas hot water heater. Billy was always complaining how old the lines were, how dangerous they were.

Almost—almost like he was hinting.

Billy was snoring softly when Dane slipped out of the bed that morning. The moonlight coming through the blinds made slashes of blue light across his torso, and he knew he shouldn't do this, but it was what he wanted, wasn't it?

And the money—the money could make such a difference. For them both.

He picked up Billy's truck keys off the kitchen table. He worried the sound of the starting engine might wake Billy, but there was no sign of life through the trailer windows once he turned the ignition key. He drove over to the little cinderblock house on Bayshore Road Kaylee had inherited from her great aunt, the moon reflecting on the smooth waters of the bay out past the backyard. Not only was there insurance, but the land was worth a lot because it fronted on the water, some Yankees would pay a lot of money for that plot of land, and there was insurance on Kaylee, too, Billy had told him that not so long ago one night he had life insurance on her.

Letting things slip, here and there. Letting him know.

Accidents happened every day, didn't they? That's what insurance was for.

The house was dark and he'd been there before, another weekend when she'd gone off to visit one of her old friends from high school, taking her beat-up little car and driving down to Gainesville. He used the pencil flashlight to unlock the door and slip inside. She was snoring in the bedroom, an empty bottle of Jack Daniels on the kitchen table next to an ashtray filled with lipstick-stained cigarette butts. She was passed out, dead drunk.

He made his way over to the stove. He knelt down and with his pencil flashlight, found the pilot light and blew it out. He stood back up and turned all the burners on.

He turned them back off.

That wouldn't work. They might be able to tell that the burners had been on. No one would believe she killed herself.

He walked through the kitchen to the Florida room and shone his light around. The hot water heater was hidden behind a screen. All the jalousie windows were closed tight. He moved behind the screen and shone his light down on the gas line. He pushed it with his foot. It looked frayed. He started to use his pen knife on it, but stopped.

No, turning the oven on made the most sense. He carefully shut the door between the rooms and turned the oven on, up to 400 degrees. He could hear the ticking of the gas line. He opened the freezer and, yes, there was a frozen pizza. He carefully opened the box, put it down on the table next to the bottle, and placed the pizza inside. He could already smell the lethal gas.

The house reeked of cigarettes, sometimes he could smell them on Billy's clothes. She'd light one when she woke up and...

Billy would be free.

She got drunk, put a pizza in the oven, and passed out, never noticing the pilot had gone out.

He got up at seven to go to the gym, and when he got back, Billy was gone. There was a note: *went to work, have to be there at eight.*

He dropped it into an ashtray and lit it with his cigarette lighter.

He spent the day cleaning the trailer and doing his laundry, eyes on his phone. But it never rang, never chimed with a text. And then he'd come to work.

Dane handed Jed his change. Jed pocketed the money, no tip. The cheap old bastard never tipped.

Kaylee was dead now. She'd never hit Billy or cut him again.

He remembered how her eyes had glittered that night she came up on him and Billy on the beach.

She'd gotten those boys to beat him, he'd never doubted that. It was the kind of thing she did and laughed about later.

He closed the bar at one, half-heartedly went over the floor with a broom, counted the money and dropped it into the safe. He'd only made about fifty bucks in tips that night, give or take, but that was fine. He locked up and walked the path back to his trailer.

Billy was sitting on the steps. He stood up when Dane came around the bend. "What did you do?" he whispered hoarsely.

Dane dropped his cigarette into the sand, unlocked his door and held it open. "What do you mean?" He said, watching Billy's ass flex in his jeans as he climbed the steps and went into the trailer. "Seems like your house blew up this morning."

"What did you do?" Billy's face was pale, his eyes bloodshot, his hair greasy and slicked back. He nervously ran one of his big hands through it, shaking his head.

"You were here with me all night," Dane said, sitting down and lighting another cigarette. "I told the cops you slept on my couch and you were here when I went to the gym at seven. Kaylee was a drunk, everyone knows it. It's not a surprise she'd blow herself up like that."

"Why?"

"I did it for you, Billy." *NO, I did it for us, but this isn't going the way I wanted it to. What's wrong with him?*

"I didn't ask you to."

"No, but—"

Billy got up. "I've got to get out of here."

"Billy—"

The door slammed against the side of the trailer and bounced back, not shutting, swinging as Billy ran down the sand path.

Dane stubbed out his cigarette.

He'd come back.

He always did.

Besides, he had that picture he'd taken of Billy's truck out in front of the house at four in the morning.

He was getting that money one way or another.

He smiled.

FROZEN IGUANA

BY DEBRA LATTANZI SHUTIKA

Thunk

Jimmy turned off the water and stood in the shower, shivering.

Thunk

Thunk, thunk thunk.

He looked up at the ceiling tile expecting a dent from the last—

Thunk

He wrapped a towel around his waist and eased out of the steamy bathroom, the trailer floor creaking with every step.

Jimmy pulled the blinds back from the front door window. The thermometer read 36 degrees, the sixth day of the Florida freeze. The iguanas had started to fall out of the trees like junkies after a hit. Across the way, a car door slammed. At midnight, Jimmy watched his neighbor Kate, wearing her scrubs, her auburn hair tied back in a ponytail, hop down from her truck and head for her trailer. For the next hour, he made the pilgrimage to the window to watch the comings and goings of the park. Three-and-a-half Buds later, Jimmy fell asleep for the night on the couch.

There is nothing more annoying than the repetitive sound of frozen iguanas hitting the roof of your trailer, with the possible exception of a man hammering at your neighbor's door. Jimmy stumbled out of bed and looked outside. It was six in the morning and there was a cop. At Kate's door.

As the unofficial mayor of Paradise Lake trailer park, Jimmy Dickson knew every resident's story. Jimmy stayed clear of the junkies and pushers, and he watched over the lost souls who somehow ended up here. Kate was one of his favorites.

He grabbed his hat and stepped outside. Kate hollered, "Calm down!" Her breath rose in small clouds.

"You Kate Lucci?" The cop towered over Kate.

"Yeah."

"You know Liza Parks?"

Kate nodded, grabbed a cigarette and lit up. "What's up?"

Jimmy guessed it was probably Liza's bastard husband. He was always giving Liza grief about visiting the kids. Everyone in the park knew about Liza's old man: a pill-pushing doctor who got her hooked on drugs, then dumped her and took her kids.

"You have a key to her trailer?" the cop asked.

"Yep."

"Can you come with me?"

"Why?"

The cop didn't answer, but motioned for Kate to follow. Jimmy watched Kate grab her sneakers and pull one on, then the other, as she hopped down two cinder block steps at her front door. The trailer door slammed behind her.

"Hey, what's going on?" Kate jumped over a trash bag that had blown onto the crushed shell sidewalk.

"When's the last time you saw Ms. Parks?"

"Yesterday afternoon, around one. I checked on her before I left for work.

"Where's that?"

"The detox clinic in Davie."

"And you left for work at around what time?"

"At two. I work the second shift."

"How did she seem?"

"Liza? Fine. She was waiting for her ex to drop off her kids. She hadn't seen them in a while."

"Did you see anyone at the trailer before you left?" he asked. She shook her head.

"Can you open the door?"

"Not until you tell me why you're asking me all this." Kate crossed her arms and took a long drag on her smoke.

"We got a call from her ex-husband saying she wasn't home last night when he came to drop the kids. He wasn't surprised, he said."

"You know Bryce Parks is an asshole liar, right?" She pointed her cigarette at him, then flicked ash and took another drag.

"Dr. Parks called Liza's mother this morning. She also can't reach her."

The cop seemed calm, but Jimmy read the tension in his neck as he spoke, a perfect balance of a man who would be happy to beat the shit out of a woman or screw her, depending.

Kate leaned toward him. "Why didn't Sylvia just call me?" She smiled when she said this. Did something about this jerk with a stick-up-his-ass appeal to her?

"She did. You didn't answer. Now, do you mind?" He pointed toward the door. Kate handed him the key. "Thank you," he said. He smiled and tipped his hat. "I do appreciate this."

He wanted to screw her.

Kate hopped up and down, trying to warm up. She checked her pockets, no cigarettes. Jimmy thought she looked out of place in Paradise Lake, where there was no lake and the park only resembled paradise if you were homeless or white trash. Kate was neither.

Paradise Lake was technically an "adult only" mobile home park. Most people moved into the park because it was cheap, they didn't want to be around kids, and were too young for "over 55," which also meant living with a bunch of bitchy blue-haired widows and old maids. In Paradise Lake, "adults only" translated into "clothing optional" and kids were allowed for weekend visitation. Kate and her buddy Liza were not nudists, but he'd heard Liza say she was happy to look at junk if it meant she could disappear from the world. In that respect, this was paradise.

Jimmy watched Kate for a long moment unnoticed, then decided to stroll her way.

At the crunch of his black boots, she turned. She'd taken to calling him Lil' Jimmy Pickens on account of the boots and white cowboy hat he wore every day. Jimmy liked that—everyone knew he was sweet on Kate, she was too young for him, and that was just fine. This morning he sported a puffy jacket that looked silly with the cowboy getup, but it was damn cold. He lifted his hat. "G'morning Miz Lucci."

"Hey there Jimmy."

"I see the poll-ice are paying a visit to Miz Parks. I hope she's okay."

"I don't know anything. I just had her keys."

He tipped his hat as Kate rubbed her arms and looked to the thermometer hanging inside the awning over Liza's patio. "Dammit, Jimmy, it's 36 degrees."

Something slammed to the earth behind Kate. Jimmy strode up beside her and they both looked over a huge iguana, belly up on the crushed shell sidewalk.

"Damn, it's been years since I seen that." Sensing Kate's confusion, he added, "They're cold-blooded creatures. When we have a bad cold snap, they freeze up an' start droppin' from the trees."

"I heard something hit my roof this morning."

"Well, you got that live oak near your lot, probably got pelted by a falling iguana. I had 'em hit my place too."

"Are they dead?"

"Some'll die. Depends on how long they're frozen. Last time we had a bad cold snap, one of them animal rescue people picked up a bunch and put them in the back of his station wagon. When they warmed up, it was like a freakin' horror movie in that car."

"What happened?"

"Poor bastard was all bit up. He hit a tree and totaled the car. The iguanas got out okay, though."

The sound of tires on gravel came from the distance. Kate and Jimmy saw a small car barreling toward them with Liza's mother behind the wheel.

"This doesn't look good," Kate said.

"No ma'am," Jimmy added.

Sylvia Garson pulled up behind the police cruiser—an ambulance followed a few seconds behind.

"Kate!" Sylvia jumped out of her Corolla and ran to her, grabbing her shoulders. "Have you seen her yet?"

"No, the cop's in there."

The officer appeared at the door as the paramedics arrived with a stretcher. "This way, please," he said.

Sylvia pushed her way through the front door. "I need to see my daughter."

"Ma'am, please let the paramedics do their job."

"What happened?" Kate asked, following Sylvia. The officer stopped her.

"You'll have to wait here. There isn't much space."

Kate conceded that point. Her teeth started to chatter and she looked at Jimmy.

"Would you mind going to my place and grabbing my jacket and smokes? They're on the kitchen table."

Jimmy nodded then ambled into Kate's trailer and returned a few minutes later with her jacket and cigarettes.

"Thanks," she said, pulling on the coat and tapping a cigarette from the pack.

A few minutes later, the officer was back outside. "Ms. Lucci, can I have a word?"

"If we can talk inside my trailer, yeah." She nodded for Jimmy to join her, and the cop followed. Jimmy paused at the door. Kate had the oldest and best maintained trailer in the park. She had an old Pan Am bag sitting on a table at the entrance. The whole place looked like a museum to the 1950s.

Kate started a pot of coffee and checked the thermostat.

"Nice place you have here," the cop said, admiring the teak paneling. He laid the keys to Liza's trailer on the counter.

"Thanks. Like some coffee? I don't think I caught your name."

"Connor Hammill. With cream, thanks."

"Jimmy, coffee?" Kate asked.

"No thanks."

Hammill turned to see Jimmy standing behind him. Jimmy sensed his annoyance.

"What's up at Liza's?" Kate asked.

"Looks like she OD'd."

"Wait—Liza's been clean for nine months. I mean religiously clean. She's a vegan now—"

"I don't know what to tell you, except that heroin is a vegetable."

Kate stopped pouring coffee to give him a look. Jimmy thought she reminded him of his mother somehow. Officer Hammill stirred under the weight of her stare.

"That's not funny," she said, slamming the pot back on the burner. "Is she okay?"

"She's not out of the woods yet, but the paramedics are hopeful." When she crossed her arms he sighed. "Seriously."

"So, what's next?"

"I guess you were unaware of the drug use then?"

"Liza is recovering. She got hooked on opioids after her last C-section. Her husband wrote her prescriptions. She's been in and out of treatment, but got serious about her recovery after her divorce. She lost her kids and that did it for her."

"Any idea when she started using again?"

"You misunderstood me. Liza. Isn't. Using."

Jimmy admired Kate. He liked a gal with moxie.

"I just found her with a tourniquet on her arm, unconscious. She had paraphernalia all over the bed."

Kate sipped her coffee. “All I know is that Liza wouldn't do that.”

“Relapse is pretty common.”

“I'm a rehab nurse. I met Liza as an inpatient and I'm part of her support team. She wasn't using.”

He flipped his notebook shut. “All I'm saying is the evidence points to OD.”

* * *

KATE PUT THE COFFEE MUGS in the sink as Hammill walked back to his cruiser. Jimmy stood behind her and they watched him drive away.

“Jimmy,” she said. “Are you busy today?”

“No ma'am.”

She grabbed the keys to Liza's place as soon as the cruiser pulled out of sight. “Want to join me?”

He nodded.

Jimmy would follow Kate anywhere.

Liza's trailer, like Kate's, was a vintage model, a turquoise *Palacio Ranchero,* but it looked every day of its fifty-six years.

“Liza slept in the back bedroom and had hopes that her kids would one day occupy the other for weekends,” Kate said as she opened the door. When they walked in, Kate stopped abruptly and Jimmy ran into her.

“Sorry about that,” he said.

“Holy shit—I know paramedics make a mess coming in and out of trailers, but this place is trashed.”

Jimmy looked around. “I don't think the paramedics did this.”

“Aren't you good with a camera?” Kate asked.

“Pretty fair.” That was modesty. Jimmy had won blue ribbons for his photography at the Broward County Fair.

“Can you use my phone to take pictures?”

“I can do one better. I'll be right back.”

He returned a few minutes later with a professional-looking digital camera. “What should I shoot?” he asked.

"I'll step out—get shots of the mess in the living room and kitchen here, then we'll go into the bedroom together. I want to look around, but I want to make sure we have evidence of what we find."

Jimmy nodded.

Kate stood in the doorway as Jimmy moved back and forth photographing the scene. "What's your story?" she asked as she smudged out her cigarette on one of Liza's ashtrays.

"Whad'ya mean?"

"I've lived in the Park for six months and aside from Liza, you're my only friend. I don't know much about you. Where are you from? How'd you end up here?"

"I'd ask you the same thing."

"You first."

"Been here near thirty years. I left home to work on an oil rig in the Gulf, didn't suit me. So I came here. I done odd jobs, then I worked at a tool and die shop. They closed down a few years ago, sent all the machines to China. I retired early."

"Do you like it here?"

"No complaints. What about you?"

"I'm a West Virginia exile."

"You runnin' from the law?" he asked, suddenly serious.

"Not at all. I had a job and a family. My daughter went off to college, my marriage fell apart, and my life kinda fell apart. I ended up here."

"Humph." Jimmy took a new look at Kate. She was a woman who had lived well most of her life, and it showed. Whatever happened in West Virginia, he figured he didn't want to know.

In the bedroom, they saw the rumpled sheets stained with blood and the remains of the tourniquet, and a few syringes, a spoon, and a lighter. Kate shook her head.

"What'd you think?" Jimmy asked after he'd clicked his last shot.

"Hammill didn't mark this off as a crime scene. He should have."

Jimmy nodded, although he wasn't sure he agreed with her. He'd witnessed other overdoses in the Park. This didn't look much different.

* * *

BACK IN HER TRAILER, KATE brewed another pot of coffee while Jimmy downloaded the photos onto her laptop. She lit another cigarette, poured coffee and joined him at the bar that served as her dining table. She pulled the laptop toward her.

She clicked through the images. "You're good at this, Jimmy."

"Just a hobby." Her praise brought a flush to his cheeks.

"I told Hammill this wasn't an overdose," Kate said. Jimmy raised his eyebrows. "Let's start with her gear—Liza was not an upscale addict. She was a mom who got hooked on opioids, then switched to heroin when she couldn't afford prescriptions. I admitted her to the detox center and she brought her paraphernalia with her." She saw Jimmy's brow furrow and added, "It's part of the admission requirement. You have to turn in your drugs and needles."

"I don't reckon I know what you're talkin' about," Jimmy said.

"This stainless steel case and syringe—" she said, pointing to one of the photos. "It's something a doctor might have at a clinic, or a Wall Street addict. Liza was a common street junkie. Plastic needles and her stash in a Crown Royal bag."

Jimmy had never considered the class status of drug addicts. He'd always thought of them as some of the people he lived among in Paradise Lake. Why would anyone with a job get hooked on drugs?

"And look at this," Kate said, pointing at the next photo. There were three small bags of white powder. "I can't believe Hammill didn't take them."

"They was on the floor under the bed," Jimmy said. "I laid on the floor to get that shot."

Kate pressed her lips together. "He didn't search the room."

“I reckon he was convinced she done herself in,” Jimmy said.

“I understand why someone who doesn’t know her would think that, but she was about to see her kids for the first time in months. It doesn’t make sense.”

Jimmy shifted awkwardly in his seat. “I don’t mean no disrespect, but I seen this before, takin’ a turn for the worse right before things should work out.”

“You’re right. It does happen. But I saw her yesterday before I left for work. Her trailer was immaculate. The kids’ room was tidy and full of toys.” She paused for a moment. “Did you see anyone over there yesterday afternoon?”

Jimmy looked away before he answered. “I saw you go in around one—”

“Right—then I left for work.”

“Then I saw her mama come around half hour later. She was there about an hour. Then her ex showed up. He has a big car, looks brand new.”

“What time?”

“Right round eight. I went outside to check the temperature. I do that during the cold spells. Can’t help myself.”

“How long was he there?”

“He didn’t stay long. The man gave me a look, like I was spyin’ or something.”

“How were the kids?”

“Kids? Naw, he was alone.”

Kate shook her head. “I need to get to the hospital to see how Liza’s doing. Would you like to come along?” Jimmy nodded.

* * *

When they arrived at the hospital, they found Sylvia on her cell, pacing in the ICU waiting room.

“Thank you for your concern, Carol. I’m sad, but not surprised. It’s happened so many times before. I hope she’ll pull through, but if not, well, I’ll help Bryce raise the kids.” Sylvia squealed when she saw Kate. "Oh Carol, I need to go." Sylvia pulled Kate into a bear hug. "I'm so happy you're here, Kate. I haven't seen Liza and no one's been out to see me."

Kate frowned. "Let me check in at the nurses' station."

Sylvia noticed Jimmy. "So nice of you to come along Mr.—eh—I'm sorry Jimmy, I don't think Liza ever told me your last name."

"Dickson. The folks at the Park call me Jimmy Dickens. They say I favor him."

"The Opry star? You do indeed, Mr. Dickens," she said, apparently unaware she misspoke. "I'm so broken up about Liza. She's been so good lately."

Jimmy didn't have anything to say, so he was quiet, watching Sylvia. The silence seemed to unnerve her and she babbled on.

"I told Bryce—that's her ex-husband—that she needed to be in a better living situation. That ole trailer park had too many druggies running around. He wouldn't give her a penny to find a decent place. Said she got herself in this situation and she'd have to get herself out. That trailer was a teetotal mess yesterday. I told her she better get a move on, clean things up before the kids arrived. I don't think people value homemaking in trailer parks. In general, that is."

Jimmy gave her a sidelong look. "There are a few bad apples, but there are some fine people in the Park. Miz Lucci here, she's a good friend. Speakin' of which, excuse me, please." He stood and tipped his hat. He strolled toward the ICU door and stood tiptoe to peek in the window. Kate was standing at the nurses' station alone, looking at a chart.

"I know Kate's a good friend, Mr. Dickens, and I don't mean to offend—" Sylvia said as he walked away. Jimmy ignored her.

"You can call me Jimmy. Or Mr. Dickson," he said, returning to his seat.

Sylvia stopped. "Isn't that what I've been calling you?"

Jimmy was about to answer when Kate reappeared. "They said the doctor'll be out shortly. Sylvia, what happened yesterday?"

"I went to see her before Bryce was supposed to drop off the kids. Liza seemed all right, but nervous. I should have known she couldn't handle it. I should have stayed with her."

Kate sat beside Sylvia, opposite Jimmy. "I feel the same way." A minute later a green-clad doctor emerged from the ICU. "Mrs. Garson?" he said.

"That's me."

"I'm sorry, but I'm afraid we weren't able to save your daughter."

Sylvia screamed and buried her head in her hands. Kate wrapped her arm around Sylvia to comfort her. Jimmy noticed that Sylvia's eyes were dry.

* * *

As they left the hospital, Kate and Jimmy saw a gurney carrying a man whose bloodied face looked like he stuck it in his Vitamix. Kate paused, but Jimmy took her arm and moved her away. "Damned iguanas," he whispered.

Once in the car, Jimmy said, "What are we doin' now?

"I want to find her ex. Wanna come?"

Jimmy nodded.

* * *

Bryce Parks' clinic was a low-slung cinderblock building, more like a payday loan center than a medical facility. It seemed deserted: no receptionist, and the lights were off. But the doors to the main offices were open, so they went in. Kate explained that he had been an orthopedic surgeon, but now specialized in pain management. Jimmy nodded. Bryce was running a pill mill.

"Bryce, you here?" Kate called. No answer. Kate walked in and around the reception desk, then toward a hall of consultation offices, all empty. Jimmy moved into a small kitchen and opened the cabinets. Boxes labeled Percocet, Vicodin, and Dilaudid fell to the counter. "Jezus, Kate, look at this."

"Jimmy, we need to get out of here."

* * *

Kate and Jimmy sat in the car in front of Bryce's clinic. "Now what?" Jimmy asked.

"I'm going to call that cop Hammill—this clinic shouldn't be wide open with all the drugs. We also need to tell him about the drugs on Liza's floor," Kate said.

They drove back to Paradise Lake and went into Kate's trailer. "I'm starved. How about I order a pizza?" Kate asked.

"That'd be just fine."

Kate called Hammill's cell. When she hung up she said, "I don't think he'll come by. He sent a patrol car to check out Bryce's clinic. I'm pretty sure he'll be out of business tomorrow. Oh, I mentioned the drugs under Liza's bed—he said he can pick them up later. He's convinced it was an OD."

When the pizza came they huddled on the sofa, looking at Jimmy's photos.

"I don't think the heater in this trailer is going to survive this cold snap," Kate said.

"What model is this place?"

"It's a '59 Spartan Carousel. When I divorced my husband, we sold our house. I walked away with some cash and I found this on eBay."

"How much d'you pay?"

"Way too much."

Jimmy smiled and took a bite of pizza. "You know, somethin' strange happened today."

"Just one thing?"

"At the hospital, Liza's mom told me that her trailer was a mess when she got there last night."

"That's impossible. I mean, the trailer is old, but Liza had cleaned it top to bottom."

"I thought you said that."

"When I went to talk to the nurses today, I was alone at the desk for a moment. Liza's chart was open and I saw her toxicology report. It was positive for morphine, but not 6-MAM—that's what shows up on a drug test when someone has taken heroin."

"I'm guessin' it was her ex-husband," Jimmy said.

"That's probably why he left the drug baggies in her trailer—he thought she'd die immediately, and with this cold snap, her trailer would be an icebox. It would be hard to know how long she'd been dead.

"One more thing—the baggies we found at Liza's—I put one in my pocket." Jimmy pulled out a small bag of white powder.

"Why'd you do that?"

"I had a funny feeling about everything, even then." He opened the bag and put his finger in, then licked it. "I thought so."

Kate dabbed her pinky in the bag and tasted. "It's talcum powder."

"Yep. Liza's trailer was staged."

Kate reached for her phone. "I'm calling Hammill—he needs to see this."

There was a huge crash overhead. "Was that an iguana?" Kate asked.

"I don't think so," Jimmy said. They walked outside and found Sylvia laying belly up on a pile of crushed shells. Bryce Parks, Liza's impossibly handsome ex-husband, was kneeling beside her in faded green scrubs, checking her pulse. Kate and Jimmy walked toward them, stunned. A small puddle of blood was gathering around Sylvia's head. A mop of synthetic hair lay a few inches from the puddle.

"I didn't know Sylvia wore a wig," Kate said.

Jimmy looked up at the sprawling live oak that stretched over Kate's trailer. "What the hell was she doin' up there?"

"Sylvia was grieving. And Liza wasn't the only member of that family with a drug problem, sadly," Bryce said.

"I'll call 911," Kate said.

"I'm afraid it's too late for Sylvia."

"Liza never mentioned her mother had a drug problem," Jimmy said.

Bryce grabbed Sylvia's purse, a few feet from her body. He rummaged through it and pulled out a small bag of pills. "Crank," he said.

"What's that?" Jimmy said.

"It's the street name for amphetamines. It can cause horrible hallucinations. Some people jump from windows. I suppose Sylvia decided follow the iguanas into the trees. My poor children, losing their mother and grandmother the same day."

"My condolences," Kate said. Jimmy had to repress a smile.

Bryce looked up, surprised by Kate's sarcasm. "That was unkind."

"So is murder."

"That's absurd. How dare you say something like that."

"Oh, I daresay. Liza's tox screen was positive for morphine, not heroin. There was only one place she could get that. From you and your *medical practice.*" Kate walked over and grabbed the bag of pills from Bryce's hands. "I'm guessing Sylvia got "crank" from the same place."

Jimmy inched forward imperceptibly.

Bryce blinked repeatedly. "You're crazy. I guess you're all a bunch of drug-addled fools. I never wanted Liza to live in this dump."

"We stopped by your office today and saw your stash."

"And we alerted the au-thorities," Jimmy added.

Bryce turned toward Jimmy "Listen, you hillbilly half-wit, Liza and her junkie mother probably got their drugs from some pusher in this place." Bryce waved his hand around.

Jimmy noticed Kate's face twitch when Bryce called him a hillbilly, but she regained her composure. "You don't need to travel anywhere to get medical-grade morphine and surgical syringes. She got them from you."

In the distance, Jimmy heard sirens blaring.

"I'm not going to stand around and listen to this nonsense," he said, and started to walk toward his car.

Kate stood rooted to the spot. She seemed to have lost her sassy tongue. Jimmy started after Bryce, but his gait was too slow to catch the much younger doctor.

THUNK!

Bryce stopped short, looking at the iguana that had crashed from the tree right above his car. It hit the hood dead-on. Jimmy barreled into him, knocking him to the ground. A few minutes later, Officer Hammill was out of his car and pointing a gun at Bryce's head. Kate helped Jimmy to his feet.

"Nice tackle," Kate said, brushing him off. Jimmy smiled.

After he cuffed Bryce, Hammill and his partner searched Liza's trailer, then came to get a statement. "How did you know Bryce and Sylvia were working together?" Hammill asked.

"I didn't until she fell on my trailer," Kate said.

"Actually, I suspected it," Jimmy said. Kate looked at him, surprised. "You see, when the doctors came out to tell us that Liza passed, Miz Sylvia put on a good show, but she didn't have a tear in her eye. I thought it was strange. Then I realized somethin' else. She said that Liza's trailer was a mess. But you had been in the trailer just two hours before, and you said—"

"It was immaculate. Yes. It was," Kate said.

"I have to think that the mess we saw this mornin' was made yesterday afternoon, when Miz Sylvia was there. Must've been a struggle, and when it was all said and done, she left the syringe and the baggies of talc to make it look like Liza had overdosed."

"But why would Sylvia do that?" Hammill asked.

"She and Liza had a difficult relationship," Kate said. "Liza had been in and out of rehab for years. Bryce had always been generous with Sylvia, and he didn't want Liza to see the kids. Sylvia had been raising them for years. They never believed she'd recovered."

Hammill wrote it down, and just shook his head. "What a mess."

Jimmy shook his head. "Officer Hammill, if we're done here, I expect I'll head home."

"That should be all. Thank you, sir." He shook Jimmy's hand.

As Jimmy walked off, he heard Hammill say, "I'm off duty at three today. Would you like to meet up for a drink?" He looked back and saw Kate smile. Jimmy could tell she liked him. Before she could answer he heard a loud *THUNK*. He looked up.

Another iguana.

THE FAKAHATCHEE GOONCH

BY JACK BATES

GOONCH IS JUST ANOTHER NAME for a catfish. A really big catfish. Sometimes it's called the devil fish or black demon because it lurks deep down there in the murkiest part of the Fakahatchee Preserve. Bottom feeders mostly. They eat gator leftovers or anything else that might get tossed into the swamps. Back in the mauve and neon *Miami Vice* days, legend had it the Everglades was a good place to dispose of a problem quick. People think that's how the goonch developed a taste for meat.

Of course, the guys who trawl for catfish say those fish are just as apt to eat water weeds and such if the pickings are slim. Sometimes they feed on their own. Had some guys drag in twenty to thirty pounders, about three feet long. That ain't no fish tale.

Neither is this one. The catfish I'm talking about is an eight-man goonch. Know what that is? That's when eight grown men stand in a line, shoulder to shoulder, and that goonch lays across all of their extended hands from tip to tail. That's how big the Fakahatchee goonch was said to be. Had a mouth like the gaping orifice of hell, or so I'm told. I ain't never seen it, but I know it's there.

There have been nights when I'm frog hunting where the frog croaking will go quiet and the swamp gets real still. Something big enough to rock my aluminum skiff passes through the water. Up ahead in the dark there'll be a splash—and a few ticks off a clock later my skiff will rock a second time, except maybe a little more treacherously, on the creature's return pass, and I'll have to sit down, clutch the sides so I don't tip out. Only way I know it's safe to leave is when the frogs start croaking again.

Sometimes though, a frog will puff its chest and blowout its braggadocio regardless of the danger it's in.

About a month ago there was a little bit of trouble down at place called Shel's Shed. People driving through West Shore on their way to the Fakahatchee Preserve might pass it if they don't know about it. Just a simple cinderblock building that faces the gulf. No actual windows except for a single glass door and a line of triple stacked glass bricks running the length of the outdoor, elevated deck. Some previous owner painted the exterior sky blue. Shel left it even though the paint chipped and cracked enough that the original light gray of the foundation peeked out.

On the inside, a scuffed, black and white tile floor waited to be mopped. Shel put in some wobbly, round, plastic tables with matching dusty, plastic chairs. The short end of an L-shaped bar greeted customers. In the back a couple of old, secondhand pool tables waited for people to play. Shel hung a big green and white sign on the bricks that said, NO GAMBLING. FOR ENTERTAINMENT PURPOSES ONLY! The tables weren't much in the way for sport, mostly just for little kids to abuse while their mommies and daddies sat at the bar drinking shells of beer and eating deep-fried frog legs or gator or chicken or whatever Shel had in the freezer.

Day trippers and tourists stayed mostly to the resort areas north of West Shore or on the well-worn path of the Interstate. West Shore sat between Bonita Springs and North Naples along State Road 41. Blink or sneeze and you might miss it.

Somebody not from the area either had to know someone who knew about Shel's Shed or had to go out of his way to find it. Back in the day we didn't have GPS or Google Maps, just good old word of mouth.

Obama was deep into his second term and it looked like Hilary was making history when the guy from Detroit opened the door at Shel's Shed. Simple looking guy in that there was nothing special about him. Jeans, bright yellow T-shirt with an orange sun over the right side of his chest. Expensive hiking boots. Told Artie the bartender he was passing through on his ways to the Keys. Mr. Detroit had some business down there and wanted to do a little fishing. He wanted to visit the spots old Poppa Hemingway had. The guy went on and on about following a literary fishing map starting with the big Two-Hearted River in Michigan's upper half on down to landing old Santiago's marlin in the turquoise waters between Cuba and the Keys.

"What are you doing way over here in West Shore if you're heading to Key West?" Artie asked.

"I got business here and there."

"What kind of business you do?"

"Consultant. Head hunter. Hatchet man. I get hired to handle situations others can't."

"Shel didn't hire you to fire me, did he?" Artie laughed half-heartedly.

About then Mr. Detroit heard the crack and smack of pool balls breaking across the worn felt on one of the tables. He sipped his beer and looked over his shoulder at the back of the room.

Jay Harmon and his buddy DT Spindle were playing a little warm-up against one another. The boys had a couple of girls with them, mostly to hold their beers or cigarettes while they took their shots. The girls were sweaty, cute, and had more than likely come over from Edison State College. They looked just fine in their short shirts and skinny jeans. DT Spindle finished his beer and asked the brunette hanging on him to go get another round.

He took a twenty out of his pocket and handed it over. The brunette smiled, all her white teeth straight and in place. The same couldn't be said for DT.

The brunette sauntered up to the bar, turning the heads of a couple of locals sitting on dusty chairs at a wobbly table as she passed. She leaned in through a space that left Mr. Detroit on one side of her and my turned back on the other. I wasn't being rude. I just didn't want trouble from DT and Jay. They'd been known to bust out a guy's teeth just because a guy had teeth. I stared straight ahead into the mirror, taking in the boys in the back and the girl next to me.

"Get a round of brews, Mr. Bartender?" The tiny brunette's voice sounded like honey drizzled over butter. Artie brought four beers out of the cooler.

"Knocking some balls back there?" Mr. Detroit asked her.

The girl quickly checked out the man ballsy enough to say something to her in front of Jay and DT. She smiled, although less of her white teeth showed this time.

"You mean the pool table?" The brunette leaned an elbow on the padded rail. Artie set the bottles down on the bar. She held up the folded twenty between her fingers. Artie took the bill. They never looked at one another.

Mr. Detroit turned on his stool. His knee kind of blocked the girl from leaving. "I guess I do," he said.

"Jay and DT are looking for someone to take on," the girl said lifting the beers. She carried the bottles by their necks, two in each hand, the bottlenecks jutting through her fingers. She'd clearly done it before. "Maybe you should join us."

"If I were you, buddy," Artie said. "I'd stick to seeing the sights and then go do your fishing."

"You down here to fish?" The girl hadn't moved much out of the narrow space, but I swear she could have turned her hips and not touched Mr. Detroit's knees or my back. That's how tiny she was.

"In the Keys," Mr. Detroit said.

She wrinkled her nose. “Then what are you doing in West Shore?”

“Hey, Darla.” DT bellowed lighting a cigarette. “You bringing us those beers or what?”

“Coming, DT.” Darla smiled and winked before she went back to the local boys.

“You want to smoke, DT,” Artie said. “You gotta take it outside.”

DT slowly blew out a long stream of smoke. At the end of his exhale, he laughed.

Darla rolled her pretty brown eyes. “Do what he says, DT. Shel’s doesn’t need any shit from the police. Neither do you.”

Mr. Detroit studied Miss Darla for a moment. When he turned back around, he had a ghost of smile on his face. He kind of shook his head and downed the rest of what was in his glass.

“You staying for another?” Artie asked.

Mr. Detroit shook his head. “I think it’s time I got to the Keys.”

I thought he escaped any confrontation with Jay and DT. No such luck. He pulled out this novelty wallet from his jeans’ pocket. At first it looked like he held a bunch of hundred dollar bills in his hand. Even Artie’s eyes lit up. Mr. Detroit peeled back the front overlap held in place with Velcro, an unnecessary eighties left over like ninety-nine red balloons and parachute pants. He pulled out a wrinkled ten dollar bill that looked like it had been dipped in tea to dye it dog-piss yellow.

“Keep it,” he said to Artie.

Now that might have been the end of it but it wasn’t. See, by then DT was standing almost directly behind Mr. Detroit. He’d seen what he probably thought was a wad of hundred dollar bills getting slipped back into the man’s pocket. When Mr. Detroit turned around, he found himself staring into DT’s beady little eyes. DT gave him a big shit-eating smile, pushing his cheeks up like a squirrel’s after it’s stuffed them full of bird seed from a feeder.

“Hey. I hear you’re here to do some fishing?” DT said, making it sound like a question.

“Yeah. I’m on my way to the Keys now.”

"The Keys, huh? Gonna go through Alligator Alley?"

"I'm taking I-75 through the Everglades."

DT nodded. "Yep. That's Alligator Alley. You want to be careful going through there."

"Because of the alligators."

"Yeah, mostly. But there's other shit in those swamps that will get ya just as bad."

I give Mr. Detroit credit. He knew how to size up a situation. Like he'd found himself on the wrong side of the tracks more than once in his life. The out-of-towner stood about an inch shorter than DT and went about thirty pounds lighter, but that didn't mean the guy couldn't recognize trouble when it stared down at him.

"Well, I'll keep the doors locked," Mr. Detroit said. He took a step to go around DT but DT countered with a slide.

"Yeah. Gators is one problem. But then there's panthers down around there sometimes. Ain't that right Jay?" DT shot a wink at his buddy.

Jay reared back on his pool stick. When the tip struck the cue ball it was like thunder in the room. Jay stood up, grabbed the beer out of the blonde's hand, and took a long drag on it.

"Let it go, DT."

"Aw, I'm just warning this fella about Alligator Alley. Gators, panthers, wild boars as big as garbage Dumpsters, Skunk Ape." DT looked back at Mr. Detroit. "You ever hear of the Skunk Ape?"

"Florida's version of Sasquatch." Mr. Detroit dug his keys out of his pocket. He held them down at his side, the fob in his palm, the jagged metal teeth of three different keys jutting out between his knuckles the way the brown bottlenecks stuck out between Darla's fingers when she carried off the beers.

People around here think I'm sundried and whiskey-drowned but I know things. I see things. I saw Mr. Detroit get ready to defend himself.

"Getting kind of late." DT said looking out the glass door. A calm, orange sun slid closer to the horizon. A ripple of its glow lit the middle row of the glass brick stripe. "You're not heading for the Keys tonight are you?"

"Thinking about it."

"Night's when the skunk ape comes out." DT slapped his own leg and laughed.

"There ain't no skunk ape in the Fakahatchee Preserve," Jay said. He leaned over the table to take another shot. Jay pulled back his large, farm boy arm and pushed the stick through his fingers like a firing pin on a 40 mm cannon. The cue ball rolled into a triangle of other balls, sending them off into two pockets and the eight ball against the rail. Jay stood up and leaned on his cue stick. "Besides. He gets into any trouble down there in Big Cypress he needs to worry about the goonch."

Mr. Detroit's head kind of ticked to the right. "Goonch?"

"Yeah. But it's been a while since anyone lost a cow or a horse so who knows, maybe it's dead."

Jay smiled and took a beer out of the skinny blonde girl's hand. He kept smiling as he drank.

About then, Darla, the tiny brunette who had first caught Mr. Detroit's eye, came out of the bathroom. She walked over to DT and stood next to him.

"DT trying to get you to play pool, mister? He thinks he's all that but if you notice, Jay does all the playing while DT does all the drinking." Darla playfully slapped DT's arm. She was playing the two off of one another.

Mr. Detroit took the bait and laid out some of his own. "Actually they were filling me in on the goonch."

Darla, that pretty little brunette, whether she was in on it or not, gave off the biggest tell I'd ever seen. She put her lips into a tight little O-shape and rolled those big, brown eyes.

"Oh, yeah. The Fakahatchee Goonch. My daddy knows this guy who was hiking through the Preserve when he heard a whole lot of splashing coming from Cochran Lake. Said he stood on the far side watching the goonch swallow a feral pig."

"All right," Mr. Detroit said. "I give. What's a goonch?"

Darla pretty much told him everything I said earlier. Mr. Detroit laughed.

"A catfish big enough to eat a wild hog? Whole?"

"I'm just saying," Darla said. She took a drink from her beer.

"And she knows." DT said. "She goes to college."

"Hey, DT. We playing or what?" Jay yelled from the back.

DT turned away from Jay and back to Mr. Detroit. "Darla said earlier you was looking to shoot some Nine Ball. Care to make it interesting?"

"I should really get going." Mr. Detroit said it in that kind of feigning tone that makes it sound like he really didn't have to go anywhere.

"Come on. Just a couple of games. You know Nine Ball, mister?"

"Hock. Charlie Hock. And, yeah. I know Nine Ball."

And he did. For the next hour, Charlie Hock of Detroit slowly took DT and Jay for whatever money they had on them plus some of the money from Darla and her skinny blonde friend. He started off slowly, losing some, then winning some back, then making it look like he was letting the boys get theirs back before he finally just wiped them out. Jay and DT weren't too happy about it and their girls were even less than thrilled seeing as how they had footed the boys' night. They were all a little sore, except Charlie Hock. He seemed pleased that he pissed them off. I thought I had the guy from Motown all figured out. The whole night had probably been just a set up for him.

"Ladies and gentlemen." Charlie Hock said, that ghost of a grin back on his face. "It's been an entertaining evening but I really need to go."

Jay pressed the tip of his cue stick against the wall. It trapped Charlie Hock between the stick and DT. Darla and her friend moved off the padded stools they had watched from for most of the night to protect their asses. Shit was about to go down.

"Not just yet, buddy." Jay said.

Hock looked from the stick to Jay. "What's the problem?"

"The problem is you have all of our money."

"You know that's how betting works, right? Someone wins. Someone loses."

"I'm just asking for ours back, mister." Jay Harmon was always more direct than his buddy DT.

"Did you run crying to your momma if someone beat you at *Halo*?"

"I'm going to bust your mouth." Jay cocked his arm back.

"Hold on," DT said. "It's not like you need ours. You got that wad of hundreds in your other pocket."

"Wad of hundreds? All I've got in my pocket is my wallet." Hock pulled it out, turned it over a few times like he was taunting Jay and DT. "I got it as a gift from my nephew when he went to the Bureau of Engraving in DC."

Jay looked at the novelty wallet in Hock's hand, then he looked at DT. No one said anything because their faces said it all. Hock grabbed the stick to move it. Jay reached out with one of his big hands and pushed Hock against the wall.

There weren't many others in Shel's at that point. Me. Artie. Darla and her friend. A couple of locals I drank with in the past. The local boys got up and hurried out the door. Darla and her friend cowered in the back by the restrooms.

Artie leaned a hand against the bar. His other hand reached below its top. I knew he was reaching for Lulu, the sawed-off double barrel Shel kept there. Illegal as all hell but highly effective. Shel called Lulu his backup plan.

"Jay. That's enough." Artie said. "Shel said if there was any more trouble from either or both of you he'd ban you from here for life."

"I want my money." Jay said. "Then I'll never set foot in this shit hole again."

"You said that last time, Jay," the blonde said.

"Shut your mouth, Candi!"

Hock slapped Jay's pool stick away from the wall. Jay just about bit the edge of the pool table. He put his palms on the diamonds to stop himself from knocking out his own teeth.

Things happened quickly after that. Jay didn't see Charlie Hock palm the purple four ball. Hock brought it up lightning quick, smashing it into Jay's nose. Hock tried to scoot passed Jay. He caught Hock by the back of his belt. Hock still holding the purple four ball, smashed it into Jay's ear. Jay howled and let go of Hock, who turned and ran into DT's hammer-cocked fist. Mr. Detroit took the punch pretty well, but I got to believe its impact wasn't what it might could have been if Jay wasn't still somewhat dazed and had thrown it himself. DT's punch carried enough force on its own because next thing I knew, DT had his arms wrapped around Hock as he dragged him outside.

First time all night I'd seen Darla out of sorts. "DT! Where are you guys taking him?"

"Fishing," Jay said. He had his gun in his hand quicker than a coral snake could sink its fangs into your ankle. "Leave Lulu on her rack, Artie."

Artie held up both of his hands. I did the same.

Jay looked at the two college girls. "You coming?"

"Hell, no." Candi said. She clung to Darla.

"All right." Jay said. He lowered the gun but kept its barrel forward. "No cops, Artie. Goes for all of you." Jay went out the door.

"Sonofabitch." Artie said. The phone was in his hand before the glass door swung closed. Did Jay really think we weren't going to call the police?

Hock's SUV was still in the lot when the Lee County sheriffs arrived. Jay's Bronco was not. The deputies questioned Darla and Candi who played like they hardly knew Jay or DT. I went back inside with Artie. A few minutes later the two girls came in as well.

"I called for ride," Darla said. "Can we wait in here?"

"That's fine," Artie said. "But I'm locking the door."

Artie brewed up some coffee. He pulled the chain on the open sign and the light flickered off and the room fell quiet the way the frogs quieted when they sensed danger. I never realized the open sign buzzed until Artie turned it off.

Took only an hour or so but eventually a pair of headlights washed over the parking lot. Darla stood up and nudged her blond friend Candi who slept with her head down on a table the way I used to in math class. Face down over folded arms. Lot of good that choice in learning did me. Sleeping, I mean.

Darla went to the door. She started to twist the lock but stopped. She stepped back.

Candi lifted her head. "What is it?"

"It's not Tammy."

"Then who is it?" Candi's voice cracked.

Darla trembled. "I think they're back."

Artie came around the bar holding Lulu. I stood up, backed down along the rail away from the door and out of Lulu' path. Darla and Candi wrapped their arms around each other and hid between the two pool tables. Artie went up to the door, one hand on the hurricane bar and the other on Lulu's dual triggers.

"Sonofabitch," Artie said.

Candi sobbed. Darla pulled her closer. "Is it them?"

Artie unlocked the door.

The two young women screamed. "What are you doing?"

Artie held the door opened and looked around the lot. Hock came in covered in mud, his clothes still wet and smelling of swamp. Artie pulled the door shut and locked it again.

"You don't have to worry, buddy," Hock said. "Those guys aren't coming back tonight." He sat down at the bar. Artie went back behind it. I moved back to my seat. Hock rested his elbows on the bar and put his face in his hands the way a man full of regrets might.

"You still open?" Hock asked. He looked at himself in the mirror. His thin smile now seemed old and tired. All of that earlier cockiness gone. He pulled out his wallet with dirty fingers he then wiped on his pant leg.

"It's on Shel." Artie said. He set down a bottle of bourbon and a shot glass. Hock knocked back two quick ones like a pro.

"Where are they?" Darla asked.

Hock smirked. "Belly up. Just not at the bar."

"What do you mean?" Darla stepped up to him. She looked at the door. "Are they coming back?"

Hock finished a third shot and shook his head. He put the back of his hand to his lips to wipe off some spittle. "No. They're not coming back."

Candi, terrified, stared at the door. "How do you know?"

"How do I know?" Hock looked at the two girls, then at Artie, and then at me. "Ever hear of a fish called the devil goonch?"

He knew we had. We told him. Hock stared coldly at us and it was right about then I got that kind of nervous twitch in my gut. The kind of twitch that says your subconscious picked up on something you didn't.

What Charlie Hock told us justified that twitch.

"Your boys took me for a ride to teach me a thing or two, as DT put it. DT drove. Jay rode side saddle keeping his gun on me. They thought I hustled them. I reminded them they invited me to play. They wanted to know why I was in West Shore."

"Why are you in West Shore?" Artie asked.

"Business," Hock said. He poured another bourbon. The man didn't have to spell it out for Artie or me.

"But where are DT and Jaybird?" Candi asked.

Hock smiled patiently.

"I swear to all of you here," Hock said. "I've seen sharks that weren't as big as that devil goonch."

" . . . Oh my God . . ." Candi grabbed her stomach like she'd felt it twitch.

"They hauled me out on a wooden boardwalk that ran along some lake. They stopped me at a spot where the split rail fence had some give. Jay told DT to give it a push to loosen it more. DT got soft feet. Said the joke was over. Jay said he wasn't joking. DT said, 'We got our money and his. Just leave him here. Rangers will find him in the morning.' Well that pissed off Jay. He pointed the gun at DT. 'He'll tell the rangers who we are, dumbass.' That pissed off DT. The two started fighting. The gun went off. The split rail gave. The dead one pulled the living one into the lake."

"Bullshit," Darla said.

Hock smiled. "Must've been that splash that woke the devil goonch because there it was swallowing DT's legs. Swallowed him right up to the chest. That fish jerked its head to the left and then to the right and then to the left then stopped so that DT looked directly at me. I thought DT was dead until he opened his mouth and said, 'Mommy?' That's something I'll never unsee."

"What happened to Jay?" Candi was getting close to hysterics. I thought Darla was going to slap her.

Hock sent someone a text. "Don't know what else to tell you." Hock knocked back his last shot. "That's what happened." I think he was trying to steady a little tremor in his hand.

"I don't believe it." Darla said. "Jay and DT grew up around here. They know the Fakahatchee and they know the gulf."

"Yeah. They said they were going to take us out on a boat," Candi said.

"Neither of them owned a boat." Artie said.

"Yeah, well, they didn't say whose boat. They just said a boat." Candi kept watching the door. Headlights lit her face. "Tammy's here."

"About effing time," Darla said.

Artie unlocked the door. Darla thanked him for letting her and Candi wait inside. She gave Hock one last look and then left.

"I should get going too." Hock said. "I smell like a skunk ape."

"Don't you think you should tell the sheriff what happened?" Artie asked.

"Shel doesn't want any connection to the disappearance of those two trouble makers."

"You know Shel?"

"Never met him. Well, face to face that is."

"We all saw what happened. Shit." Artie thought about what he said. His hand went below the bar.

"Leave Lulu alone, Artie."

Artie looked at me like he forgot I was there. Hock kept his eyes on Artie.

"Two days from now when someone cares enough to report one or both of them missing, a sheriff or a deputy will show up. They'll ask the two of you if those boys were here on this night and you'll say—" He pointed at me, his finger and thumb making a gun.

"Yeah. I saw them. They were shooting pool with a couple of girls. One was a brunette. One was a blonde. Good-looking girls. Too smart for those idiots. The boys got into a disagreement with the girls and left. The girls called for a ride. Ain't seen none of them since."

"Bull's eye." Hock said. He tossed me DT's keys. "I'm betting you know a guy who will know what to do."

"I know a couple of guys."

"Don't shop it around. Dump it quick. Cash is yours."

"I appreciate that."

I think all that talk bothered Artie somewhat. He pointed at the black bubble in the ceiling tile. "You guys are forgetting the security camera."

Hock shook his head. "Shel turned it off before he left. He's upgrading. Had to shut down the old system."

"How do you know so much about Shel if you never even met him?"

"I said I never met him face to face." Hock stood up. "Look. You're going to tell the cops what you saw. I get that. But all you can tell them about me is I was a guy from Detroit those two bubbas tried to make disappear after he took their money playing pool. Or you can keep it simple. Go with this guy's story. I mean, I'm covered in swamp muck. Can you even describe me, Artie?"

Mr. Detroit brought a gun out from under his shirt and laid it on the bar. It was Jay's gun. Mr. Detroit's backup plan. Robbery gone bad, maybe. At least he didn't have to execute it or us.

"Describe who?" Hearing Mr. Detroit say his name probably spooked Artie more than Jay's gun.

It was almost like I could hear the frogs croaking from the swamp. The danger passed. That twitch in my stomach was gone and so was Mr. Detroit.

Artie and I stood there for a few minutes before we went out to DT's four-door pickup truck. I dropped down the tailgate on the cap-covered payload. I think we both expected to find Jay and DT tied up with duct tape over their mouths.

The truck bed was empty.

Artie stepped back. "What kind of business does this guy do?"

"The kind that's none of yours." I said. "I'll tell you this, though."

"Yeah? What's that?"

"The devil goonch ate well tonight." I closed the tailgate.

Artie laughed. "You and I both know there isn't any goonch out in the Fakahatchee Preserve big enough to eat a couple of full grown men."

"You know what, Arnie? There is now." I got in the driver's seat.

"Wait a minute. What are you doing?"

"You heard what I said. If DT and Jay left, DT's truck can't be here."

"So what are you going to do with it?"

"I know a guy, right?"

Artie started to get it. "Is that guy you?"

"See ya in a few days, Artie. When I get back we'll go fishing."

Artie didn't find that as funny as I did.

THE CASE OF THE MISSING POT ROAST
BY BARB GOFFMAN

LOOKING BACK, I SHOULD HAVE known something was wrong when the pot roast disappeared. Sure, everyone misplaces something sometime. I once searched for the remote control for an hour till I spotted it in the bathroom. And for years I've found my husband, Charles's, false teeth all over the house—they've never fit quite right so when they bother him he takes them out and puts them down, never paying attention where. But the pot roast? I was sure I'd left it defrosting on the counter when I went to get my hair done, yet when I came home, it was gone.

I searched for it in vain. It wasn't in the fridge or freezer. Not in the garbage. Not in the oven. Charles was clueless. There was no way he'd cooked and eaten it in the hour I was gone. So what happened to that pot roast was a mystery. In the back of my mind, I wondered if I'd only dreamed I'd bought the roast. But I couldn't admit my faculties might be failing. So I dismissed the missing pot roast as weirdness and whipped up some pasta.

That was a month ago. Perhaps if I'd forced myself to figure out what happened to the pot roast, I wouldn't be in this position now. But back then, I had bigger problems. Charles had started suffering from short-term memory loss and personality changes, and he was getting worse every day. One minute he'd be the man I'd loved for decades, optimistic and kind; the next, he'd be surly and paranoid, acting like a wary stranger. He'd accused me of stealing from him—me, his wife of fifty-one years. And then, in a heartbreaking moment, he'd accused me of trying to kill him.

"Alzheimer's," his doctor had diagnosed.

I'd figured that was the problem, but having it confirmed was a terrible blow. His doctor gave me all kinds of pamphlets and urged me to look into long-term care for Charles. I cried when he did that. I knew eventually such care would be necessary. But not yet. I was only seventy-one years old and in relatively good health. I was determined to care for Charles in our home for as long as I could. He was my husband. My love. I owed him that.

* * *

A WEEK AFTER THE POT roast vanished, I came back from the library late one afternoon with a stack of books—Charles and I both loved to read—and found him banging his fist against the wall of windows on our lanai. Charles's mind might have been fading, but his body was strong. I feared he'd break the glass.

"Charles, stop!"

"You stay away from me!" he screamed at the window. "You'll never get me!"

I stared outside. Our house backed to a lake, with a golf course on the other side of it. We had a good view of the fifth tee. But no one was out there right then.

"Charles, who are you talking to?"

He veered toward me and began muttering and pacing. "He wants to kill me. Wants me dead."

My eyes watered. "No one wants you dead, darling."

"Are you blind, woman? He's right there, taunting me." He pointed toward the lake. "Romeo!"

I looked closer. Charles was partly right. Romeo, the alligator who lived in the lake, was floating out there, his snout skimming the water's surface. But Romeo wasn't taunting Charles. How could he? And he certainly didn't want Charles dead. Alligators can live just fine with people as neighbors as long as we don't feed or disturb them. It was a blessing, I realized, that our backyard sloped down to the water. Because of his bad knee, Charles would never walk down to the lake because the incline made him unsteady, so I didn't have to worry he'd bother Romeo.

I approached Charles. "Let's go in other room. I got us some great books to read."

The doctor had said that when Charles became agitated, I should try to remove the source of his stress. It broke my heart that Romeo was a new source of stress for Charles. He'd always loved that alligator. All wildlife, in fact. It was one of the reasons we'd retired to southwest Florida, near the Everglades. There was so much wildlife around.

"No. If I don't watch him, he'll come after me."

"That's not going to happen." I laid my hand on Charles's arm. "C'mon. I've got the newest Adrian McKinty."

"No!" he yelled and pushed me hard.

I fell back, slamming against a table before landing on my side on the tile floor. Sparks of pain exploded from my hip. I screamed.

After I lay there for a couple of minutes gritting my teeth, I looked up to find Charles standing over me. His eyes were wide. Concerned. "Bev, what happened? Are you okay?"

My Charles was back. "Call an ambulance," I said.

The paramedics arrived quickly, and Charles let them in. He was like his old self. Polite and caring. When they asked what happened, I told them I'd tripped and fallen. I didn't want Charles to be blamed. He'd never have hurt me if he was in his right mind. Besides, he didn't even seem to remember doing it.

The good news, we learned a few hours later, was that my hip wasn't broken. All those calcium pills I'd been taking for years had paid off. But I was badly bruised. The doctor recommended rest and medication for pain and swelling. The hospital gave me a cane for support.

I was relieved to go home and sleep beside my husband that night. When you're my age and you land in the hospital, terrible thoughts flit through your mind. Is this the beginning of the end? Will I need to go into an assisted living facility? Or worse? What would happen to Charles? I desperately wanted us to stay together in our own home.

So the next morning, I pulled out the pamphlets Charles's doctor had given me. If we were going to continue living independently, we'd have to hire some in-home care, at least until I got better. I called one of the services that provided aides. The next afternoon, Gabriela arrived.

She was about twenty-five years old, tall, and lean. She wore her wavy, dark hair in a bun, had a friendly smile, and seemed eager to help. Immediately she had a good way with Charles. I'd been afraid any aide we'd hire would treat Charles like an invalid, but Gabriela treated him like family, and Charles responded positively. We agreed she'd come each day at three for an eight-hour shift. Alzheimer's patients tend to get worse as the day goes on, so it made sense for her to start mid-afternoon. I could handle Charles each day until then, especially since Gabriela would help with the cooking and cleaning, so I wouldn't have to put pressure on my hip doing those chores. All in all, she was a godsend.

* * *

"THAT'S A BEAUTIFUL PIN," MY friend Margaret said, nodding toward a porcelain butterfly I'd clasped to my shirt where I usually wore my favorite cameo—a gift Charles had given me years ago. We were at the country club playing bridge with Lois and Anita two weeks after I hired Gabriela.

"Thank you." I picked up my new hand, hoping Margaret wouldn't ask about my cameo. She had an uncanny ability of raising the one issue you'd like to avoid.

"What made you change?" Margaret said. "You always wear your cameo."

Darn it. My cameo had disappeared two days ago. I'd debated not wearing any pin today, but of course Margaret would have picked up on that too. I shrugged and bid.

"Come on, Bev," she said. "Why the secrecy? Did it break?"

Lois glared at her. Chat during bridge was frowned upon, but Margaret acted as if she hadn't noticed and kept staring at me, clearly waiting for an answer. I felt like she somehow already knew the truth.

"If you must know, I misplaced it," I said, hoping that would be the end of it.

"You misplaced it?" Margaret quickly bid, then returned her attention to me. "You never misplace anything."

This was true, as far as Margaret knew. I hadn't told her—or anyone—about the pot roast. I didn't want people to think I was losing it. I shrugged again, trying to concentrate on my cards. We began to play the hand, and the talk died down. But as soon as we tallied the score, Margaret started in on me again.

"How are things working out with that girl you hired?"

"Just fine," I said.

Margaret's eyes narrowed. "Just fine, huh? And it's just a coincidence that right after you allowed this girl to start roaming around your house, your beautiful cameo goes missing?"

I felt my cheeks flush. When I'd mentioned the prior week that I'd hired Gabriela, Margaret had pounced, warning me not to trust her. "They all steal," she'd said. I'd defended Gabriela, telling Margaret she was a nice woman, and that it was wrong to generalize like that. But of course now my cameo had disappeared.

"Margaret, it's your turn to deal." Lois sounded annoyed.

"Chill," Margaret said. Her granddaughter had taught her that term a few months before, and Margaret loved to use it. "Bev is in crisis. We need to help her."

I pursed my lips. I wasn't in crisis. "You don't need to worry. I've got everything under control."

Margaret snorted. "If I were you, Bev, I'd keep a close eye on that girl. First she'll steal your jewelry. Next it'll be your husband."

* * *

I WAS SO AGGRAVATED BY Margaret's comment that I left the club early and drove home. Sometimes I couldn't stand Margaret. She was such a negative busybody. Gabriela was no femme fatale. I must have misplaced my cameo. Or the clasp broke, and I lost it. Either way, Gabriela surely hadn't stolen it. I wasn't going to become one of those people who believed the worst of everyone else.

The house was still as I walked in. I spotted Charles sleeping on a lounge chair on the lanai, so I stepped quietly into our bedroom to search once more for my cameo. But I stopped short, squeezing my cane hard. Gabriela was standing on the far side of the room, reaching for my jewelry box.

"Gabriela?"

She twirled toward me, her mouth ajar.

"I . . . how is Charles?" I asked. I was so embarrassed that Margaret had been right—Gabriela was stealing from me!—that I couldn't bring myself to confront her about it.

"He's having a good afternoon," she said with a smile. "I didn't expect you home so soon."

I could tell. "My hip was bothering me."

"Oh, I'm sorry. Anything I can do to help?"

"No, nothing."

I went to sit on the lanai, feeling so foolish. I'd trusted Gabriela. Given her a key to my home. Let her—as Margaret said—roam my house. I should fire her. But Gabriela had such a good way with Charles. He lit up around her. I had to think about him, about what was best for Charles. If Gabriela helped him, then I could put up with a stolen cameo. Tomorrow morning I'd put our valuables in our safety deposit box. Everything else Gabriela could have. It would be worth it.

* * *

THE BIRDS WERE CHIRPING EARLY the next morning, and Charles was in a good mood. After breakfast he went onto the lanai to read the newspaper, and I went into our bedroom to go through my jewelry and decide what to bring to the bank. I opened the box, and my hand flew to my mouth. My cameo was sitting in the top tray. Not in its usual spot, but it was there.

I backed up and sat on my bed. Gabriela hadn't gone anywhere near the jewelry box again yesterday. I'd kept my eye on her. So the cameo must have been there the whole time. How had I missed it?

I bit my lip, suddenly afraid that Charles wasn't the only one with dementia. Then I shook my head. *Snap out of it, Bev. One misplaced cameo doesn't mean you're losing it.* Besides, it was a huge relief to realize my first instincts had been right. Gabriela hadn't been stealing from me. There was no reason to store my jewelry after all.

With a smile, I went out to the lanai. Charles was staring out the window as Romeo glided by.

"Isn't he beautiful?" I said.

Charles glared at me. "You say beautiful. I say deadly."

It felt as if a dark cloud had suddenly blocked the sun. My Charles was slipping away again, replaced by this fearful man. I had to find a way to improve both our moods.

"How about I cook a nice dinner tonight? Pot roast with onion, carrots, and the little potatoes you love?" My hip was hardly stiff anymore, and the cane really helped, so I could do it.

"Pot roast?" Charles grinned as bright as a full moon reflecting off the lake. "That's a perfect idea."

"Wonderful. I'll go pull one out of the freezer."

I set the roast on the kitchen counter to defrost, then returned to the lanai to read. I used to read only dark mysteries, but since Charles had gotten sick, I'd found myself gravitating to lighter cozies. They made me feel better. A few times as I turned the page, I caught Charles watching me out of the corner of his eye and smiling. I was so glad that the decision to cook one of his favorite meals had improved his mood. And mine. It was going to be a good day after all.

* * *

AROUND TWO THIRTY, I WENT to Publix to pick up the vegetables for our dinner. Charles was still doing well, and Gabriela would be arriving soon in case he needed anything.

I returned home an hour later, eager to start cooking. I always loved how the house smelled after the roast went into the oven. Gabriela met me at the door and carried the groceries into the kitchen.

"Mmm. These carrots look good," she said. "What would you like me to make for dinner?"

"No need," I replied, setting my purse on the counter. "I'm feeling spry today, so *I'm* going to cook the roast."

"What roast?" Gabriela stared into the bag she'd just emptied.

"That one." I pointed to the side counter, where I'd left the pot roast. Except it wasn't there. I blinked repeatedly and quickly scanned every counter in the kitchen. No roast. Charles's teeth were sitting out, but no pot roast. I looked at the table. Not there either.

Had I left it defrosting in the sink? Not there. Maybe it was in the refrigerator. No, it wasn't in there either. Not in the freezer. Not anywhere.

"Bev, are you all right?" Gabriela asked.

"I don't understand," I cried. "It was here. I left it right there!" I pointed again at the counter.

"There wasn't any roast sitting out when I arrived," Gabriela said softly.

"No. That can't be. Charles," I called. He ambled in from the lanai and grabbed his teeth. "Have you seen the pot roast?"

"What pot roast?"

"The roast I'm supposed to make for dinner. The one I set out to defrost."

"You didn't set any roast out."

My heart began pounding. Charles was looking at me vacantly. His memory wasn't necessarily trustworthy, but Gabriela's was. She stared at me with concern, her forehead wrinkling. Was I going crazy? How had a second pot roast disappeared?

Tears splashed my cheeks as I hurried to my bedroom. I slammed the door, lay down, and cried. At one point I rolled over. Charles wasn't there to hold me, so I hugged his pillow instead.

Something hard pressed against my arm. Confused, I turned the pillow sideways and shook its case. One of my gold necklaces slid out onto the bed. Oh my stars. I didn't even remember wearing it recently, but I must have, and instead of putting it away in the jewelry box, I'd put it in the pillowcase.

It was true. I was losing my mind, just like Charles.

* * *

My mood over the next few days matched the weather: dark and dreary. A hurricane was coming. The newscasters advised people in our area to evacuate. All of our neighbors were leaving, but Charles was being obstinate, not wanting to go. Considering I could barely get out of bed, I had no energy to fight him.

"Don't worry," I told Gabriela over a tuna salad dinner. "We'll be fine."

She looked doubtful.

"We've been through storms before. They say this will only be a category three. A little one. We'll latch down the hurricane shutters and ride it out."

"The words *little* and *hurricane* seem like an oxymoron," Gabriela said.

"Look how smart she is." Charles beamed at Gabriela. "Bev's right. Everything's going to be just fine. Don't you worry your pretty, pretty head."

Gabriela looked from Charles to me and sighed. "If you say so."

* * *

I SPENT THE EVENING READING on the lanai, trying to distract myself from my worries, while Charles kept staring out into the darkness. Gabriela was busy as a bee, making meals to get us through the storm, replacing batteries in the flashlights, and picking up refills of Charles's medication. She was like the daughter we'd never had, and I was ashamed I'd ever doubted her.

Charles went to sleep around ten. An hour later, right before leaving, Gabriela came over and sat beside me.

"Please don't stay here during the storm," she pleaded.

"We'll be—"

She held up her hand. "I know. You think you'll be fine. You've been through storms before."

I nodded.

"But you haven't been through storms before with an Alzheimer's patient. Between the wind and the rain, Charles might become very agitated. You're in no position to help him or protect yourself should he become aggressive."

"Charles would never hurt me," I said, even as the day he pushed me down flashed through my mind.

Gabriela laid her hand on top of mine. "I'm worried about you too."

She was referring to the pot roast, I knew, but she didn't say the words. "I'm all right. I get a little confused sometimes."

"Have you told your doctor?"

"Not yet." Gabriela squeezed my hand. "I'll tell him. I promise. After the storm's over."

Nodding, she pulled a piece of paper from her pocket. "This is the phone number and address of the local Red Cross, in case you need help. I'm heading home to pack, and then I'm driving to my sister's in Jacksonville. I'll be back as soon as I can after the storm. And I'll try to call to check on you."

"Thank you, Gabriela."

She kissed my cheek, and in mere moments she was gone.

* * *

Gabriela had been right about the storm riling Charles up. He usually was easygoing in the morning, but the next morning, after I showered, I found him pacing on the lanai. The hurricane had sped up during the night, and the moaning wind was whipping leaves off the palm trees out back.

"Where have you been?" he demanded. "Who were you with?"

"I was just getting dressed," I said calmly, hoping to soothe him.

"You're lying. You're all twitchy. You're hiding something."

I stifled a sigh. The only thing I was trying to hide was my sadness.

"We should pull the hurricane shutters down before the wind gets worse," I said.

Charles shook his head and blocked the door. "No, it's not time yet."

As if there were a set time. But okay. The shutters could wait. Best to calm him down first.

"How about I get you some water. Maybe you're thirsty." I pushed a plastic cup under the fridge's water dispenser, hating the tone I'd used in my voice. I was treating my husband like a child. But I didn't know what else to do when he got like this.

I held the cup out to him as I stepped back onto the lanai, and he knocked it out of my hand. "You're trying to poison me! I saw you put something in there."

"Water." I sighed. "The only thing in that cup was water."

I sopped up the mess with a towel, then threw it into the hamper. When I returned, Charles seemed calmer. He was staring out toward the rippling lake.

I decided to make use of it. "I wonder what happens to the fish during a storm. If they were in the ocean, they could swim somewhere safe, but here, they're stuck."

I hoped focusing on wildlife would bring my Charles back, but he merely grunted.

Okay. I'd try a different tack. "Look at all those birds." There were so many moving in tandem that the sky seemed to be swaying. "They must know something's up."

"Now!" Charles said. "We need to pull the shutters down now."

Talk about mental whiplash. "All right."

"Hurry. It's time."

I grabbed my cane, wanting to be sure I'd remain steady on the grass. Then I pulled the sliding glass door open and stepped outside, with Charles practically pushing me onto the patio. It had already started raining, and the sweet smell of ozone hit me. I paused a moment to breathe it in.

"You should grab the birds first," he said.

We had three small iron statues of pelicans standing in the soil surrounding some of our trees. They each weighed about eight pounds, so they could fly about in a strong wind and strike the house. We'd brought them in before previous storms, and the wind was already gusting.

Halfway down the lawn, I reached for the first pelican. That's when someone shoved me. I fell on my bad hip and rolled a few times down the incline, stopping several yards from the water. I cried out, but no one would be able to hear me over the wind, even if anyone were around. Which they weren't. Everyone with sense had evacuated. Everyone but me and my husband, who was now standing over me with a gleam in his eye.

"You want to kill me, but I won't let you," he said.

Sharp pain prevented me from sitting up. "I don't want to kill you. I love you. Look at me." Charles's attention had turned to the lake. I shook his pant leg. "Look at me."

He did.

"It's me. Bev. Your wife. I love you."

"No, you've been trying to kill me because you know I've found someone else."

Someone else? "There's no one else. Not for you or for me. Please, Charles, help me up."

"There is! The pretty girl. Where is she? Why isn't she here now?"

The world spun for a moment. "Gabriela?"

"What did you do to her?"

"I didn't do anything to her. She's gone to her sister's place until the storm passes."

"When she comes back, you'll be gone, and I'll be able to give her everything she deserves." He reached into his pants pocket and pulled out my cameo.

"*You* took my cameo?"

"It's not yours. It's mine. I paid for it. And I can give it to anyone I want to."

The rain was picking up. I had to get back into the house. I tried to crawl but only moved a few feet before my screaming hip stopped me. My cane remained out of reach. Why had I thought I could care for Charles on my own? Why hadn't I insisted we evacuate? What was I going to do?

Calm yourself, Bev. Charles will snap out of this eventually, and then he'll help you up. You just need to wait.

In bad times, I often gave myself a good talking to. And as usual, it worked. I took a deep breath and hoped my Charles would return soon, before the storm really intensified.

"There's my pretty boy," Charles said.

Pretty boy?

I followed Charles's gaze. Romeo had emerged from the lake and was slowly crawling toward me. Alligators often sought dry land like our patio during storms. As long as we didn't bother them, they shouldn't bother us. Of course, that was easier to believe when I wasn't lying there defenseless.

"C'mon, boy," Charles said. "I've got lunch for you. I know she won't be as delicious as those roasts I tossed to you over the last few weeks, but she does have some meat on her bones."

In that moment time seemed to stop. I hadn't been going crazy. Charles had accused me of stealing from him, but he'd really been stealing from me. The necklace and the cameo and the pot roasts too. He'd been feeding Romeo, which meant the alligator would likely come after me now. He'd be used to humans and see me as easy prey. Charles had accused me of trying to kill him, when really that had been his plan all along for me.

I grabbed his pant leg and shook it with everything I had. "Charles!" I screamed as the rain mixed with the tears streaming down my face. "Charles. It's Bev. I'm hurt. Help me!"

I had to get through to him before Romeo reached me. "Charles!"

Romeo was only a few yards away. *Oh, God, please help me.*

At that moment something zoomed over my head, landing a few feet from Romeo. It began tumbling toward the water before easing to a stop in the grass. What the heck? It was a pot roast. Romeo snapped it up and slid back into the lake. I twisted toward the house as Gabriela rushed to us, her hair pasted against her cheeks.

Charles's eyes bulged. "What'd you do that for? You've ruined everything."

Gabriela smiled gently. "Nothing's ruined. Everything's going to be fine. But you need to go back inside, and I have to help Bev."

"Help her? You're on *her* side? You're all against me!"

Charles lunged at Gabriela, his hands tightening around her throat. As she tried to fight him off, I used all my strength to inch up the lawn and grab my cane. My hip felt like it was on fire while I pushed myself into a sitting position and swung the cane as hard as I could at the back of Charles's bad knee. He cried out in pain and fell. Gabriela stumbled backward, wheezing.

With my strength spent, I flopped onto the grass as the rain poured and Charles moaned. Soon Gabriela kneeled by my side.

"Are you all right?" she asked.

"Me? What about you?"

She squeezed my hand. "I think we'll both be okay. I've called an ambulance."

I stared at her, my guardian angel. "Not that I'm complaining, but what are you doing here?"

"I got halfway to Jacksonville before I turned around. I was the only idiot on the highway heading toward the coast. But I couldn't let you stay here alone. I thought you'd need me, though I didn't realize how much."

"How could you know?" She had no reason to suspect Charles was violent. Few Alzheimer's patients were.

Gabriela nodded. "Charles gave me a cameo a few weeks ago. He said it was a promise pin, until we could be together. I should have told you, but I didn't realize what he'd planned. I thought it was a crush, and I didn't want to hurt you."

"So the day I caught you by my jewelry box?"

"I'd just put the cameo back inside."

"And the pot roast just now?"

"I grabbed it at Publix an hour ago, right before they closed. I figured I'd make it for dinner tonight if the electricity held out. You've been trying to have one for weeks."

At that I laughed until tears sprang from my eyes. For the first time in months, they were tears of happiness.

* * *

CHARLES AND I BOTH SPENT the storm in the hospital, and Gabriela didn't leave our side. It turned out the hurricane wasn't as bad as had been predicted, which was good, because we never got our shutters in place.

Our home is now up for sale. Gabriela's living there, taking care of it until it sells. Charles and I have moved into an assisted living facility. He's in the memory-care unit, where he can get the attention he needs. And I'm in a small apartment where I can get help when I need it, which I sometimes do because of my hip.

I don't get to sleep next to my husband every night anymore, but I do get to see him every day, and that's enough. I'd made a huge mistake trying to care for Charles on my own. I'd said I was doing it for him, so he could have the continuity of living at home, but really, I'd been doing it for me. I was the one who didn't want things to change. And I'd nearly paid for my selfishness with my life. At least now I don't have to worry that Charles is trying to kill me. He's taken a shine to one of his new nurses, and I don't interfere.

As for Romeo, I hear he's been spotted near Margaret's place. She likes to eat on her patio at night. I'm thinking of sending her a pot roast.

HOW TO HANDLE A SHOVEL

BY CRAIG PITTMAN

THE GREEN FORD PICKUP TRUCK jounced along the washboard road, a cloud of dust swirling in its wake. The radio was on. Carrie Underwood faded in and out of the static like she was about to disappear.

Billy, the skinny kid sitting in the passenger seat, peered over his shoulder into the bed of the truck to check on their load. As the truck rumbled on, the twelve gopher tortoises were bouncing around in their shells and probably wondering what the hell happened to them.

The driver, a heavyset man everybody called J.T., noticed what Billy was doing and smiled to himself.

"It ain't fair," Billy said, turning back around.

A sunburn blossomed on Billy's cheeks. The wind from the open truck window plucked at his straw-colored hair. Sweat bled through his T-shirt, and globs of dirt stuck to his ragged sneakers and the sweaty parts of his shirt and faded jeans. It even adhered in spots where the sweat had run down his face, creating splotches of salty mud.

"What ain't fair?" asked J.T. He wore a sweat-stained camo cap pulled down low on his bald head. His short sleeve shirt strained at its buttons. It had once been dark blue but it had faded until it matched the sky. J.T. kept the shirttail untucked to accommodate his bulk, and now it lay across his lap like a tablecloth, parted in the middle for the spit cup he held between his meaty thighs. J.T.'s graying beard started around his earlobes and hung down to his belly like a pennant, and around one side of his mouth were a few stray flecks of tobacco. He kept his sun-baked elbow leaning on the truck window, steering with two fingers on his left hand. With his right, he grabbed the cup and held it up to spit a stream of brown juice into it, still keeping his eyes on the road. Then he shoved the cup back where it had been.

"What ain't fair is how I'm doin' all the work and takin' all the risk, and you keep on about all the money, that's what," Billy said. He knew he sounded like a whiner. He didn't care. He was just trying to persuade J.T. one more time to hand over his money before he was forced to off the fat man.

Billy spit a stream of tobacco out the window. He knew J.T. didn't like finding tobacco juice splattered on his fender. They had discussed it twice already, a week ago. Today, he did it anyway. He wasn't concerned about keeping J.T. happy anymore, just with keeping him distracted until Billy found the right time to kill him.

From the corner of his eye J.T. saw what Billy did, knew it was done on purpose. J.T. kept the anger out of his voice anyway, used the same tone of voice he used when his little snot-nosed grandkids didn't listen to him.

"We been over this—how many times now, Billy?" he rasped. "Sure, you the one down in the hole pulling out the gophers. That's 'cause you're still young and strong and quick. But *I'm* the one knows where the burrows is, and I'm the one that knows where the buyers is, and I'm the one showed you how to hook them gophers and get 'em out in the first place. Seems to me a 70-30 split's more than fair."

Suddenly J.T. glanced over at Billy with narrowed eyes.

"Anyway, what risk you talkin' about?" he asked. "Cops after you? Somethin' you need to tell me about?"

"No, man, ain't no cops," Billy said, and spit out the window again, twisting his body so J.T. wouldn't see him fingering the switchblade in his pants pocket, making sure it would be easy to reach when he was ready. "I'm talking about all the snakes down in them burrows. I'm liable to get bit and we out here in the scrub miles from any doctor."

J.T. chuckled, spit in his cup. "Boy, them rattlers ain't studyin' you. They out lookin' for food and you too scrawny. Listen, you want to talk about risk? I'm the one takin' a risk. I'm already on probation for two counts of illegal possession of gopher tortoises. We get pulled over, I'm looking at felony jail time."

J.T. spit. "It ain't *my* fault them gophers is endangered. It ain't us gopher hunters that put 'em on the list. It's all them developers that wrote a big check to the state so they could get permits to pave over the burrows and suffocate 'em. But who's all them grouper troopers after? Me."

"Naw, they just want you 'cause you got such a sweet personality," Billy joked. "You're the girl of their dreams."

J.T. snorted. "More like a nightmare, you ask me. I never did have much use for cops, and right now I want to avoid 'em at all costs."

"Now hold on. Ain't your nephew a wildlife officer?" Billy nodded at his own statement. "Yeah, I seen his picture on the news. They were callin' him a hero for shootin' that crazy guy waving a machete around tryin' to kill some woman."

"Some hero," J.T. said, frowning. "Knife versus gun, the gun's gonna win every time, ain't it? Don't matter how big the knife is."

Billy wasn't sure how to take that. He knew J.T. kept a sawed-off shotgun tucked under the driver's seat for killing any rattlers they might run across. That's why Billy had already decided to wait to kill him outside the truck. Now he casually looked J.T. over, checking for a telltale bulge from a pistol tucked somewhere. He only saw the regular bulges of fat, so he decided it was safe to tease J.T. a little more.

"So was you the one who talked your nephew into goin' into law enforcement? Figured you'd get you a source on the inside?"

"Haaaaaaayyyy-ell no," J.T. said, and spit. "When his daddy died, I took that boy out in the woods and taught him everything I know. Showed him how to hook gophers and pick palmetto berries and dig up a loggerhead nest to collect all the eggs, and how to keep clear of the law while you're doin' it. I showed him how to live off the land just like I do, just the way my daddy did and his daddy before him. I even give him a share from everything we hauled in so he could help support his mama. So what did he do when he grew up? He got *religion*." His voice took on a mocking tone. "He said *Jesus* didn't want him breakin' the law, Jesus wanted him to *enforce* the law!" J.T spit again, and followed that up with a few choice words.

"On the other hand," J.T. added with a sideways look at his passenger, "if it hadn't been for that, I wouldn't have any need of *you*, now would I, Billy?"

"Guess so," Billy said. "But there's another reason why you oughta cut me in for more of the profit."

Before he could start in, J.T. was already shaking his head.

"Listen, I know you need money, Billy. But it ain't my fault you got sloppy and got caught selling pain pills at the phosphate mine and lost your day job. And it ain't my fault you're in Dutch to ol' Hermano as a result."

Billy swallowed hard, trying to keep a poker face. He didn't know J.T. knew that he'd lost his job.

J.T. gave him a slow smile that showed off yellow teeth and plenty of gaps. "I saw how you was looking at my roll when I paid for the ice for the beer cooler. But I ain't runnin' a charity here."

"Well if you ain't gonna give me more of the money, how about you pickin' up some more of the work?" Billy asked, an idea dawning on him. "How about you do the hookin' this time?"

J.T. was silent for a few miles, mulling it over and then said, "OK, tell you what. You hook him, and we'll split the diggin'."

Now it was Billy's turn to snort.

"I don't believe I've ever seen you handle a shovel, J.T."

"Shit, I been handling a shovel since before you was born, boy. I know how to handle a shovel."

J.T. spun the wheel, turning the truck down a short dirt path among a stand of spindly pine trees. He stopped the truck in front of a padlocked metal gate and handed a slip of paper to his passenger.

"Here's the combination. Don't dawdle—we don't want to be tryin' to find our way outta here after dark."

Billy hopped out, unlocked the gate and swung it open. After J.T. drove through, he closed and locked it again, then climbed back into the truck, wiping his palms on his jeans. His palms were sweaty because he knew the time for sticking J.T. with his knife was close. He'd used the knife a couple times in barroom fights, doing some damage but nothing fatal. He'd never killed a man in cold blood before, and he could feel his nerves twanging like a clothesline in a high wind.

J.T. drove more slowly now, the truck yawing and teetering across a series of gouged-out holes as they crept between hammocks of twisted oaks and thick stands of prickly pears. Scrub jays chirped in alarm and flew away, and an armadillo that had been scouring the ground like an armored vacuum cleaner quickly scurried back into the brush.

"How you even know about this place?" Billy yelled as the truck's springs creaked and groaned. "We so far out now it's like we done drove to Mexico."

J.T. stopped the truck at a clearing in the oaks, turned off the engine and twisted sideways to look Billy full on.

"It's them developers," he explained. "All these places we been to this week was supposed to be turned into little cul-de-sac houses set around a big ol' golf course. The developers' wrote the checks and got permits to pave over the gopher burrows, but then they run out of money to even clear the land. So these gophers, they been living on borrowed time anyway. A fella I know had a map showing all these places where they had permits already and suggested I could go get 'em. Ain't nobody miss these gophers we been hookin' out of their holes. We get this one here and we're done for today."

"Even this place way out here in the boonies? They was gonna build some golf course place out here too?"

"Yep, it was gonna be a whole new city out here—not just houses but choke-and-puke fast-food joints and quickie marts and what have you, just like you see all over this damn state now. Think they was gonna call it 'Renaissance' or 'Rendezvous' or somethin' French like that. Now enough yappin. Let's get to trappin'."

Billy thought this might be his chance—but then he realized J.T. was standing by the side of the truck with the door open, his shotgun in easy reach. No way to get him fast enough. Instead Billy grabbed the metal hook out of the back of the truck and walked over to the tortoise burrow. He laid down on the pine needles and fed the line into the burrow, shifting it this way and that, trying to snag his prey. Thirty minutes later he was sweatier and dirtier than he'd been before but the tortoise had avoided the hook.

"Looks like we gotta dig him out," Billy said, getting up and dusting himself off.

"Looks like," J.T. agreed, then spit. "You already dirty, so how about you take the first shift. You dig for fifteen minutes, then I'll take over."

Billy eyed him for a minute, about to object. After all, he'd been doing all the work for the past thirty minutes. But then he had an idea. He eagerly grabbed the shovel from the truck and started tossing hunks of dirt out. In fifteen minutes he had excavated enough of the burrow to stand up in. He climbed out and told J.T, "Your turn. I still ain't even seen this gopher."

Billy decided this was it. He would stick J.T. with his knife three or four times, rob him, roll the fat man's body into the hole, cover it up, and drive off in J.T.'s truck. He could sell the truck for cash and pay Hermano everything he owed, and if anybody asked, he'd claim J.T. drove off by himself and disappeared. Or he could just keep going, living on the cash as long as he could, leave everything behind and start over. He liked that idea a lot.

As J.T. reached for the shovel, Billy pulled out the switchblade, popping it open with a sharp "snick!" as it came free of his jeans, starting an upward swing at J.T.'s thick belly. Billy had a flash in his mind how this would go, the knife sliding in, a look of surprise spreading on J.T.'s face as the blood spread across his shirt, as the knife went in over and over.

But J.T. didn't stand still and take the blade, the way Billy had pictured it.

Instead, the fat man sidestepped the arc of the knife and as he did so, he tossed the empty beer bottle straight at Billy's face.

Billy flinched backward. When he did, J.T. swung the shovel at Billy's ankles, hooking the back of the blade behind his feet. Then J.T. yanked it toward him.

Billy felt his feet fly out from under him. The next thing he knew he had landed on his shoulder, hard. Dust puffed up around him, choking him, and he lost his grip on his knife. He reached for it but suddenly J.T. was standing on it, keeping it under his left boot while his right boot began kicking at Billy's ribs, over and over, hard. Billy yelped, curled up in a ball.

Suddenly it dawned on him: I'm losing a fight with a fat tub of goo. He uncurled, made a grab for J.T.'s feet, but J.T. jolted him with the hardest kick of all.

Suddenly Billy realized something was happening even worse than losing the fight. He realized J.T. wasn't just kicking him. With each kick, he was booting Billy closer to the edge of the hole. A couple more kicks and he'd be close enough to topple into it.

Billy started scrabbling in the dirt for a handhold, looking for a way to hang on. He grabbed a handful of sand to throw in J.T.'s eyes, but as he raised up to throw, J.T. planted his boot in Billy's midsection and rolled him like a log over the edge of the hole.

When Billy landed at the bottom, he landed hard. Something snapped in his left arm and he screamed.

Billy twisted around to look up, tears springing from his eyes. J.T. stood silhouetted at the edge of the hole, the glare of the sun behind him.

"Listen," J.T. said, his voice sounding far away. "You 'bout as slow as them gophers in my truck, man. I knew you was gonna jump me the minute I saw you eyeing my bankroll. Then I saw you fingering that pig-sticker at least three times today, waitin' for your chance. If it was up to me, I woulda just banged you up a little, teach you a lesson about fuckin' around with your boss. But ol' Hermano told me yesterday he wanted you gone. Said he wanted to make you an example to his other dealers about what happens when you screw up. Plus he was willing to pay good money. That roll of cash you saw? Most of that was what he paid me to get rid of you."

"What?!" Billy screamed. He didn't believe it. "You broke my fuckin' arm, man! Stop clownin' around and get me outta here! I need a doctor!"

J.T. shook his head.

"Sorry, Billy, you done. Hermano wants you gone, you gone. You been livin' on borrowed time today, just like them gophers."

Billy dug his shoulders into the dirt, trying to prop himself up. He was full-on crying now, snot running out of his nose. His voice shaking, he asked, "You gonna bury me here, let me smother to death like them gophers? Or you just gonna leave me for the rattlers to get?"

"Jesus, what kinda cruel sumbitch you think I am?" J.T. asked, sounding wounded.

He lifted his shirttails, reached under one of the rolls of fat on his belly, and pulled out a .25 caliber Browning. As he pointed it down into the hole, the chrome glinted in the rays of the setting sun. Billy screamed again and squeezed his eyes tight just as J.T. squeezed the trigger. The flat crack of the gun faded away quickly as a soft breeze riffled through the scrub oak leaves.

J.T. tucked the gun into his back pocket and started shuffling around with the shovel, raking the dirt back into the hole. He'd let this go on a little longer than it should have. He wanted to get the gophers in his truck over to Hermano's house pronto so they could be cleaned and they could have a couple for dinner—and he could get the other half of his payment.

He sighed. That Billy was an annoying little shit, but he'd miss having him around for company. He'd have to find him another new assistant. Maybe this time get one who wasn't such a fuck-up.

In ten minutes J.T. was done. He tossed one more load of dirt on top, spread it around, patted it down, then turned and headed for the truck.

"Told you I knew how to handle a shovel," J.T. muttered as he climbed behind the wheel. Then he spit.

A POSTCARD FOR THE DEAD

BY SUSANNA CALKINS

West Palm Beach, Florida
July 1921

LILY BAKER PEERED INSIDE HER mailbox before reaching in to retrieve her mail. Back when her half brother had been West Palm Beach's postmaster, he had delighted in leaving snakes in mailboxes as pranks. Of course, the last laugh had been on him, when he had died of a snake bite last Christmas.

There was only one piece of mail today, though—a postcard featuring a swanky hotel in Orlando, a city she'd never been. She turned it over to read the message but was surprised to find it blank. Only her name and address had been printed on the postcard, in careful block letters.

Curiously, she studied the card. The stamp had been cancelled in Orlando two days before. July 27, 1921. Flipping the card back over, she looked at the picture more closely. The hotel was the San Juan, which the postcard informed her had been built in 1885 by C. E. Pierce. Built for the filthy rich, from the looks of it.

* * *

LILY WAS STILL BY HER mailbox when she saw Officer Danny Jamison coming down the street on his bicycle. She had known Officer Jamison since they were kids—he'd been just one year ahead of her in school. After high school they'd gone in different directions, although on occasion their paths crossed. She was about to wave as he passed by, when instead he stopped in front of her and dismounted his bike in one easy move.

"Hey Lily," he said, leaning his bike against her palm tree. "Your sister around?"

Lily shifted from one foot to the other. Why was Danny asking after Junie? Though she and her older half sister had lived together since their parents had passed away a few years before, Junie tended to be tight-lipped about her goings on. But Lily would catch whispers about illicit gin, late night séances, Ouija parties, and other secret doings connected with West Palm Beach's furtive Bohemian scene. A far cry from her day job heading the town's post office, which Junie had taken over from their brother some eight months before. "She must have left for work early," Lily said. "I didn't see her this morning."

"I see. But you saw her last night?"

Lily hesitated again. The truth was, she hadn't seen Junie since last Friday, three days before. Her sister had left the house in a hurry, carrying a small valise. *If anyone calls for me,* she had said, *tell them I'm very ill and may not be home for a few days.*

Where are you going, Junie? Lily had called out, startled. Despite her increasingly wild ways, Junie had never missed a day of work.

But Junie had just shrugged. *Never you mind.*

Not wanting to rat Junie out, Lily just offered a non-committal nod before countering with a question of her own. "Why are you asking about Junie?"

Officer Jamison shuffled his feet, and Lily suddenly remembered him as a fourteen-year-old with tousled hair, embarrassed to tell the teacher that he had failed to complete his homework. "What is it?" she asked more sharply. "Danny, tell me straight."

The policeman squared his shoulders. "It's Mr. Montafort. The former assistant post master. He's just been found murdered in Orlando. At a hotel called the San Juan."

Lily gasped, her fingers tightening around the postcard in her skirt pocket. She remembered Mr. Montafort. In his mid-forties, handsome in his own fashion. Junie, flirting with him. "I know he quit the post office a few days ago," she said. "He was planning to open a store in Orlando, wasn't that it?"

"That's true."

"What do you need from Junie?"

"The Orlando police would like to speak to her. They believe that Junie may know something about Mr. Montafort's death."

"Why would they think that?" she asked, trying to suffocate a memory of Junie blowing Mr. Montafort a kiss after church.

"The hotel room in which he was murdered was registered to Miss Junie Baker."

Lily's thoughts flew back to the postcard. Had Junie sent it? But why no message? Sweat began to spread under her armpits. And if Mr. Montafort had been murdered, then what about Junie? "Danny," she said, looking right into her old friend's eyes, "Is my sister all right?"

"I don't know," he said, studying her face. "If you saw her last night, then—"

"I didn't!" she exclaimed, starting to tremble. "I haven't seen her since Friday!"

Officer Jamison grabbed her arm and helped her sit down on the wooden porch steps.

"Lily, I think you'd better tell me what you know."

* * *

Down at the West Palm Beach police station, Lily clutched a cup of black coffee that Officer Jamison had brought her. In the meantime, her former sister-in-law Martha Baker had arrived. Since her half brother Orville's death eight months before, she had barely seen Martha. After a thin brittle embrace, Martha sat in an adjacent chair in the station waiting room, her slender legs entwined around the rungs of the chair. As usual, she looked habitually drab in a navy checked gingham day dress. "So what's that dreadful sister of yours done now?"

"Please, Martha. I'm worried about her."

"Pfft. That one. She always lands on her feet." The woman stood up and began to pace about the small waiting area. "So what was she doing in Orlando? Not taking her postmistress position very seriously, that's for certain."

Lily sighed. "I don't really know."

Martha scowled down at Lily. "You do know. It's obvious that she was having an affair with Mr. Montafort." She tsk-tsked. "Poor dear Mr. Montafort. *Orville's* right-hand man, you remember that, don't you?" She shook her head. "Now I see why he didn't mind that your sister was given my dead husband's position. Postmistress, pfft."

Annoyed, Lily turned away from her former sister-in-law, but it was harder to cast away the disturbing images elicited by Martha's words.

How *had* her sister become postmistress so quickly? Everything had happened so rapidly last winter after Orville had succumbed to the snake venom. A gift, he had said, but he never told them who had given him the snake.

Just a week after Orville had been buried in Woodvale cemetery, Junie had sent around a petition to all their neighbors, essentially demanding that their brother's position be passed on to her. Back then, in January, Junie had still appeared to be an upstanding member of the community, playing for the church and directing the choir. This was of course before she'd started spending her nights in the local speakeasy. At the time, the community had rallied around her petition and named her postmistress of the West Palm Beach post office.

Officer Jamison opened the door then, causing both women to start. "I just got off the telephone with the Orlando police." He looked concerned. "They located your sister."

A chill flooded over her. "Is she all right?" she whispered.

The officer looked startled. "Oh, yes. My apologies. Yes. She's well. They found her at a boarding house in Orlando."

"Oh thank God," Lily said, putting her face in her hands. But then she looked up. "What happened? Do you know who murdered Mr. Montafort?"

Officer Jamison took the other chair and drew it close to Lily. Martha looked askance at the movement, but the other two ignored her. "Did you know that nearly $27,000 had been stolen from the post office last week? Did your sister tell you that?"

"Why, no, she hadn't." Lily paused. "What do you mean? How did that happen?"

Martha sniffed. "Embezzlement. It's obvious. Most people don't realize how much money the post office takes in every day."

"It seems that the theft was recently discovered," Jamison said, licking his lips. "A few days ago, the Federal Reserve Bank in Atlanta received two packages from the National Bank in West Palm Beach that were supposed to contain cash. Nineteen thousand dollars and $8,000 respectively. But when the bank clerks opened the packages, they discovered that someone had wrapped a few dollar bills around stacks of pages cut from a magazine, and that the rest of the money had been stolen."

Lily gave a low whistle. "That's a lot of dough!"

Martha looked annoyed. "That theft could have taken place at any point. Did they search the clerk in Atlanta?"

Officer Jamison nodded. "Yes, the police there questioned her. The Feds too. Those bags were kept under constant scrutiny after they were picked up from the post office."

"Well, maybe the theft occurred before the money arrived at the Post Office," Martha persisted. "Maybe an employee from the West Palm Beach bank stole the money. Plenty of opportunity."

The officer shook his head. "The bank clerk claimed that she signed the money over to Mr. Montafort, who then signed for both packages. This was corroborated by another bank employee.

In fact, that was one of the last packages Mr. Montafort signed for on his last day of work."

"Then it would most certainly appear that Mr. Montafort stole the money," Martha declared, heaving a great sigh. "We all knew he planned to open that store in Orlando." She looked down at the officer. "Oh, he must have been desperate to steal the cash. If only I had known! Orville would have wanted me to lend his friend the funds, I'm sure of it. He was my husband's right-hand man."

"Maybe he was murdered for the money?" Lily asked. "Perhaps someone knew about it." Was that why Junie was in Orlando? To track down the money, and Mr. Montafort? Surely, she'd be doing whatever she could to get the money back.

Officer Jamison scratched his ear. "The fact of the matter is that a great deal of the money was found on Mr. Montafort's person, at the hotel room."

"That doesn't make any sense," Lily replied. "Why wouldn't the murderer just take the money?"

Officer Jamison made a gesture like he was going to touch her hands, but then didn't. "I'm afraid that you must prepare yourself for a different explanation all together."

"Which is?" Martha and Lily asked together, in surprising unison.

"That your sister embezzled those funds herself. And then tried to frame Mr. Montafort for the theft, after she killed him."

"No!"

"I'm sorry to tell you that Junie has been arrested by the Orlando police, on charges of embezzlement, fraud, and murder."

* * *

THE NEXT AFTERNOON, LILY WALKED into the Orlando jail with some trepidation. Officer Jamison had driven her and Martha the 170 miles in his own Ford Model T. She didn't know if he was doing this out of professional obligation, curiosity, or a long-ago friendship, but right now, she didn't really care. She was glad that she didn't have to make the trip with just Martha.

After they were met by a white-haired deputy, Officer Jamison disappeared to speak with the Orlando station chief. The deputy led them down a corridor to a row of cells, stopping when he reached the last one on the right. Lily could see figures huddled on the benches.

"Junie Baker!" he called, running his baton along the iron bars. "Visitors!"

Her sister popped up from the bench to their right, and hurried over, looking a little more unkempt and frazzled than usual, an observation she heard Martha note under her breath. "Darling!" Junie called, reaching her hands through the bars.

Instinctively, Lily reached out and caught them in her own.

"You brought *her,*" Junie said, flicking her eyes towards Martha.

Lily shrugged. "She insisted."

Martha sniffed. "I suppose I shouldn't have expected you'd be grateful."

Behind Junie, the woman on the other bench stirred. "Who's the sour puss, Junie?" the woman called out, her voice sounding a bit slurred as if she were drinking.

"Mind your own apples," Junie said, before tightening her grip on Lily's hand. "How did you get here?"

"Officer Jamison drove us from West Palm Beach. My old friend Danny," she added, hurriedly, trying to put off the questions she could see rising to Junie's lips. She glanced at the deputy who was standing by the door about thirty feet away, and lowered her voice. "We don't have time to talk about this right now. What we do need to discuss is—Junie, what *happened?!* Do you know who murdered Mr. Montafort?"

Junie closed her eyes. "Oh, dear Phillip." Then she opened them again, gazing into Lily's eyes. "I saw it all, you know that?"

"What?!" Martha exclaimed. "Whatever do you mean?!"

"Shhh! You saw the murder?" Lily whispered, feeling uneasy. Junie's face had taken on an odd dreamy look. "You were there?"

"In a way," her sister replied. "I saw it in my crystal ball. When I was still at home."

"Oh, brother," Martha replied, not even bothering to hide her snort. "The murder's made her mad."

Lily shushed her sister-in-law again. She spoke to Junie slowly, as one might speak to a child. "Junie, I need you to explain from the beginning."

Junie took a deep breath. "Last Thursday, Philip sent me a telegram asking me to join him in Orlando, at the *San Juan*. He told me a key would be in my name at the front desk.

Martha tsk-tsked. "That's a 'New Woman' for you. Throwing herself at a man. Disgraceful."

"I was very surprised to receive Phillip's telegram, to be honest," Junie said, speaking only to Lily. "Before he had left West Palm Beach, he had told me that I shouldn't expect to see him again. His plan was to move to Orlando, start a new life."

"He changed his mind, it seems," Lily said, still watching Junie's face.

"He said in his telegram that he wanted to discuss our future. I was so happy." Here her sister frowned. "But then, later that same day, the West Palm Beach police came by the Post Office and informed me about the theft." Her lips trembled slightly. "I just knew in my heart that Philip must have taken the money. For us."

She took a deep breath. "When I peered into my crystal ball though, it was dark. I couldn't see anything at all. That told me something bad would happen. So I decided to join him at the San Juan, and read our future there."

"Is that what the postcard meant?" Lily asked, side-stepping her sister's wild talk.

"What postcard?" Junie asked.

"Never mind that," Martha said, irritably. "Tell us what you 'saw.'" Again, the contempt in her tone was palpable.

Lily scowled at Martha, trying to regain the narrative that Junie had begun. "You came to Orlando," she prompted, "and registered at the San Juan. Did you call on Mr. Montafort then and—"

"No," Junie interrupted. "I didn't register at the San Juan. Philip had left a key for me at the front desk."

"Was there a message?" Lily asked.

"No. Just the key. So I took the lift to the third floor and walked up to room 323 and knocked on the door."

"And?" Lily asked.

"He didn't answer so I thought I would go in and wait." Junie's face paled. Stepping as close as she could to the bars, she gripped Lily's hands. "It was awful. Phillip was on the floor. I could see a knife in his chest." She gulped. "I remember falling to my knees, and crawling over to him, thinking I could pull the knife out."

"Oh!" Lily whispered, trying to imagine the scene.

"I don't know if I screamed or cried. Lily, my mind went numb." She looked at the ceiling. "Then I heard someone else screaming. A maid. She must have come in. I ran off, right past her. I ran down the stairs and out of the hotel. I didn't know where to go. I walked for miles, and then I finally came to my senses and just checked into the first boarding house I saw."

"Why didn't you stay and try to explain yourself?" Martha asked, her eyes narrowing.

"I panicked. I knew I couldn't stay in the room."

"You ran out of the hotel. With blood all over your coat," Martha said, her tone mocking. "No wonder they locked you up. Sounds pretty suspicious to me."

Junie's eyes filled with tears. "I didn't murder him! I loved him!"

"Why not just have a séance for him?" Martha asked, rudely. "Can't you just ask his *departed spirit* who killed him?"

"I will!" Junie replied. "As soon as they let me go."

Martha sniffed again. "Why don't you check your crystal ball for the likelihood of *that* happening?!"

* * *

BACK IN THE WAITING ROOM, they found Officer Jamison waiting for them, accompanied by another officer who introduced himself as Chief McKinley, the head of the Orlando police. He ushered the three of them into his office.

"My sister did not murder Phillip Montafort," Lily stated.

The chief nodded like he expected her to say that. Opening a package on his desk, he pulled out a telegram and laid the yellow sheet in front of her. "Perhaps you can explain *this.* We found it in the deceased's coat pocket."

Lily leaned forward to read the telegram, and to her annoyance, the other two did as well. Martha couldn't refrain from reading it out loud. "*Dearest Phillip. We have much to discuss. I look forward to your explanation. Remember there are many futures. Bus arrives in Orlando tomorrow at two. —J.*"

"Well, it makes sense," Lily replied, trying not to feel faint. "She sent this in reply to Mr. Montafort's telegram. I imagine she wanted an explanation about the missing money."

"Uh-huh," Chief McKinley said. "And how would you explain this?" He pulled out a postcard similar to the one Lily had received, depicting an image of the hotel. In block letters, several words had been written. *Rm 323. Noon. Bring champagne. —Junie.*

"The hussy!" Martha murmured, venom in her voice. "So brazen."

"The timing is different," Lily said, tapping first on the telegram, and then the postcard. "Did her bus arrive earlier than expected?"

The chief shrugged. "She might have taken an earlier bus."

That was certainly possible. Lily remembered how her sister had run around that Friday morning, clearly flustered.

Still, something seemed strange. From her handbag, she pulled out the postcard she had received in the mail and laid it beside the other. The images of the hotel were the same.

"I received this in yesterday's post," Lily said, turning both postcards over to examine the hand-printed words on the back.

"Same hand," Officer Jamison noted.

"Junie said she didn't send me a postcard. Besides, I can tell you, neither of these are in Junie's handwriting. Junie writes with more sweeping curls and looping letters."

"Hmm . . . " Neither officer seemed convinced. "Just because she printed these two cards instead of using cursive doesn't prove anything."

"Sir," Lily said, turning back to the chief, "Junie told me that Mr. Montafort had left her a key to room 323 at the front desk. She said she never registered for her own room at the hotel."

"The room was most definitely registered to her though," he replied, just as the telephone on his desk rang. He picked up the receiver. "Orlando Police, McKinley speaking." Then he covered the mouthpiece with his hand, and nodded towards the door. "The secretary will show you out."

* * *

As they moved out of the police station, Lily stopped, shielding her eyes from the bright Florida sunshine. "We need to speak to that clerk at the San Juan."

"For heaven's sake, why?" Martha cried, pulling the brim of her hat low over her face.

"Something just isn't right," Lily replied, looking up at Officer Jamison. "Please. Danny. You've brought all this way. Surely you feel that too."

He gazed down at her, before nodding. "The San Juan is over on Orange and Central, just a few blocks away. We can make our inquiries there." He glanced at his watch. "Then we can grab a bite to eat. I'm starving."

* * *

The inside of the San Juan was as impressive as its exterior. Lily blinked a bit at the opulence of the lobby, but she did not let the grandeur deter her in her mission. She strode up to the lobby desk, where two clerks in bright red suits with gold buttons were waiting. Martha murmured that she needed to find the lavatory, and Lily just nodded, suddenly wondering too late how to go about getting answers.

Fortunately, Officer Jamison knew what to do. "Pardon me," he said to the clerk, flashing his West Palm Beach police badge. "I wanted to make some follow-up inquiries related to the *incident* that occurred this past Saturday morning."

Although the clerk was probably pushing forty, his face still lit up. Clearly the murder had been a highlight. "Yes, sir, anything you want to know, sir." He stood up straight, with military building. Probably a retired soldier, Lily thought.

"Were you working when Junie Baker checked in last Friday morning?" Officer Jamison asked.

"Yes, sir. I mean no, sir. I'm sorry I—"

"It's a simple enough question—" he peered at the shiny metal pin on the man's uniform, "Samuels."

Mr. Samuels stood up straight. "Yes, sir. What I meant is that Junie Baker checked into her room on Thursday evening, not Friday morning."

"What? No, that's not right," Lily said, confused.

Officer Jamison nudged her with his foot. "Why do you remember her specifically?"

The man grinned, showing dull yellow teeth. "I remember that she had this fantastic hat, and I thought 'that's rather to-do for someone named 'Junie Baker.' And, of course, the name stuck in my head after the police asked me the name of the guest in Room 323." He lowered his voice. "Heard it was a real bloody affair. Couple people saw her run right through the lobby, too, after the murder. Covered with blood, too, but no one had thought to stop her. Wish I had been there. I'd have stopped her. But I wasn't there until later."

Lily pressed down a wave of nausea that had arisen with the man's words, and she moved a few steps away.

Officer Jamison leaned in towards her. "Are you all right?" he asked, looking concerned. "Do you need to sit down?"

"What he just said doesn't make sense," she said in a low voice. "I know Junie was home on Friday morning. I saw her before she left. I mean, I know now that she came to Orlando, but still it's strange that he says that she checked in on Thursday evening. And what hat was she wearing? Junie hates hats."

"Yes, something is definitely odd here," he replied, stepping back to the counter and addressing the clerk again. "We've spoken with Miss Baker. She said that you two conversed on Friday morning."

"Wasn't me. Like I said, I came in later. Missed all the excitement," Samuels said, and then gestured to the other clerk at the end of the counter. "Marty Oliver's your man. Hey, Marty!"

The other clerk looked up. "Yeah?"

"Cop here wants to know about Junie Baker."

"What about her?"

"She told us she talked to you on Friday afternoon," Officer Jamison said, watching the man closely.

"Nah, she didn't check in. She asked if there was a message for her. '*Junie Baker,*' she said." He wiped the sweat on his lip. "I gave it to her. It was a key."

"Was that unusual?" Lily asked.

"No, it happens sometimes," Samuels jumped in, after giving a curious look at his colleague. "Sometimes people leave a key for a relative . . . or a lover."

There was something sly about his tone. "Did you know Phillip Montafort? The man who was murdered?" Lily asked. "Was he the one who left Miss Baker the key?"

Mr. Oliver crossed himself. "Yeah, I knew Mr. Montafort. He's stayed with us before. It wasn't him. In fact, it was a woman who left her the key."

"A woman?" Lily replied. She and Officer Jamison exchanged glances.

"Yes, she'd come by that morning. She told me that she wanted to leave a room key for someone who'd be arriving shortly. She also said she had hurt her hand and asked me to address the outside of the envelope for her."

"Did you tell the police this?" Officer Jamison asked.

The clerk shrugged. "No. I just told them how I'd seen a woman walk out of the lift, with blood all over her coat and an odd look in her eye. Told them it was Junie Baker they were looking for, and that was the last I'd heard of it."

* * *

"They were all quick to pin this on Junie," Officer Jamison commented to Lily.

"That's for sure," she replied.

They had moved over to two overstuffed chairs, waiting for Martha. They could see she was now pouring herself a glass of cucumber water from a great pitcher on a wooden sideboard.

"What should we do now?" Lily asked. Tears welled in her eyes, thinking about Junie in jail.

Officer Jamison touched her hand. "Lily," he started to say, before being interrupted by the desk clerk clearing his throat.

"Yes, Samuels, what is it?" Officer Jamison asked, scowling.

To their surprise, the clerk leaned over, close enough that they could smell tuna on his breath. "The woman, she's here."

"What woman?" They asked in unison.

"Junie Baker. The one I checked in last Thursday evening. Oliver said she was the same one who had him write the name on the envelope. She's right over there."

They followed his finger and Lily gasped. He was pointing straight at Martha, as she walked towards them, cucumber water in hand.

* * *

"What in the world?" Lily cried, even as her mind began to reel. "That can't be the woman. That's Martha Baker, my sister-in-law."

But Martha's eyes had widened as she took in Lily staring at her, with the clerk still standing behind them. She looked toward the great glass doors of the San Juan at the gleaming sunlit street beyond.

Sensing what she was about to do, Officer Jamison jumped up from and grabbed Martha's arm. He turned to the desk clerk, who was watching everything with astonishment. "Samuels! Ring the police at once! Ask for Chief McKinley."

"Yes, sir," the clerk said, before hurrying away.

"Martha, is this t-true?" Lily asked. "These men said you posed as Junie. Why ever would you have done that? Unless, does that mean—" She couldn't finish the thought.

Officer Jamison finished it for her. "—that she killed Mr. Montafort. Yes, it seems quite likely. The question is *why?* Not for the money, it would seem since she left it there. No, it's clear that she wanted to frame your sister for murder."

"What? Why?"

Martha's face grew dark. "Your sister! She killed my husband! Took my Orville away from me!"

"No!" Lily exclaimed. "He died of a snake bite!"

"Mr. Montafort was the one who bought the vile creature. He's the one who put it in the box, for my Orville to unwrap. Junie put him up to it, I'm sure of it. I found the card they left for him, a few weeks ago. I waited for them to come forward, to confess their actions, but they never did."

Lily stared at her sister-in-law. The woman was mad. But a faint memory stirred in her.

Junie, in Mr. Montafort's arms, weeping at her brother's funeral. Whispering together. A sense of shame? Remorse? Is that why Junie was so determined to carry on her brother's work? She shook her head. "It was an accident. A prank gone bad, I'm sure of it."

She frowned. "But you planned all this? How?"

Now Martha looked smug. "I was there, Phillip's last day of work. I knew that those bank shipments were likely to come in. When I was in his office, I saw his hotel information. He must have made the reservation at the *San Juan* earlier that day."

"You took the money and travelled to Orlando a few days later. You wanted to be there by the time Mr. Montafort would have arrived at the San Juan," Officer Jamison said, clearly trying to puzzle out the details. "Then you sent the telegram to Junie, pretending to be Mr. Montafort, inviting her to come."

"You didn't realize that she would send you a telegram in return," Lily added, picking up where Officer Jamison had left off. She tried to imagine what had happened next. "Then you booked a room in Junie's name, and the next morning you left a key at the front desk for Junie."

"After asking the desk clerk to address it for you," Officer Jamison added.

"Then you sent a note to Mr. Montafort, inviting him to come to 323. Is that when you killed him?"

Martha sniffed. "He didn't even put up a fight. Dropped like a lamb."

"He was already dead when Junie arrived a few hours later," Lily said, tears beginning to slip down her cheeks. "Oh poor Junie. She loved him, you know."

"She should have known he'd be dead," Martha said. "Didn't she *foresee* this in her glass ball?! Your sister's a real dumb Dora, you know that?" Her face grew dark again. "I didn't expect Junie to send that stupid telegram back to Montafort. Messed up everything."

One thing still wasn't clear to Lily. "But why send *me* the postcard?"

Martha gave a harsh laugh. "Call it a whim, I guess. Thought it might help you believe the lie."

"Quite the opposite actually," Lily said, pulling herself together. "I never thought Junie would send me a blank postcard." She picked up a handful of the hotel postcards from the counter. "Since *you* like them though, I'll mail these . . . you can use them to decorate your jail cell."

HANGOVER

BY JOHN D. MacDONALD

He dreamed that he had dropped something, lost something of value in the furnace, and he lay on his side trying to look down at an angle through a little hole, look beyond the flame down into the dark guts of the furnace for what he had lost. But the flame kept pulsing through the hole with a brightness that hurt his eyes, with a heat that parched his face, pulsing with an intermittent husky rasping sound.

With his awakening, the dream became painfully explicable—the pulsing roar was his own harsh breathing, the parched feeling was a consuming thirst, the brightness was transmuted into pain intensely localized behind his eyes. When he opened his eyes, a long slant of early morning sun dazzled him, and he shut his eyes quickly again.

This was a morning time of awareness of discomfort so acute that he had no thought for anything beyond the appraisal of the body and its functions. Though he was dimly aware of psychic discomforts that might later exceed the anguish of the flesh, the immediacy of bodily pain localized his attentions. Even without the horizontal brightness of the sun, he would have known it was early. Long sleep would have muffled the beat of the taxed heart to a softened, sedate, and comfortable rhythm. But it was early and the heart knocked sharply with a violence and in a cadence almost hysterical, so that no matter how he turned his head, he could feel it, a tack hammer chipping away at his mortality.

His thirst was monstrous, undiminished by the random nausea that teased at the back of his throat. His hands and feet were cool, yet where his thighs touched he was sweaty. His body felt clotted, and he knew that he had perspired heavily during the evening, an oily perspiration that left an unpleasant residue when it dried. The pain behind his eyes was a slow bulging and shrinking, in contrapuntal rhythm to the clatter of his heart.

He sat on the edge of the bed, head bowed, eyes squeezed shut, cool trembling fingers resting on his bare knees. He felt weak, nauseated, and acutely depressed.

This was the great joke. This was a hangover. Thing of sly wink, of rueful guffaw. This was death in the morning.

He stood on shaky legs and walked into the bathroom. He turned the cold water on as far as it would go. He drank a full glass greedily. He was refilling the glass when the first spasm came. He turned to the toilet, half falling, cracking one knee painfully on the tile floor, and knelt there and clutched the edge of the bowl in both hands, hunched, miserable, naked. The water ran in the sink for a long time while he remained there, retching, until nothing more came but flakes of greenish bile. When he stood up, he felt weaker but slightly better. He mopped his face with a damp towel, then drank more water, drank it slowly and carefully, and in great quantity, losing track of the number of glasses. He drank the cold water until his belly was swollen and he could hold no more, but he felt as thirsty as before.

Putting the glass back on the rack, he looked at himself in the mirror. He took a quick, overly casual look, the way one glances at a stranger, the eye returning for a longer look after it is seen that the first glance aroused no undue curiosity. Though his face was grayish, eyes slightly puffy, jaws soiled by beard stubble, the long face with its even undistinguished features looked curiously unmarked in relation to the torment of the body.

The visual reflection was a first step in the reaffirmation of identity. You are Hadley Purvis. You are thirty-nine. Your hair is turning gray with astonishing and disheartening speed.

He turned his back on the bland image, on the face that refused to comprehend his pain. He leaned his buttocks against the chill edge of the sink, and a sudden unbidden image came into his mind, as clear and supernaturally perfect as a colored advertisement in a magazine. It was a shot glass full to the very brim with dark brown bourbon.

By a slow effort of will he caused the image to fade away. Not yet, he thought, and immediately wondered about his instinctive choice of mental phrase. Nonsense. This was a part of the usual morbidity of hangover—to imagine oneself slowly turning into an alcoholic. The rum sour on Sunday mornings had become a ritual with him, condoned by Sarah. And that certainly did not speak of alcoholism. Today was, unhappily, a working day, and it would be twelve thirty before the first martini at Mario's. If anyone had any worries about alcoholism, it was Sarah, and her worries resulted from her lack of knowledge of his job and its requirements. After a man has been drinking for twenty-one years, he does not suddenly become a legitimate cause for the sort of annoying concern Sarah had been showing lately.

In the evening when they were alone before dinner, they would drink, and that certainly did not distress her. She liked her few knocks as well as anyone. Then she had learned somehow that whenever he went to the kitchen to refill their glasses from the martini jug in the deep freeze, he would have an extra one for himself, opening his throat for it, pouring it down in one smooth, long, silvery gush. By mildness of tone she had trapped him into an admission, then had told him that the very secrecy of it was "significant." He had tried to explain that his tolerance for alcohol was greater than hers, and that it was easier to do it that way than to listen to her tiresome hints about how many he was having.

Standing there in the bathroom, he could hear the early morning sounds of the city. His hearing seemed unnaturally keen. He realized that it was absurd to stand there and conduct mental arguments with Sarah and become annoyed at her. He reached into the shower stall and turned the faucets and waited until the water was the right temperature before stepping in, just barely warm. He made no attempt at first to bathe. He stood under the roar and thrust of the high nozzle, eyes shut, face tilted up.

As he stood there he began, cautiously, to think of the previous evening. He had much experience in this sort of reconstruction. He reached out with memory timorously, anticipating remorse and self-disgust.

The first part of the evening was, as always, easy to remember. It had been an important evening. He had dressed carefully yesterday morning, knowing that there would not be time to come home and change before going directly from the office to the hotel for the meeting, with its cocktails, dinner, speeches, movie, and unveiling of the new model. Because of the importance of the evening, he had taken it very easy at Mario's at lunchtime, limiting himself to two martinis before lunch, conscious of virtue—only to have it spoiled by Bill Hunter's coming into his office at three in the afternoon, staring at him with both relief and approval and saying, "Glad you didn't have one of those three-hour lunches, Had. The old man was a little dubious about your joining the group tonight."

Hadley Purvis had felt suddenly and enormously annoyed. Usually he liked Bill Hunter, despite his aura of opportunism, despite the cautious ambition that had enabled Hunter to become quite close to the head of the agency in a very short time.

"And so you said to him, 'Mr. Driscoll, if Had Purvis can't go to the party, I won't go either.' And then he broke down."

He watched Bill Hunter flush. "Not like that, Had. But I'll tell you what happened. He asked me if I thought you would behave yourself tonight. I said I was certain you realized the importance of the occasion, and I reminded him that the Detroit people know you and like the work you did on the spring campaign. So if you get out of line, it isn't going to do me any good either."

"And that's your primary consideration, naturally."

Hunter looked at him angrily, helplessly. "Damn it, Had . . . "

"Keep your little heart from fluttering. I'll step lightly."

Bill Hunter left his office. After he was gone, Hadley tried very hard to believe that it had been an amusing little interlude. But he could not. Resentment stayed with him. Resentment at being treated like a child. And he suspected that Hunter had brought it up with Driscoll, saying very casually, "Hope Purvis doesn't put on a floor show tonight."

It wasn't like the old man to have brought it up. He felt that the old man genuinely liked him. They'd had some laughs together. Grown-up laughs, a little beyond the capacity of a boy scout like Hunter.

He had washed up at five, then gone down and shared a cab with Davey Tidmarsh, the only one of the new kids who had been asked to come along. Davey was all hopped up about it. He was a nice kid. Hadley liked him. Davey demanded to know what it would be like, and in the cab Hadley told him.

"We'll be seriously outnumbered. There'll be a battalion from Detroit, also the bank people. It will be done with enormous seriousness and a lot of expense. This is a pre-preview. Maybe they'll have a mockup there. The idea is that they get us all steamed up about the new model. Then, all enthused, we whip up two big promotions. The first promotion is a carnival deal they will use to sell the new models to the dealers and get them all steamed up. That'll be about four months from now. The second promotion will be the campaign to sell the cars to the public. They'll make a big fetish of secrecy, Davey. There'll be uniformed company guards. Armed."

It was as he had anticipated, only a bit bigger and gaudier than last year. Everything seemed to get bigger and gaudier every year. It was on the top floor of the hotel, in one of the middle-sized convention rooms. They were carefully checked at the door, and each was given a numbered badge to wear. On the left side of the room was sixty feet of bar. Along the right wall was the table where the buffet would be. There was a busy rumble of male conversation, a blue haze of smoke. Hadley nodded and smiled at the people he knew as they worked their way toward the bar. With drink in hand, he went into the next room—after being checked again at the door—to look at the mockup.

Hadley had to admit that it had been done very neatly. The mockup was one-third actual size. It revolved slowly on a chest-high pedestal, a red and white convertible with the door open, with the model of a girl in a swimming suit standing beside it, both model girl and model car bathed in an excellent imitation of sunlight. He looked at the girl first, marveling at how cleverly the sheen of suntanned girl had been duplicated. He looked at the mannequin's figure and thought at once of Sarah and felt a warm wave of tenderness for her, a feeling that she was his luck and, with her, nothing could ever go wrong.

He looked at the lines of the revolving car and, with the glibness of long practice, he made up phrases that would be suitable for advertising it. He stood aside for a time and watched the manufactured delight on the faces of those who were seeing the model for the first time. He finished his drink and went out to the bar. With the first drink, the last traces of irritation at Bill Hunter disappeared. As soon as he had a fresh drink, he looked Bill up and said, "I'm the man who snarled this afternoon."

"No harm done," Hunter said promptly and a bit distantly. "Excuse me, Had. There's somebody over there I have to say hello to."

Hadley placed himself at the bar. He was not alone long. Within ten minutes he was the center of a group of six or seven. He relished these times when he was sought out for his entertainment value. The drinks brought him quickly to the point where he was, without effort, amusing. The sharp phrases came quickly, almost without thought. They laughed with him and appreciated him. He felt warm and loved.

He remembered there had been small warnings in the back of his mind, but he had ignored them. He would know when to stop. He told the story about Jimmy and Jackie and the punch card over at Shor's, and knew he told it well, and knew he was having a fine time, and knew that everything was beautifully under control.

But, beyond that point, memory was faulty. It lost continuity. It became episodic, each scene bright enough, yet separated from other scenes by a grayness he could not penetrate.

He was still at the bar. The audience had dwindled to one, a small man he didn't know, a man who swayed and clung to the edge of the bar. He was trying to make the small man understand something. He kept shaking his head. Hunter came over to him and took his arm and said, "Had, you've got to get something to eat. They're going to take the buffet away soon."

"Smile, pardner, when you use that word 'got.'"

"Sit down and I'll get you a plate."

"Never let it be said that Hadley Purvis couldn't cut his own way through a solid wall of buffet." As Hunter tugged at his arm, Hadley finished his drink, put the glass on the bar with great care, and walked over toward the buffet, shrugging his arm free of Hunter's grasp. He took a plate and looked at all the food. He had not the slightest desire for food. He looked back. Hunter was watching him. He shrugged and went down the long table.

Then, another memory. Standing there with plate in hand. Looking over and seeing Bill Hunter's frantic signals. Ignoring him and walking steadily over to where Driscoll sat with some of the top brass from Detroit. He was amused at the apprehensive expression on Driscoll's face. But he sat down and Driscoll had to introduce him.

Then, later. Dropping something from his fork. Recapturing it and glancing up to trap a look of distaste on the face of the most important man from Detroit, a bald, powerful-looking man with a ruddy face and small bright blue eyes.

He remembered that he started brooding about that look of distaste. The others talked, and he ate doggedly. They think I'm a clown. I'm good enough to keep them laughing, but that's all. They don't think I'm capable of deep thought.

He remembered Driscoll's frown when he broke into the conversation, addressing himself to the bald one from Detroit and taking care to pronounce each word distinctly, without slur.

"That's a nice looking mockup. And it is going to make a lot of vehicles look old before their time. The way I see it, we're in a period of artificially accelerated obsolescence. The honesty has gone out of the American product. The great God is turnover. So all you manufacturers are straining a gut to make a product that wears out, or breaks, or doesn't last or, like your car, goes out of style. It's the old game of rooking the consumer. You have your hand in his pocket, and we have our hand in yours."

He remembered his little speech vividly, and it shocked him. Maybe it was true. But that had not been the time or place to state it, not at this festive meeting, where everybody congratulated each other on what a fine new sparkling product they would be selling. He felt his cheeks grow hot as he remembered his own words. What a thing to say in front of Driscoll! The most abject apologies were going to be in order.

He could not remember the reaction of the man from Detroit, or Driscoll's immediate reaction. He had no further memories of being at the table. The next episode was back at the bar, a glass in his hand, Hunter beside him speaking so earnestly you could almost see the tears in his eyes. "Good Lord, Had! What did you say? What did you do? I've never seen him so upset."

"Tell him to go do something unspeakable. I just gave them a few clear words of ultimate truth. And now I intend to put some sparkle in that little combo."

"Leave the music alone. Go home, please. Just go home, Had."

There was another gap, and then he was arguing with the drummer. The man was curiously disinclined to give up the drums. A waiter gripped his arm.

"What's your trouble?" Hadley asked him angrily. "I just want to teach this clown how to stay on top of the beat."

"A gentleman wants to see you, sir. He is by the cloakroom. He asked me to bring you out."

Then he was by the cloakroom. Driscoll was there. He stood close to Hadley. "Don't open your mouth, Purvis. Just listen carefully to me while I try to get something through your drunken skull. Can you understand what I'm saying?"

"Certainly I can—"

"Shut up! You may have lost the whole shooting match for us. That speech of yours. He told me he wasn't aware of the fact that I hired Commies. He said that criticisms of the American way of life make him physically ill. Know what I'm going back in and tell him?"

"No."

"That I got you out here and fired you and sent you home. Get this straight. It's an attempt to save the contract. Even if it weren't, I'd still fire you, and I'd do it in person. I thought I would dread it. I've known you a long time. I find out, Purvis, that I'm actually enjoying it. It's such a damn relief to get rid of you. Don't open your mouth. I wouldn't take you back if you worked for free. Don't come back. Don't come in tomorrow. I'll have a girl pack your personal stuff. I'll have it sent to you by messenger along with your check. You'll get both tomorrow before noon. You're a clever man, Purvis, but the town is full of clever men who can hold liquor. Goodbye."

Driscoll turned on his heel and went back into the big room. Hadley remembered that the shock had penetrated the haze of liquor. He remembered that he had stood there, and he had been able to see two men setting up a projector, and all he could think about was how he would tell Sarah and what she would probably say.

And, without transition, he was in the Times Square area on his way home. The sidewalk would tilt unexpectedly, and each time he would take a lurching step to regain his balance. The glare of the lights hurt his eyes. His heart pounded. He felt short of breath.

He stopped and looked in the window of a men's shop that was still open. The sign on the door said OPEN UNTIL MIDNIGHT. He looked at his watch. It was a little after eleven. He had imagined it to be much later. Suddenly it became imperative to him to prove both to himself and to a stranger that he was not at all drunk. If he could prove that, then he would know that Driscoll had fired him not for drinking, but for his opinions. And would anyone want to keep a job where he was not permitted to have opinions?

He gathered all his forces and looked intently into the shop window. He looked at a necktie. It was a gray wool tie with a tiny figure embroidered in dark red. The little embroidered things were shaped like commas. He decided that he liked it very much. The ties in that corner of the window were priced at three-fifty. He measured his stability, cleared his throat, and went into the shop.

"Good evening, sir."

"Good evening. I'd like that tie in the window, the gray one on the left with the dark red pattern."

"Would you please show me which one, sir?"

"Of course." Hadley pointed it out. The man took a duplicate off a rack.

"Would you like this in a box, or shall I put it in a bag?"

"A bag is all right."

"It's a very handsome tie."

He gave the man a five-dollar bill. The man brought him his change. "Thank you, sir. Good night."

"Good night." He walked out steadily, carrying the bag. No one could have done it better. A very orderly purchase. If he ever needed proof of his condition, the clerk would remember him. "Yes, I remember the gentleman. He came in shortly before closing time. He bought a gray tie. Sober? Perhaps he'd had a drink or two. But he was as sober as a judge."

And somewhere between the shop and home all memory ceased. There was a vague something about a quarrel with Sarah, but it was not at all clear. Perhaps because the homecoming scene had become too frequent for them.

He dried himself vigorously on a harsh towel and went into the bedroom. When he thought of the lost job, he felt quick panic. Another one wouldn't be easy to find. One just as good might be impossible. It was a profession that fed on gossip.

Maybe it was a good thing. It would force a change on them. Maybe a new city, a new way of life. Maybe they could regain something that they had lost in the last year or so. But he knew he whistled in the dark. He was afraid. This was the worst of all mornings after.

Yet even that realization was diffused by the peculiar aroma of unreality that clung to all his hangover mornings. Dreams were always vivid, so vivid that they became confused with reality. With care, he studied the texture of the memory of Driscoll's face and found therein a lessening of his hope that it could have been dreamed.

He went into his bedroom and took fresh underwear from the drawer. He found himself thinking about the purchase of the necktie again. It seemed strange that the purchase should have such retroactive importance. The clothing he had worn was where he had dropped it beside his bed. He picked it up. He emptied the pockets of the suit. There was a skein of dried vomit on the lapel of the suit. He could not remember having been ill. There was a triangular tear in the left knee of the trousers, and he noticed for the first time an abrasion on his bare knee. He could not remember having fallen. The necktie was not in the suit pocket. He began to wonder whether he had dreamed about the necktie. In the back of his mind was a ghost image of some other dream about a necktie.

He decided that he would go to the office. He did not see what else he could do. If his memory of what Driscoll had said was accurate, maybe by now Driscoll would have relented. When he went to select a necktie after he had shaved carefully, he looked for the new one on the rack. It was not there. As he was tying the one he had selected, he noticed a wadded piece of paper on the floor beside his wastebasket. He picked it up, spread it open, read the name of the shop on it, and knew that the purchase of the tie had been real.

By the time he was completely dressed, it still was not eight o'clock. He felt unwell, though the sharpness of the headache was dulled. His hands were shaky. His legs felt empty and weak.

It was time to face Sarah. He knew that he had seen her the previous evening. Probably she had been in bed, had heard him come in, had gotten up as was her custom and, no doubt, there had been a scene. He hoped he had not told her of losing the job. Yet, if it had been a dream, he could not have told her. If he had told her, it would be proof that it had not been a dream. He went through the bathroom into her bedroom, moving quietly. Her bed had been slept in, turned back where she had gotten out.

He went down the short hall to the small kitchen. Sarah was not there. He began to wonder about her. Surely the quarrel could not have been so bad that she had dressed and left. He measured coffee into the top of the percolator and put it over a low gas flame. He mixed frozen juice and drank a large glass. The apartment seemed uncannily quiet. He poured another glass, drank half of it, and walked up the hallway to the living room.

Stopping in the doorway, he saw the necktie, recognized the small pattern. He stood there, glass in hand, and looked at the tie. It was tightly knotted. And above the knot, resting on the arm of the chair, was the still, unspeakable face of Sarah, a face the shiny hue of fresh eggplant.

MUSCLE MEMORY

BY ANGEL LUIS COLÓN

"You don't like it." Katie gives me this look I'd swear her mother used to give me whenever I lied but it's been so many years that a passing glance could evoke the same memory.

Got a laundry list of reasons why I don't like it here but I keep my mouth shut. I'm sitting on a bed that reeks of old piss and medicine—room's about the size of a nice bathroom, so it makes sense. Better than a jail cell but not much better. I don't feel this old. I don't like Florida.

Single window behind me with faded curtains. Laminate floor. Don't think there's a word for the color but if depression had a color, this floor would suffice. Wood panel walls. Framed photographs of people I love without me in them. I shift on the bed. Back hurts. Knees hurt. Head hurts. All the pills I take and not one seems to dull things enough for me to focus.

I raise a hand and find myself wondering if I'm always so slow or if my perception's fucked from the new pills. "It's fine," I slur, "Besides, this is where I sleep. They got a bunch of tables and shit out there where I can occupy myself."

Katie frowns. "I tried to find a spot at the nicer place a few miles up the highway, you know, by the girls' school. They—"

"Ain't about to let in a man who pulled a nickel on first-degree manslaughter. I get it." I motion behind my Katie, a woman now. A woman who shouldn't have to look at me the way kids look at a dead pet. "You got the kids to worry about." I smile when I think of them. Two girls. Both got my way of pissing all the wrong people off—a blessing. "When you lugging them here?"

"This weekend?" Less of a suggestion and more of a maybe. Katie and I aren't the closest but we've come to the conclusion—silently—that we're all each other really have anymore.

Katie collects her things and presses the little button that's supposed to summon a caretaker in case I fall or forget how to tuck my dick into my pants. We wait a solid ten minutes—enough time for me to be dead on a bathroom floor and cooling—before some bumbling idiot waddles on into the room. I barely pay attention. Katie asks questions, a laundry list of bullshit she needs to confirm so she can feel comfortable on the ride back to her apartment. I stare at my tiny TV and try not to let the anger gnaw at me. I remind myself she owes me nothing and I'll never find the time to change that.

Katie finishes her talk with the idiot and walks over to me. She leaves a kiss on my forehead as an afterthought, mumbles a goodbye, and walks out of the room.

I'm left with the idiot, of course. "Are you OK Mr. Clarke?" he asks.

I shrug. "Making my peace as we speak." Point to the TV. "We got a remote in here?"

The idiot nods and walks to the TV. Finds the remote behind it and turns the set on. "You like action movies? Comedies?"

"Baseball. It's baseball season, right?"

"Indeed it is. Marlins fan?"

"You hit your head? I sound like the kind of man roots for a team named after something people eat?"

The idiot laughs. "Yankees it is."

"You're goddamn right." I point at him. "You got a name?"

"Derrick. I'm your daytime help."

"Well, Derrick, I'm Sean but you keep calling me Mr. Clarke. Get the game on and fuck off for a little while. I need the quiet."

Derrick finds a game—Boston against The Nats—and smiles at me. He pours me some water and leaves it on the nightstand. "Just ring if you need anything, Mr. Clarke."

I wave the kid off and pretend to care about the game. Try not to think about Katie. Try to push the hope that she forgot something and needed to come back out of my mind. Try to stop wondering if that was the last time I saw her and didn't get to tell her how much I loved her.

So I go to sleep. I learned that in prison; sleep had a hell of a way of making the time fly on by. Need that a lot more than I used to.

* * *

"How old are you?" Manny stares at his nails and bites at the edge of his middle finger.

Manny's an old queen from Miami. Same situation as me. His background check came up with all sorts of fucked up bullshit and his relatives had to dump him in the shithole that is Palm Heights Senior Assisted Living Center. I like Manny because he's around my age and he tells funny stories. He's uncomplicated and doesn't scream or moan or cry like everyone else does. And it's not like I don't understand. This is a miserable place and sometimes misery can infect to the bone marrow—I know that personally—but a little sunshine helps.

Manny is a sliver of sunshine on a pitch black day.

"Never said," I answer, "But if it matters, I'm pushing seventy-five. Shocked as anyone else God hasn't struck me down yet."

Manny shakes his head. "We too young and pretty to be in here." He thumbs through a gossip rag. "Man forgets to turn off his oven three maybe four times and all of a sudden he needs to be locked away in a place like this. The simple act of living longer than these assholes wanted us to is our only crime."

Manny was 'locked away' by his only nephew. Won't speak the kid's name he's so pissed at him for leaving him at Palm Heights. Still, and I'd never say it to Manny's face, the man forgets things constantly. Even eating. Only three weeks here and I've had to remind him when he hasn't started or that he's already finished his food at almost every meal. I'm no slouch in the not realizing my shirt's on inside out department but it seems worse for Manny. I wonder if it's this place, though. If Palm Heights plants its roots into every person living here and makes us even more hollow. I'd be the densest motherfucker alive to not realize I should have died in prison. It isn't like I traded up once I got out, is it?

I only nod at Manny. I learned fast that it wasn't wise to speak when he waxed on about what led him to this place. "Wanna watch the game tonight?" I ask instead. It's easy to send him on a better path of conversation. Manny hates the Yankees and they're playing the Red Sox. Only perk of this dump is the satellite service with the baseball package. Pretty sure we only have it because the management likes betting.

Manny nods. "After dinner."

"It is after dinner."

Derrick walks over and smiles. "Mr. Gutierrez, we got an appointment." He waves to me. "Evening, Mr. Clarke."

"What appointment?" Manny always gets short with Derrick. Probably looks at all young men as potential scapegoats without the evil nephew around.

I wave at Derrick. "Maybe get this guy a little reefer to take the edge off. He's grumpy as hell today."

"Manny's always grumpy." Derrick smiles.

"For you? Always." Manny frowns and leans towards me. "This kid's a scumbag with a flashy smile. Don't listen to a word he tells you." He doesn't whisper. Just wants to be a dramatic ass.

Derrick smirks and helps Manny onto a wheelchair. "Say goodnight to Mr. Clarke, Manny."

"Fuck you." Manny flips Derrick the bird as he's rolled away.

I finish reading a magazine article about the fifth movie in a series I've never seen and decide to call it a night. Nobody else necessarily wants much to do with me—my past was a topic of discussion within days of moving in—and frankly, I don't want anything to do with anyone else. Manny's a fine distraction but I can only stomach a single friend at a time. I leave the magazine behind since I don't need it anymore and slowly stand. My knees creak and pop. Sound like old leather straps about to give. I take a breath, steady myself, and move forward. The first few steps are always stiff but I loosen up enough to ignore the little nagging pains that shoot up and down my legs. I stop a moment when I think I hear someone call my name but it's just in my head.

I steal an extra bottle of water on my way back to the room. Need a little something exciting to happen while I wait to die.

* * *

"ARE YOU MAKING FRIENDS?" KATIE sits on the sofa in my room. She looks like its burning her, as if sitting any longer would be a torture she never experienced before.

The body language makes me angry. Makes me want to throw it all out in the open. Not my place. Besides, my granddaughters are climbing all over my bed; annoying each other in tiny ways—a finger poke, a stuck out tongue. They make me smile.

"You know I ain't the sociable type," I say. "How's work? Everything going well?"

"Taking more shifts." A crack in that wall. "Got a friend watching the girls every Wednesday. It helps."

"You know you can dip into the money I put aside for you."

"Dad, we agreed we wouldn't talk about that money."

"Pop-Pop are you rich?" The older one, Kaylee, grips her sister Becca in a bear hug and smiles sweetly at me.

"Don't listen to Pop-Pop, sweetheart. He's joking." Katie stares daggers at me.

I ignore her. "Then dip into my pension check. Union had to be good for something."

Katie shakes her head. "All of that goes to pay for here, Dad. Your social security leaves enough in case of an emergency." She straightens her posture. "You should give the other money away to charity. It's—" She frowns. "It's no good."

No good. The money I hoarded for years working under the thumb of some tertiary Mafioso is no good. So much suffering and so many terrible decisions. I did it all for some greater good and now it sits in a checking account untouched for who knows how long. It was never my money, I figured. It was an investment in Katie; in the little girls running around my cramped room in this shitty old folks' home.

"No more money talk." I slowly stand up. Kaylee runs over and gives me a useless push to help me onto my feet. I brush her hair aside with my palm and smile. "Thank you sweetie." I turn to Katie. "Let's talk a walk. I think there's bingo if the kids would enjoy that."

Katie sighs. "Sorry, Dad, we need to leave. The girls have tae kwon do and it's literally the only time I have to do laundry this week."

My heart breaks but I've learned to ignore that. "Sure. Look, though, I understand why you want nothing to do with the other thing but maybe take enough to get the laundry done elsewhere. Treat yourself to a dinner out with the kids. Just—"

Katie stands and walks over to me. She takes the crook of my arm and leads me towards the door. "We're fine. I promise. It isn't only about where that money came from, you know."

Her own past. I get it. Katie doesn't want to think of the life she had before she found meaning in her children. Doesn't want to think about her dead mother. She doesn't want to think about the drugs or why I went to prison. The time before she realized she could take the hard road to raise those girls right. Katie learned a lot from me—all the things not to do. As much as she hurts me, I'm always so damn proud of her.

"I'll stop. I swear. Feel bad is all." I point to the door. "I'll walk you all out." Grab the little one—I can still pick her up with momentum—and kiss her as many times as she can bear before squealing. The bigger clings to my leg and I go soft inside. Best goddamn drug in the world. "Maybe I can see how the pension flows. There's gotta be a way to put a little extra money in your pockets." I laugh. "Ain't like I'm living it up here."

"Worry about you, Daddy. I can do this." Katie leads the way out.

I believe her.

Outside my room, we bump into Manny alone in a wheelchair. He seems down. Doesn't say hi.

I kiss the girls goodbye. "Pop-Pop needs to talk to his friend," I explain and they leave me with smiles. I turn my attention to Manny. Grab his shoulder when he doesn't look at me. "Hey. You doing okay? Pretty far from your room."

Manny's eyes are wet. "I'm in trouble," he chokes back a sob, "So much trouble."

"What happened?"

"I fucked up. I fucked up and he's going to be so mad at me." Manny licks his lips. They're chapped—frayed at the edges.

I notice there's a neat set of fading bruises on Manny's neck. They hadn't been there the last time I saw him. Last time I saw him was when Derrick was wheeling him off for what I thought was a doctor's appointment.

"Manny, what did you fuck up?" I give him a gentle smack on the cheek. "What, you shit the wrong bed?" Keep it light. Calm him down. I know how to do this—how to make a man talk. One of the only things I was ever good at. Damn good at spotting the kind of bruise that ain't from a slip and fall too. "This about Derrick? What happened with Derrick?"

Manny lowers his head. Grabs the lapel of my shirt. "I'm in so much trouble. The doctor didn't give me what I needed to bring.

He wouldn't listen to me. They're going to be mad. I promised them and I fucked up." He looks up at me. "What am I going to do? They'll kill me."

I'm at a loss. What the hell kind of old folks' home is this? Why is this man so scared? What could someone like Derrick possibly have him doing that would provoke this kind of response? We're old men. We're no longer useful. I find a rage building inside me. A taste for the past that I pretend not to miss day in and day out; as if the memories of me in my prime, of me when I held some kind of fucking control in my life should be something I'm ashamed of. I think of the girls, though. I think of the fact that there are two human beings on this planet with no prior knowledge of the poison their grandfather is to this fucking world. That their mother looks at her father with equal parts pity and pure disdain. It should be enough to make me stop and call someone else to handle Manny.

That anger burns me and that feeling is so goddamn familiar and so very comforting in its own special, fucked up way. I can't fight it, not anymore. I'm so tired of feeling useless again. Exhausted of feeling like a piece of trash on the side of the road. So that heat boils in my gut, rises up my chest, and drifts out my throat.

"What do you need me to do, Manny? Tell me how I can help you." The words give me strength and suddenly my knees don't hurt so much anymore.

Manny smiles at me. He breathes a sigh of relief and collects himself. I crouch as best I can using the arm of wheelchair to balance.

Manny says, "I need you to see Doctor Anderson. Tell them you have stomach upset . . . "

* * *

I TELL THEM I HAVE stomach upset. That something I ate is shredding my guts and making me piss out my backside. The appointment's scheduled and there I am, sitting in an examination office and watching a doctor opening a cabinet with two locks on it.

"I'm going to give you a few samples and prescribe a full dose of loperamide. It should help your stomach settle." He turns to me and smiles. "Otherwise, Mr. Clarke, everything else seems fine. We'll call you soon with any lab results if we need to."

I nod and try to give the impression that I'm a harmless, weak old man. "I'm sorry, doc, but is there any way I can get a little water? I'm parched to high hell. Probably a little dehydrated."

The doctor nods. "Of course. Give me a second." He steps out of the room in a hurry—eager to please.

I stare at the open cabinet and ask myself if shit like this was always so easy or if the creases all over my face have given me some kind of newfound helplessness. No wonder little old ladies love shoplifting. Why wouldn't a person give it a shot if they were deemed invisible and harmless?

Moving as fast as I can, I shuffle to the cabinet and grab a few boxes of the loperamide from the back, taking care to give the impression that nothing has changed at first glance. Will someone notice that I've taken about seven boxes of free samples? Probably. But I'm hoping to be in my ambulette by then and the memory of me to be a smudge after the next four or five old timers come in complaining about pissing forty times a night.

I slip the boxes into the lining of my jacket. I smuggled a steak knife into my room the night before and set it all up. Thankfully, the boxes are thin and shouldn't bulge—hopefully. I make sure to safety pin the slits shut in a way that won't let a box fall out and get dressed all before the doctor walks back in with a paper cup of water.

"Thanks," I say as I take the cup and sip it. I wonder if I'm being too slow with it—suspicious. Why am I overthinking something like that? Am I nervous? I have no idea. I thought this would feel like it used to but I find it hard to remember what things like this really felt like. I convinced myself there was control and strength and all I'm getting out of this is shaky hands and a tongue too dry to drink a cup of water like a normal fucking human being.

The doctor examines his chart in the way a person would when they're ready to move on. "Okay then, Mr. Clarke. We'll be in touch. Have a good day. The ambulette's waiting outside."

I hightail it out of there and get onto the ambulette. The driver gives me a hearty hello and it looks like I'm the only fella he was waiting for, so we're off on the way back to Palm Heights. The ride's pleasant. No small talk. A Marlins game on the radio that I give fleeting attention to. Only thing that gets the heart rate up is the occasional rattle from my jacket when we hit a pothole coming off our exit. Nearly shit myself in fear but my driver doesn't notice.

We're a mile out from home when the driver gets a call—which he shouldn't take but does. He laughs a little and gives me a short glance. I know that kind of look—he knows. I'm not being paranoid. They noticed the missing boxes when I left—I know this and now the driver does as well. We pull into the drop off area of Palm Heights and now I'm faced with walking past the son of a bitch without issue. Not like there's anything in my hands. If anything, there's nothing to prove so long as I can get in the building. Hell, and so what if I nicked some extra diarrhea medicine? I can play the old and stupid card, can't I?

The driver stops the ambulette but doesn't open the doors. "Mr. Clarke?" The inflection is loaded with a follow up. "The doctor's office just called."

"They need more piss?" I ask.

The driver lowers his head. Rubs his eyes with his thumbs. He's been here before. It tires him. Not a good sign. "They're missing some medication, Mr. Clarke. Got any idea why?"

I shake my head.

The driver sighs. "Look, man. Give me what you took and I'll find a good excuse. I'm not in the mood." He talks to me like a fucking child. "We can say it was a mistake. You got confused or whatever."

I shake my head and stand up. "I need some rest."

The driver stands and blocks my path. "Mr. Clarke." He holds up his hands.

It's muscle memory and what I heard called 'old man strength' while I was locked up. You spend decades of your life doing the same motion over and over again and it comes back with no effort. Your body knows which way to bend and flex—even if the exertion isn't the same. Doesn't matter. If the task is programmed into your bone marrow the way it is mine, it all happens without even thinking—like a goddamn bird taking flight.

This is why the poor driver's index and middle fingers of his right hand bend back and snap so fucking easy. The shock registers on his face before the pain does. I pull the hand down once I hear the snap and twist his wrist as hard as I can. I feel the ligaments stretch but nothing rips—I'm either merciful or a little weaker than I used to be. I maintain the hold until he yelps and steps away from me; snatching at my hand but unable to muster the conviction to break my grip.

"Let me out," I growl, "Let me out and you forget all of this."

The driver lurches backwards to grab at the little handle that opens the door. I let go of his hand and he slumps onto the driver's seat and holds it like a newborn child. I hurry out of the ambulette and walk right into a group of three nurses waiting for me—Derrick at the head of the group.

"Mr. Clarke—Sean. What happened?"

I turn around and point at the driver. "This little motherfucker accused me of stealing," I yell. Try to ramp up the drama. Bring attention to the event in order to divert from what I did. "He physically assaulted me."

Derrick keeps his distance. "Mr. Clarke, your doctor called us and mentioned there were quite a few boxes of anti-diarrhea medicine missing from their office. I understand if you got confused but they prescribed—"

"I'm not fucking confused." I raise my hands. "And what fucking medicine, you assholes? What medicine. I'm empty fucking-handed." I thrust my arms up—bad call—and a box of loperamide falls out followed by another, and another. The struggle loosened the safety pins I used to hold my jacket together.

Derrick shakes his head and motions to me. "Come on, Mr. Clarke."

"No." I point at him. "This is your fault. Manny needed help."

Derrick arches an eyebrow. "Mr. Gutierrez? He's perfectly . . . oh . . . " He sighs and turns to his coworkers. "I got this." Derrick walks over to me and empties the rest of the medicine from my jacket lining. "Let's call your daughter and have a quick talk, Mr. Clarke."

"But Manny. He needed this. He said he needed this or they were going to kill him."

"Let's go inside, Mr. Clarke. Please. We can talk about it inside." Derrick leads me into the main building and directly to the front desk. He guides me into a little office to the right of the desk and pulls out a chair. "Sit please."

I do as I'm told. I realize I'm sweating.

Derrick leans on a desk and smiles. "What did Manny tell you?"

"He was in trouble," I say.

"And he needed seven packs of loperamide, right?"

I nod.

Derrick points behind me. "Manny's eating ice cream right now. Not a care in the world. He still thinks it's Tuesday but it's Friday. He also tends to slip back a few years sometimes. I think you two have a lot in common when it comes to your shared past endeavors."

"Oh yeah? How's that?"

"Manny used to steal pharmaceuticals back in the day. Stuff to use when they make meth or fuck with pain pills for folks to drown themselves to death out there. You know they use loperamide for that? To cut OxyContin?"

I shake my head. "No."

"Yeah, it's what they caught Manny with at the last home he lived in. He said the same thing too: that he was in danger."

"But he wasn't?"

Derrick nods. "But he wasn't."

Far past dementia-addled. Manny's plain nuts and maybe I am a little too. Time was I would've noticed if the story was loose, if the desperation stank of something other than sincerity. I realize that maybe all that confidence and effort was something else—my own desperation.

Something clicks. "What about the bruises?"

"On his neck?" Derrick shrugs. "No clue, really. We've got someone to look at Manny on Monday. Maybe a blood clot or something. I mean, he seems to be okay. You, though, Sean. You stole a bunch of medicine and broke a man's hand. I have no idea what we should do next but I think we've all got a tough day ahead of us." He frowns. "I know you're not a bad person but I'm not sure you're a good fit here and I think my bosses are going to agree." He pulls his phone from his pocket. "Let's call your daughter."

* * *

KATIE STARES STRAIGHT AHEAD AS she drives. She breathes through her nose. The girls are in the back sleeping. It's past 10 pm and they have school tomorrow according to their mother.

I shift in my seat. Hear the rattle from the little trailer hitched to the back of Katie's car with all of my things.

"I'm sorry," I say for the hundredth time.

"Not now, Dad. Go to sleep, please." Her voice is cold. Reminds me of the way her mother spoke to me before the end of everything—before the world ended.

"You can use my checks now. Sort of a blessing in disguise, right?"

Katie pulls the car over. She shifts into park and turns with the speed of a viper. "A blessing? A fucking blessing?" she hisses the words quietly, her face reddening. "You broke a man's fucking hand and tried to steal medicine for fucking diarrhea? What? Did you miss cell bars? Did you miss hurting people? Like you hadn't done enough, Dad?"

"I thought my friend was in trouble."

"Bullshit. You thought you could do what you always did: make yourself feel big and important."

"I never wanted that. I wanted to make everything better."

Katie's shoulders slouch. "I can't do this." She pulls the car back onto the road. "You were with Bank of America, right? Same as me?"

"What do you mean?"

"The money, Dad. Your dirty money."

I nod slowly. "Yeah, I have a card."

We drive in silence for a few more miles and Katie pulls into a parking lot for Bank of America. She shuts the car off and holds a hand out. "Give me your wallet."

I do as I'm told.

"My birthday or Ma's?"

"Both. Yours first then hers"

Katie nods and gets out of the car. I watch her at the ATM as she angrily jabs her finger at the screen and wipes tears from her eyes with her free hand. She stomps back over to the car and sits down. Holds my wallet out. "Here."

"What did you do?" I ask.

"I moved some of the money to my account to handle taking you in for a few weeks while we find a new place for you to live."

"You can take extra for the girls."

"Stop talking before I scream."

Katie gets back on the road and I watch her drive. I watch the rage and disappointment wash over her the same as the passing headlights from the other side of the highway. How she grips the steering wheel; I can imagine her fantasizing it's my neck that she's wringing. The thoughts that must be playing in her head: how she'll have to explain this to the girls. How I'll be an extra body in an apartment that probably doesn't have much room left to begin with.

"I'm sorry Katie." It's all I know to say. "I'm so fucking sorry." I gave the same words to her mother all the time. She's inherited things nobody should want; those old words and this old man. Best favor I ever did for that girl was get locked up but I should have known better, I should never have walked out of there alive.

I know all those things but I don't say them—I can't. Instead, the tears well up easier than they used to and I croak out, "I'm so sorry."

Katie doesn't answer.

THE UNIDENTIFIEDS

BY J. D. ALLEN

Saturday 2 p.m.—The Funeral

FOR JIM, A FUNERAL WAS about as appealing as removing his own appendix. Two funerals in as many weeks had him planning a stop at the liquor store on the way home and a look at his choice of occupation. Jim Bean squinted as the Vegas sun reflected off his cousin's silver casket. Jim had picked out the coffin and planned the service. With the recent experiences, he'd learned obituaries should be seventy-five words, and lives could shatter in a moment.

He now stood over the proceedings. He fought Vegas sweat and tears as Alexis's casket thumped to the bottom of the rectangular gave. She was the only person left from his old life he still called family. The girl in that box had been shot in the chest and burned to cover the identity of her remains.

Jim glared across the casket as the words meant to soothe and heal drifted over to the deceased. He hoped they helped her.

Andrew Zant stood opposite that death divide. His dark glasses and darker suit complemented the smirk on his pale, pointy face. Jim read victory in that smug look. Maybe it didn't show his eyes, but it was displayed in his presence. Jim wasn't surprised to see someone from his organization here to confirm the death. The shock was Zant showed up in person. He even let himself be photographed on the way to the graveside service.

A hum of rage and hostility was ready to bust from Jim's chest as he openly stared at the Vegas tycoon. The man thought himself superior. Thought he'd gotten away with it.

He thought wrong.

Wednesday Morning—Three Days before the Funeral

"I NEED TO SEE HIM now." Jim was not about to back down from the pit bull of a receptionist outside Zant's office in the Americana hotel.

An Andrew Zant owned hotel and casino on the Las Vegas Strip. Zant's office was on the twenty-third floor. She snarled, but typed a message on her computer, presumably an instant message to the boss man on the other side of the steel door. Only Vegas casino owners locked themselves in safe rooms like it was a usual way to do business. There was a buzz, and the door unlatched.

The Persian rug Jim walked on was dead ugly and probably cost more than his townhouse. The wall to his right was a room-length glass terrarium. The thing was ceiling height, maybe fourteen feet floor-to-ceiling, complete with living trees and a small pond. The oversized tank was home to a hulking snake. Zoro, as the gold plaque read, was the most massive boa constrictor Jim had seen outside a B horror film.

There was an entry in the glass near Zant's desk. Jim wondered how many of bodies of his enemies the beast had constricted and ingested. He wished he hadn't contemplated that given the reason for his visit. He'd have scotch-addled nightmares of wrestling the yellow-white reptile.

"Well, well, well. Mr. Bean." Zant lit a cigarette and leaned back in his chair. "Now that I've dropped everything I was working on, what can I do for you?"

His small features and tiny fish-like mouth gave Bean the creeps every time he had to talk to the man. Which, since his cousin Alexis had taken up with the hotel owner, had been more than one time too many.

"I'm looking for Alex." Jim didn't want to show his concern for her for fear that Zant would clam up. They'd met before on business. He knew Jim was a private investigator. Jim wanted to have a conversation, see what the jackass had to say before he thought he was being interrogated. Jim watched his eyes and body language.

"You think I hold her schedule? Perhaps I'm her secretary? Because my time is so invaluable that you come up here presuming I'll check her calendar for you?" He glared, waiting for a confirmation of his importance and inconvenience.

He got neither. Jim's turn to shrug. "You are her latest boyfriend." Alexis and Zant met when she was the headline dancer in a show in the Americana Lounge. Zant had taken her in, impressed her with money and local celebrity. Alexis quickly got in over her head. The money and the glamour of being Zant's girl hooked her as fast as any drug could. Jim had worried then. He was even more worried now.

A tiny bit of anger slipped in the rat-faced man. "She went to Texas. Or that's what I was told. Something about a friend in need."

That was bullshit. Alexis had texted Bean the night before. One word.

Help.

"I didn't know she had friends in Texas." Jim was standing with his hands clasped in front of his body. Legs relaxed. Ready to move if needed. Zant was also relaxed, but lying and deceit were this guy's bread and butter. He wouldn't give it away too easy.

"She mentioned the chit's name a time or two. Glenna, Gina? I don't know." He sucked on the imported cigarette, blew the smoke out, turning his attention to his disturbingly large snake. "I'll tell her you stopped by when I talk to her."

Dismissed.

"When do you anticipate you might talk to her?"

"How should I know? The girl's in Texas with my credit card. Could be she stays for a while. Now get the hell outta here."

Jim left on that note, not pushing his luck. If Alexis was in danger, poking Zant's buttons could make it worse on her. He headed down to the casino floor, making a note of the cameras along the way. Likely Zant had contacted security to track Jim's way to the exit. He stopped at a quarter slot and fed it a fiver. The two minutes it would take for him to lose that cash would be just enough to check out staff. He was casual about it, pretending to watch a girl in a short skirt strut past.

Yahtzee!

Big Al was working a blackjack table. Al was a great guy and had a soft spot for Alexis. Jim hit the Play All button on the machine and promptly lost his five.

Slipping up to the blackjack table, he felt the buzzing sensation of eyes on him. Took him about two seconds to see a security goon had eased into the warning zone. Close enough to be recognized, not so close as to make a scene.

Al looked up and didn't give him a hint of recognition. Traded the cash Jim laid on the table for chips. Jim tossed in his bet. A ten spot.

Al dealt to Jim and the other player at the table. He was not into chatting either.

Jim busted. Twenty-four.

"So. Any good dancers in this place?"

Al slightly hesitated. His glance darted to Jim's face and then back to the shoe to pull more cards.

"There was one girl. But she seems to have lost her job."

Jim felt his gut tighten. "Really?" He said it slow.

Blackjack.

He collected his winnings. The other player vacated his chair taking his little stack of chips along.

Jim had changed the flow of the table with his presence. Too bad.

"Yeah. I heard she made a scene in front of wrong big deal player and they took her to the Ranch."

Damn.

"Any clue where the ranch might be?"

"Out behind that old tire place off 95 on the road to Corn Creek . . . or so I hear that's where problems go to die or fade away."

He dealt the cards again. King. Queen. Nine.

Bust.

Jim slid his remaining chips to Big Al as a tip, a nice one, and gave him a slight nod of the head. "Thanks."

"I hope you find her in time." It was as much of a whisper as one could use in a bustling casino.

Wednesday Afternoon—Three Days before the Funeral

JIM HAD TRACKED DOWN THE location on his mapping software. It was well-removed from town, looked like an abandoned flop-house. He surveyed it from the remote side which he accessed by a borrowed four-wheeler. There were several wooden structures. He couldn't identify their former uses but upon searching, he found the floors had been ripped open in two of the buildings and the boards carelessly replaced. Maybe if Zoro had trouble digesting all of his human snacks, this is where the remnants came to rest.

He eased a little closer and used his binocs to zoom in. He could see people moving around in the house. He hoped Alexis was one of those silhouettes. Being in a place like this meant she might not be in great condition, but hopefully, she was alive.

There was no way to move in closer without being spotted. No real foliage or terrain to hide behind. His worry compelled him to rush the castle, but he needed a plan first. You didn't walk away from Andrew Zant if he'd decided your time was up. She'd have to disappear. Zant's reaper-like fingers greased the wheel of every illegal or immoral venture in the city. She had to be killed and buried to be forgotten.

Jim backed off. Time for a visit with Ely.

Wednesday Evening—Three Days before the Funeral

At Ely's place, he took a swig from a cheap scotch. "I know it sounds crazy, but . . . "

"Dude. I'm all about the crazy, but this one will get you hard time and maybe a Bellvue visit."

Ely was an old Vietnam vet with an extensive association with computers and the tech world. The guy existed in the stoned-out-of-his-skull state, but Jim didn't care. Ely could find the most obscure things. And thus the visit.

"It's your cuz, so I'm there."

He tackled the keys in front of one of his wall of workstations. Jim felt a little like he was in the Bat Cave in Ely's renovated stone building. The guy grumbled, tapped keys, and cursed as he worked. Jim looked at the clock. Figured it might take him some time to find a suitable body.

"Gotcha." Ely kissed the monitor. "Pretty good match."

Bean chuckled. "Four minutes. I guessed seven."

"Alexis's body type fit a couple of the unidentifieds at the morgue. One was interred into the Remembrance Mausoleum at Wedgewood Park today." Ely spun in the chair to face Jim. "But getting the body outta there is up to you, my man. May I suggest a crowbar with an ergonomic handle." He handed Jim a slip of paper with a number and a letter on it. *G 125.*

Thursday Later at Night—Three Days before the Funeral
Wedgewood Park

Jim struggled to get the poor girl's body into his SUV. Brash move to back up to the mausoleum and rob the above-ground grave, but it was the best he could do in the time he had. Alexis could be dead, beat up or worse. Taking this poor woman would be hard by himself, but he was not about to ask for help and implicate anyone else in the madness. He had three slugs from a flask before he got the nerve to pick the lock on the crypt and take the body.

The empty casket was back in the tomb, the crypt relocked, and every step of the way, Jim kept trying to justify his plan by assuring himself that at least this would give this unidentified girl's death some meaning.

Wednesday Even Later at Night—Two Days before the Funeral

BEAN WASN'T A BIG FAN of guns. A shock and awe plan without firepower added to the madness of the idea. Going in alone with nothing but a knife, a slap jack, and a string of old fire crackers.

He pulled up in front of the paint-peeling front stoop. Never hurt to ask first. If he could talk them into giving Alexis up he could still right his wrongs. He walked without worry right to the front door. Knocked. Waited.

Knocked again.

The door swung open. A dazed-looking kid already missing two teeth glared at him. Said nothing.

"I need to see Alexis."

"Nobody here wants to see you." He started to close the door.

Jim put his boot in the door. Pays to have the steel-toed boots on occasion. He showed the Las Vegas PI license this scheme would most likely get revoked if he fails. "Jim Bean. I'm a private investigator, not a cop. My client is looking for her daughter. I don't give a shit what else you got going on in there."

The man's face pinched. "Ain't no bitch here named Alexis." He tried to shut the door again. He cursed when the boot still stopped the process.

"What's your name?"

The asshole tried the use his second-hand hundred-dollar running shoes to push out the size twelve Redwing. Jim wanted to laugh at the guy's rising panic.

"If I leave without her, I will stop at the end of the block and call the cops. Seeing as I can see paraphernalia from here, they'll have probable cause to come up in here and crawl up your ass. Right?"

The kid sucked his lips between his teeth in an apparent struggle to think it through. Maybe he was smarter than Bean had given him credit for. His darting eyes indicated that he was thinking through all the ramifications.

"They will come down here and take care of this situation. They'll come busting in here and whatever you guys have going on is going to get your picture on the police blotter by morning. And if I have my facts straight . . . Zant will consider you a problem moving forward."

That got his attention. He straightened, his bloodshot eyes bulged.

"I'll say it one more time. All I want is the girl, that girl."

He gave Jim the once over for the third time. "Wait here."

The door closed when Jim moved his foot, but he had no intention of waiting. He counted to three and opened the door, walking in as if he paid the rent. A quick scan as the second goon entered the room and found Jim the back door, a hall to the left and a black-and-white tiled kitchen to the right. There was a girl passed out on the couch and another staring at a soundless fishing show not comprehending a shit thing around her.

Neither girl was Alexis. Both would have to be protected. Good thing he started with the less messy choice.

The kid from the door rushed at Jim with a small knife, but his state of mind wasn't much better than fishing show girl. Jim took his stance. He dispensed with the pocket knife with a block from his left hand. A right elbow to the throat left the kid sucking air on the matted red carpet. He matched the flopping fish in the boat on TV.

The new guy produced a gun. It was silver and pointed at Jim, center mass. Model and caliber were irrelevant at the moment.

New Guy fired regardless of the girl on the couch. Jim fell behind the sofa as a couple of rounds blasted through the back, spewing foam and fabric fragments in to the air. The shots exploded through the back near Jim's feet. The girl would be sacrificed without hesitation.

The hallway was closer, but trigger-happy New Guy was in the way. He lit the firecrackers, and Jim hoisted the cheap couch up, dumping the now screaming girl to the ground underneath it. He bolted for the protection of the old tile and tossed the firecrackers in the hall behind New Guy.

The loud popping echoed in the narrow hall, giving the impression there was firepower coming from behind. The rapid fire was a more significant threat than Jim. New Guy scrambled for the door scooping up the doorman on his way. He mumbled something about these girls and the value of his own hide.

Jim shook passed-out girl. She roused and grumbled. Not dead was all he cared about at the moment.

A scream came from down that little hall. Jim moved in low and slow. Smoke met him in the doorway at the far end on the left. One of the firecrackers had ignited some sheer curtains and then the bed. Near the closet door, Alexis squirmed in a chair. Her hands were duct-taped behind her back and her feet were taped to the chair's legs.

The tape was quick work. She looked unharmed. Questions would come later. "Get the girls into the truck." Jim ordered to get her to move. She did so without question.

He rushed to the back of the SUV.

"Is that a body?" One of the girls screamed when he pulled the package from the back of the vehicle.

"Stay put." He said to the three of them.

"Jim? What the hell have you done?" Alexis' pale, makeup-less face made her look so young.

"You have to disappear. We have to make Zant believe it." He hoisted the wrapped body up on his shoulder and carried her into the house then put her in the same chair. The flames were dancing closer as he taped the poor girl in Alexis's place.

He found the gun New Guy had dropped on his way out and put a single bullet in the girl's chest. He said a word of prayer to a god he no longer believed in over her twice-dead body.

Saturday—2:30 p.m. The Funeral

THE SERVICE WAS WRAPPING UP. Zant had stayed longer than needed just to confirm that Alexis was dead. Of course Alexis was in South Florida trying out her new identity as a bartender. New IDs are pricey. She gave the guy the jewelry Zant had given her to make up the costs. Jim hoped she was enjoying the sun and sand during her funeral. He felt even a bit smug about it. Alexis had confided in him that she was pregnant with Zant's child. The man didn't know. And he never would.

Zant approached as the few attendees began to disperse.

Jim gritted his teeth.

"I gotta say, you get points for the high production value, Bean." He glanced over at the cemetery plot, and then looked back to Jim. "The obit was a beauty" He shook his head. "And all the trouble of putting on a service." Zant cracked a smile.

"Love the theatre of it all." He made a circle with his index finger then removed his glasses and those beady gray eyes locked on Jim's face. "I'll let her go, Bean. But you have to know all you did was put yourself in debt."

He held those dark glasses folded and tapped them on his other fist, looking up as if to contemplate his words carefully. "It took me two nights thinking about it. Playing it over. You made a mistake. And I had to pull a string or two but I figured out how you did it. I even managed to scrounge up a bit proof."

He pulled a picture of Jim loading the body in his SUV at the mausoleum. "I'd hate for this to make a serious dent in your future ability to earn a living. Or her future ability to stay living."

Jim tried to keep his poker face. But he wasn't at all confident.

He'd been caught. He felt ill. His mind raced on options to extract Alexis from Florida.

"So, this is how we play this out. You owe me, Bean. Let's call it a favor for a favor. If I need info or something that falls under your expertise, you come running. No questions and nobody else finds out about our little arrangement. You do that, and pretty Miss Alexis can stay hearty and hale wherever you tucked her."

Zant didn't wait for the reply.

"I won't even bother to look for her."

ALL ACCOUNTED FOR AT THE HOORAY FOR HOLLYWOOD HOTEL

BY ELEANOR CAWOOD JONES

MONA, LINGERING OVER A THIRD cup of coffee, flipped through her collection of vintage postcards while the all-consuming sound of crunching cereal across the table grated increasingly on her nerves.

She took a sip of lukewarm coffee, gritted her teeth, and reminded herself of her husband's many good qualities—of which turning mealtime into crunchtime was not one. Things were easier when she had to dash off to her accounting job. In those days, there was never time for another cup of coffee, much less prolonged crunching noises.

"Rodney!"

Rodney looked up from the *Racing Times*. "Mmmm?" At least he wasn't speaking with his mouth full.

"I wonder if this hotel is still around?" She held up a '50s postcard with a modestly clad bathing beauty posing in front of a diamond-shaped, brightly painted sign advertising the Hooray for Hollywood Motel. In the photo, an appealing, pink building featuring a bright blue swimming pool practically beckoned vacationers. A single-story structure in a horseshoe shape provided easy access to drive in and unload luggage. The fine print mentioned another pool in the back of the motel, as well as an onsite restaurant. Nothing about ocean front, but Mona knew the area well enough to know the motel would be right between the coastal road A1A and highway 95 in the heart of Hollywood, Florida.

Rodney perked up. "Alexa, phone number for Hooray for Hollywood Motel in Hollywood, Florida."

Mona shuddered, once again, at having to share her vintage, mid-century kitchen with Alexa the interloper. But Rodney had retired two years before her and had spent his spare time acquiring gadgets, of which this conversational internet talkie was the latest.

Rodney pushed a piece of paper across to her. "Here's the phone number. You ready for a trip?"

On the day she retired six months before, Mona had sworn she was going to do nothing but enjoy sitting at home, taking walks in the neighborhood, and reading books. Which, for the first four months, had been paradise. Now she was getting restless, and Rodney knew it. He was always ready to go at the drop of a hat, and had even acquired a tiny, vintage, twin-axle Airstream trailer. It was shiny and always waiting in the driveway of their split-level Ohio home. He was dying for a chance to hook it to their big Buick sedan and take off for parts unexplored.

Rodney's brown eyes twinkled at her over his newspaper. "There's a little racetrack 'round Hollywood, you know. I could take you out for a few two-dollar bets." It was their inside joke, that they derived just as much excitement over picking a two-dollar winning horse as they would have wagering much more. They'd figured that out more years ago than Mona cared to count, when they stopped by Gulfstream Park during their Florida honeymoon. They'd had so much fun they stuck around for an extra three days at a little family motel just south of Hollywood, spending days at the beach and nights at Gulfstream, enjoying the lavish buffet suppers between modest bets. They'd been sad when they found out the motel was torn down a few years after their trip. And though they'd been to Florida several times since, that early trip lived on in Mona's memory as the best of the lot. It would be fun to recreate it.

Besides, that twinkle in Rodney's eye reminded her why she'd fallen for him in the first place; it might be the perfect time to take a late-in-life second honeymoon. They were a childless couple and with no work commitments, they could stay as long as they liked, maybe even all winter long.

She smiled back at Rodney and put down her coffee cup. Her spirits lifted as she picked up the new, much-loathed, bells-and-whistles cell phone her husband had presented to her the day after she retired, and dialed the Hooray for Hollywood Motel.

"What?" a voice rasped on the other end of the phone.

Taken aback, Mona held her hand away from her ear and looked at the phone as if she could see what the presumed was the grumpiest man in the world on the other end. A goblin, perhaps?

"Any vacancies the week after next?" She picked a date at random.

"Got two prime rooms open starting November sixth." He sounded a bit more cheerful, and about a thousand years old. "How long you stayin'?"

Mona negotiated a room and price to stay for a week, hung up, and turned her thoughts to packing while Rodney grinned at her across the table. She thought about buying a bathing suit and spared a moment to recall wistfully the size she wore on their honeymoon. But no matter. That charmer across the table (now thankfully cereal-free) seemed to like her okay like she was.

* * *

MONA WAS GLAD TO PULL up at last at the Hooray for Hollywood Motel. So the sign wasn't as brightly painted as on her vintage postcard. If she looked close enough, it might even be peeling. But the glass-fronted lobby was still intact, the building still flamingo pink, and even the round swimming pool in the middle of the horseshoe-shaped structure looked clean.

She stood and stretched in the gorgeous sunshine while Rodney backed the Airstream trailer into a parking place and unhitched the Buick, which he backed into the spot next to it. Not a lot of cars, but it was midday on a weekend and probably most tourists were on the beach or at the racetrack. They'd spent the night at a slightly grubby roadside inn outside Atlanta on the way down, and she couldn't wait to get into their room for a quick change of clothes, then maybe some lunch.

She walked into the lobby and came face to face with the gnome behind the desk, and was certain before he even opened his mouth this was the same Grumplestiltskin she'd spoken to on the phone. He humphed at her, looking up from an oversized laptop atop a beat-up, paper-strewn desk he'd placed behind the check-in counter. He struggled up from his chair and lurched over to meet her. They were the same height, just over five feet, and she decided she'd underestimated his age at one hundred. He had to be 101 if he was a day.

"The Johnstons from Ohio," she said cheerfully, tucking a loose strand of her newly highlighted hair behind one ear. "We're here for—"

"Yeah, yeah." The gnome waved a gnarled hand in the air. "Only folks from Ohio I'm expecting today." He shoved a sheet of paper at her. "Sign here, list the license plate. And that'll be an extra twenty-five dollars for the trailer for the week, since you're taking up two parking places."

Mona raised one eyebrow and opened her mouth to make a retort about the number of spaces currently available in the parking lot, but felt Rodney's hand gently pressing into the middle of her back.

"That'll be fine," Rodney boomed cheerfully. "We'll just get unpacked and grab a bite at the restaurant." He looked around. "Where *is* the restaurant, by the way?"

The gnome grinned at him, perfect dentures gleaming in the light. "Don't know that there's been a restaurant here in this building since about the mid '70s, now's I think about it. We turned that area into the bingo hall and meeting room. Used to have lots of political meetings and book clubs there in between the bingo games. Of course that was before the bingo got ruled illegal for us, and I guess the politicians' ladies who read moved on to bigger pastures." He gestured behind them to a glass-fronted room filled with tables and chairs. It looked lonely and unused. In fact, the whole motel had an air of disuse.

Mona studied him. He was wearing a pair of neatly creased blue jeans, a pressed sport short, and a clean pair of white sneakers. What was left of his snow white hair was parted neatly in the middle of his head. Down, but now out, she decided.

"I'm afraid we're at a disadvantage." Rodney was bringing out his best retired public affairs officer voice. "We're Rodney and Mona. And you are?"

The gnome sized Rodney up and decided to break out a few manners of his own. "Well, I'm Harvey, aren't I? Harvey Sebastian. Florida born and bred. Welcome to The Sunshine State." He pushed the slip of paper toward Rodney, along with a pen. "Sign here and we'll put you in a room on the back side, away from the road. Just walk drive around behind to room 107 and that's yours for the week. Anything you don't find, you call me. I'm the owner. Maid service too, now you mention it." He turned around to search a drawer in the old desk, looking for their key, Mona assumed.

She saw a familiar box on the gnome's—Harvey's—desk. "Oh, look!" She said before she could stop herself. "Fasten software! That's the best home accounting program around. How do you like it?"

Harvey looked at her and scratched his left eyebrow. "Well, the truth is, I'm used to being self-sufficient, but I'm having a little trouble getting it to work just perfectly. No background in computers, just hotel management, and the paperwork's got a little beyond me. I thought this new-fangled software program would help, but I reckon I'm gonna have to hire me some help to get it set up, and that'll be tough 'cause I'm not really a people person."

No kidding, Mona thought.

Rodney finished filling out the form and, seeing what was coming, put his hand back on his wife's back and pressed again. Hard.

"But that's what I do! Or at least I did until six months ago. I know all about accounting and software programs, both for home and business. I worked for a private financial consulting firm." Mona felt a pang, remembering her old job fondly.

Rodney groaned softly. "We're on *vacation*, honey."

Harvey studied her. "So, you any good?"

Rodney removed his hand and gave up.

Mona felt her hackles rise. "I ran the office, dealt with clients, automated businesses, and saved everybody a ton of money along the way. Yes, I'd say I was *good*."

Harvey made up his mind. "So maybe I give you a reduction in the price of the room and you give me a few lessons, then. What do you say, want to barter?"

"Even better," Mona said. "You give us the room for free and I spend six hours a day helping you organize and set up. That desk looks a mess and I shudder to think how much paper you've got hiding in the back room. I can at least get you started."

She heard Rodney sigh beside her and turned to him, smiling brightly. "But I need evenings off to watch sunset on the beach and hit the track at Gulfstream with my husband."

And just like that, Mona had a job, free room and board, and a week's worth of dates with the handsomest husband she knew. She reached over and squeezed Rodney's hand and felt him squeeze back, which she knew meant he was fine with it all.

"I just didn't realize how much you missed working," he told her that night. "I knew you were worried you were retiring too soon, but I know you didn't like the new boss much. I'm sorry if I pressured you to quit, honey."

"I thought I was ready, too," Mona said. She unpacked a new pink dress printed with big blue flowers. Very Floridian, she thought, smoothing it on the hanger. "But it's just a week, and I'll have him set up right as rain. You'll see. We get a free vacation, too." Not that money was that tight, but they had talked all the way down about maybe pulling up stakes in Ohio and trying to afford a little place of their own in Florida. And with a little luck, they'd need their money to stretch through many more years together, with lots of sunsets and two-dollar bets in their future.

She smiled and turned to Rodney. "Need more coat hangers, dear?" He was still a snappy dresser, she thought fondly. He'd brought more clothes and shoes than she had.

* * *

A MONTH LATER, THEY WERE relaxing at the pool behind their room, enjoying a couple of drinks topped with sliced pineapple. Rodney had set up a makeshift bar in their room and kept ice, lemons, and pineapples in the little refrigerator.

"Any closer to being done?" Rodney asked lazily.

Mona smiled at him and looked around their little slice of heaven. Their room wasn't overly large, but it was all they needed. The pool was empty and sparkling in the sunlight, since Harvey had just finished his daily swim. It was the pool that had turned out to be the real gem. Surrounded by tall coconut palms, the water was shaded and a comfortable temperature. Just right for floating or swimming short laps. Even better, she, Rodney, and Harvey were the only ones allowed to use it. The other guests, what few there were, were relegated to rooms and the larger pool in front of the motel, by the highway.

"Well," she replied slowly. "We've got all the bills automated. Everything comes right in and right out of Harvey's business account now like clockwork, right on time. He just has to click a few buttons and remember a few simple passwords. He can use the software perfectly. We have it set up that all the room payments go direct to the checking account, too. In fact, he really doesn't have to leave this place to do any banking at all, unless someone gives us cash. And Harvey isn't big on reporting cash. He's got a stash in a drawer in his room."

Rodney looked at her in astonishment. He hadn't missed the use of the words *we* and *us*. "And you're okay with him not reporting cash?"

Mona shrugged. "I'm his accounting consultant, not his conscience. No higher ups to report to and, frankly, he's not bringing in a whole lot of income. When his parents were alive and he was their manager, they brought in a pretty penny and it's all salted away in checking and savings accounts. He's not a big believer in the stock market so it's all pretty simple, cut and dry. Besides, he uses the cash to pay for the paper delivery, milk man, and grocery deliveries. He just leaves it out on the front desk for them."

Rodney grinned at her. "You've mellowed out, Mona. And I kind of feel like we've slipped back into a simpler time. Imagine getting fresh milk delivered every other day, and all the cottage cheese and yogurt you could want." He paused. "You have any desire to head back up north any time soon? We may have some banking of our own to do, sort the mail from the post office, that kind of thing. And is Norma tired of watering the plants yet?"

Mona stretched luxuriously. "No hurry if you're not. I took a little personal time to set up all our accounts to pay automatically last week, and Norma doesn't have enough to do so she doesn't mind at all taking care of the plants and making sure the pipes don't freeze." She hesitated. "Any chance you're good with having our mail forwarded down here for a little while, too?"

Rodney though about it. "I like it," he said slowly. He gestured around them. "Feels right. And, hey, maybe semi-retirement isn't so bad, is it? Not with a free room, six or seven restaurants with buffets and a strip of Florida beach within walking distance, and all the swimming and relaxation we could want. No, I'm okay with stretching this out. Just take the time you need to help Harvey get all set up. In fact, maybe take a little more time than you need."

"Glad you think so." Mona stretched again and Rodney could see she was losing weight. The swimming and sunshine suited her. "I've got Harvey paying me a small retainer now. And I'm starting to talk to him about maybe doing some marketing, opening back up the restaurant and meeting room, maybe a few extra staff to help him spruce up the rooms so he doesn't have to do it all, once the people start coming. In fact, since he found out you're a PR man, he seems interested in seeing what you can do to help out in those areas."

She squinted at him, watching him take that in.

"I'll think about it," he said.

And a week later Rodney had placed fliers in the local grocery stores and churches advertising free space for book clubs and Bible studies, with snacks, tea, coffee, and soft drinks for purchase. He'd cleaned and repaired old tables and chairs and set them up with attractive tablecloths from the dollar store on the next block. He'd turned the Airstream trailer into a working toolshed and a place to store odds and ends, so the meeting area didn't look cluttered. He was also planning to turn a corner of the meeting area into a small gift shop carrying hats, Hooray for Hollywood Motel shirts, flip flops, notecards, and magazines. Mona had it set up so he could run credit card purchases straight through his cell phone into Harvey's account.

She'd set Rodney up with a small retainer, too. Automatically transferred from one of Harvey's accounts straight into his, regular as clockwork.

And two more months went by before everything changed abruptly. It was the day after Harvey had been talking to Mona about changing his will, and the milkman had dropped an entire glass quart of milk all over the front stoop outside the open front door, sending a crashing interruption of breaking glass to interrupt the conversation just when, she told Rodney later, it was starting to get good.

Because Harvey was starting to see results. Reservations were coming in. Three book clubs and a women's Bible study group had booked the meeting room on a regular basis. Harvey was beginning to see a second life come into the beloved vintage hotel his parents had built and run successfully, and he was thinking they might make perfect permanent caretakers, as he put it. They hardly saw him. He was admittedly a hermit, and liked nothing more than to hang out in his room with his several hundred cable channels, cook dinner on his hotplate, and go for the daily swims he credited for his long life and good health. Mona had taken to spending day hours at the front desk, and had a knack for customer service.

And just when it was all going so well, Mona got up for an early morning swim one weekend day after a violent rainstorm the night before, and saw an alarming sight in the pool. "Rodney, come quick! It's Harvey!" Rodney came rushing out of the room, took one look at Harvey floating face down in the pool, and jumped into the pool with his clothes on. He splashed through a few floating coconuts into the deep end and pulled Harvey's motionless body to the side, where Mona helped pull it over the edge.

Rodney climbed out and held Mona back as she leaned over to start resuscitation. "Look at his head."

Mona took one look and almost passed out on the concrete. A deep indentation in Harvey's head told the story that any efforts at first aid would be pointless. She teared up. "I told him to get those coconuts off the trees. I knew they'd hurt someone with all that wind! Damn him. It was just one more thing he didn't want to pay for, and he had plenty of money!"

Rodney reached out for her. "Let's call an ambulance."

She stiffened in his arms.

"What is it, Mona?

She turned her tearstained face up to look at him. "Maybe not quite yet."

"What in the world are you talking about?" Rodney was starting to get concerned. His wife had gone deadly calm.

"Do you really want everything to change?"

"Mona, you're not making any sense. Let me get my cell phone and call emergency services."

She clutched his arm. "Just hear me out. I've been happy here. Useful, happy, warm, comfortable. We've got this motel singing again. I know Harvey would want it to keep going. We call the ambulance, they take him away, we're out of our room and out of jobs and out of what I've come to think of as home." She sat back on her heels. "I don't *ever* want to go back to Ohio, Rodney. Hollywood has become our home now."

Rodney shook his head at her. "Nothing we can do about this. We'll find another hotel, or a little house somewhere down here. Not to worry."

Mona spoke slowly, as she would to a five-year-old. "Where else would we find money to live for practically nothing, as long as we want? We've got people coming in, all the groups coming for the meeting room, we've applied for the liquor license to get the restaurant up and running again—and, Rodney, Harvey has enough money going into his accounts that with what's already there, we can keep this place going for years. Years, Rodney."

Rodney gave her a blank stare.

"Don't you see, honey? I've got all his accounts automated. He doesn't even need to do anything but push a few buttons every month. He doesn't owe any debt or have any credit cards. I know all his security codes. *He doesn't even have to be here to run this place!*"

Rodney sat and thought. It made sense. In some weird, frightening way, it was true. Harvey didn't even need to be around for this place to grow and prosper. "What do you propose, Mona?" Then a frightening thing occurred to him. "You didn't have anything to do with this, right? I mean, it was an accident, right? The coconut hit him while he was swimming, right?"

Mona was horrified. "Of course not! I'm just thinking what's best, for Harvey, for us, for this motel. And I don't think having him hauled off in an ambulance and this place sold or shut down or even knocked down by a developer is best for anyone." She burst into tears. "How could you even think that?"

Rodney reached for her, pulled her to her feet. "I don't know. I think I just panicked." He wrapped her in his arms while Harvey lay at their feet. "Now come on with me." He let her go and bent down to scoop up Harvey, cringing while he did it, but it had to be done. "And bring the coconuts from the pool, too. Just in case one of them has blood, or worse, on it."

"Where are we going?" Mona couldn't imagine.

"To the deep freeze in the restaurant, Mona. Till I think can of something else, anyway. I was thinking we could put him in the Airstream but that's out front, and it's too hot. So this is better. Now come on. You know the combination to the freezer door, right? You can go ahead of me and get the door, clear some space in the back behind the soft drinks. Oh, and get a blanket or a bedspread. We don't want to leave any traces of Harvey in there once we figure out what to do."

That night, Rodney began work on the rock garden he'd been planning to build in the back garden, near a little fountain he'd found while clearing some overgrown plants. If he got the fountain working, it would be a cool, shaded resting place for Harvey. The rocks would serve as a marker.

It would be perfect.

And while he worked, Mona sat at her desk, going over the accounting files and passwords to make sure everything was in good working order. It, too, was perfect. She must remember to tell Rodney never to change anything. She'd write down the passwords for him, just in case, and teach him where everything was, just in case she got sick or something unexpected happened, but he must never change anything. Not a single inventory order, a single grocery list, a single deposit or withdrawal. In a sense, they had to become Harvey and adopt all his straightforward, dependable habits. Harvey wouldn't be missed. Except, she had to admit to herself, she'd miss him a bit. He had a way of growing on you.

If only he'd gotten around to changing the will, formally hiring them as caretakers and permanent residents. She knew that was what he wanted and intended. And the more she told herself that, the more she believed it.

Surely they were doing the right thing. It was just what Harvey would have wanted, after all.

* * *

BUSINESS WAS BOOMING A YEAR later when Mona found out Rodney had doubled the milk order. She found out when the milkman came around asking if the order was right, since Harvey had never spent an extra cent on extra quarts of milk in his life. He wanted to talk to Harvey directly and Mona could only pawn him off for so long by saying Harvey was unwell and recuperating in his room.

She was furious at Rodney, who then sneaked back to the desk and changed the milk order back to the original amount, but by then Mona's guard was up. The milkman had been back, bringing chicken soup for Harvey, and insisting his old acquaintance give him a call. Not that they'd ever been close, he told Mona, but he'd started thinking it over and was worried about the old geezer. The old geezer, he reminded Mona, who'd never changed his milk order once in the whole time he'd been delivering this route, or before. He'd checked.

Mona didn't like the way the milkman looked at her and she told Rodney that night to start packing the Airstream. The next day they'd empty some bank accounts and be gone. She told him he'd be lucky if she didn't leave him for being so stupid and cheating her out of her new home at the Hooray for Hollywood Motel.

"We'll talk about it later, on the road or at the airport," she told him. "I can't believe an intelligent guy like you did something so stupid. You'll be lucky if I don't kill you myself."

Rodney was practically in tears himself, and she relented a bit. "We didn't kill Harvey, but even though we know he'd want us to go on running the hotel, no one else will understand. They might call it theft. And if they find the rock garden, we're really in trouble. I think we need to leave right away. And don't worry, I'm not going anywhere. We're in this together."

And while they were putting the last of their things in the Airstream, the police came. The milkman had come to report a route regular he hadn't seen in some time. He'd explained about the milk order changing and all about how a new couple seemed to have taken over the hotel. He told them he'd walked the grounds the night before and found what looked like a new garden in the back grounds. Not a garden that was there back when he was a kid and used to swim in the back of the hotel, since his parents had been friends of Harvey back then.

A policeman without a lot to do on a lazy Florida morning decided the story was interesting, and stopped by the hotel. He marked Mona and Rodney back inside and sat them behind the front desk, where they clung to each other.

Their Hollywood fantasy, which had seemed so harmless, would be over soon.

* * *

Very late the night before, the milkman had taken one of his empty milk bottles to a deserted beach south of Hollywood—unless you counted the few drunks and homeless sure to be snoozing nearby. He'd smashed the milk bottle on the rocks beside the ocean and thrown the larger pieces into the water. The tide would take the care of the rest. He'd washed the bottle at home, but you never know what DNA would stick around, and he couldn't afford to keep it at home anymore while he decided what to do with it.

It had been a shame to have to do the old guy in, the childhood friend of his parents, but his mom had told him long ago Harvey was leaving him all the money he had in the world, and the hotel, because there just wasn't anyone else. Harvey had enjoyed the boy coming around when he was young, and even though they no longer had a relationship, he was sure the will was still the same, because Harvey was such a creature of habit.

When the new people came around and he'd overheard Harvey talking about making changes to the will, he knew he had to do something. It was easy enough to hit the old guy from behind while he was walking to the pool for his morning swim; even easier to toss a few coconuts into the water to make it look like a dreadful accident. Then, he waited.

His acting job at the police station had been superb. Concerned senior milkman worried about an old friend of his parents who he'd been prevented from seeing.

Sorry, Harvey, he thought. But what's done is done, and no use crying over spilled milk.

SOUTHERNMOST POINT

BY NEIL PLAKCY

IT STARTED WITH A SELFIE, and the drag queen who photobombed my boyfriend Lester and me.

Lester represents single-batch whiskeys, based out of Fort Lauderdale, where we both live. His region extends all the way to Key West, and one weekend in January he had a couple of promotions set up at bars on Duval Street, in the center of the entertainment district. I had a couple of days' vacation coming to me from the FBI, where I work as a special agent attached to the Violent Crimes Task Force, so I took them and went along for the ride.

And a beautiful ride it was, once we ran out of highway, then cleared the urban congestion of Key Largo. All of a sudden there was water on both sides of the road, the dark blue-green of the Atlantic to our left, the lighter green of the Gulf of Mexico to the right. The long emptiness of the Seven Mile Bridge was liberating, even with the skeleton of the old railroad bridge beside us.

We made it to Key West late on Sunday afternoon, and after we checked into a bed-and-breakfast on Duval Street, we rented bikes and cycled over to the Southernmost Point, a big marker striped in yellow, orange, and black that indicated we'd reached as far as you can go on the US mainland.

"Imagine living down here," Lester said. "Only ninety miles to Cuba, and nearly twice that back to Miami."

"I think there's a kind of person who likes to live at the edge," I said. "So far from everything else. Like you can leave all the troubles you had wherever behind you and kick back with a margarita and a pair of flip-flops."

"Thank you, Jimmy Buffett," Lester said. "Come on, let's get a picture of us with the marker in the background."

I held up my phone to take a selfie, and then Lester and I walked down to the water's edge, where we looked out at the choppy ocean. After a moment or two of contemplation, I pulled out my phone and looked at the photo. I realized that a drag queen with an enormous floral headdress and bright red cupid's bow lips had passed behind us just as I snapped the shutter, and photobombed the picture.

Especially with the drag queen behind us, it was a great shot, so before Lester and I got back on our bikes to head to Mallory Square to catch the sunset display, I uploaded the picture to Facebook and made it public. I'd only been in South Florida for six months by then, and I liked to use my Facebook feed to show my brother, my college buddies and my friends back home in Scranton what life was like in the area a wag had called the capital of the Caribbean.

Lester and I cycled along Whitehead Street, past the Six-Toed Cat Café, Straw Hat Mama's gift shop and Mel Fisher's Maritime Museum, and I stopped periodically to take and upload more photos. It was a beautiful afternoon, temperatures in the low seventies, the sun beginning to sink behind the tall trees.

We got to Mallory Square about fifteen minutes before sunset, locked up the bikes, and began to wander past magicians, jugglers, and performing cats, eventually positioning ourselves with a good view of the sinking sun.

It was a clear, cloudless evening, and the sun put on a great show for us, dipping below the horizon in a pink and red glow. The audience applauded, as every guide book mentioned, and Lester and I shared a quick kiss. As we stood up to head back to the bikes, my phone burped with a notification from Facebook. I had a new message from someone named Merrick Davidson.

Since I only accepted friend requests from people I know in the real world, I was surprised that I didn't recognize the name. I cocked my head and thought for a minute. Couldn't place him.

I gave in to my curiosity and clicked through to the message. *Angus, I need to talk to you as soon as possible about the young man in the picture behind you. I think he's my son, who has been missing for several weeks.*

It still wasn't clicking. Who was this guy, and how did he recognize a drag queen as his missing son?

"What's up?" Lester asked.

I showed him the message. "I feel like I ought to know who he is but I can't place him."

"Somebody from work?"

I shook my head. "I deliberately haven't friended any of the other agents. Trying to keep a little bit of personal life."

"Look at your mutual friends," Lester suggested, and I clicked through.

The first photo I recognized was Tom Laughlin. He was an older guy I'd met at Lazy Dick's, the gay bar near my house. "I know," I said. "Remember the time that Tom invited me to his book group meeting? Davidson was one of the other guys in the group."

"Sounds like he needs to talk to you. You want to make the call?"

"I guess." I held my finger over the phone number in Davidson's message, and a window popped up allowing me to dial it. "This is Angus Green. Can I speak with Merrick Davidson?"

"Thanks so much for getting back to me so quickly," he said, the relief evident in his voice. "I've been worried sick about Jeffrey and your photo was the first time I've had any idea he's all right."

"Slow down," I said. "First of all, how can you tell it's your son in the picture?"

"I bathed and diapered that boy. I went to his soccer games and his school plays, I taught him to drive a stick shift. I know that's his face."

"Even in makeup with that funky hat on his head?"

"Especially that way," Davidson said. "He was a shy kid in high school so his mother and I encouraged him to join the drama club. Turns out he has an amazing singing voice, and he starred as Edna Turnblad when his high school did a production of *Hairspray*."

Could a kid be any gayer? No wonder he'd ended up doing drag in Key West.

"He and I have always had a great relationship. I waited until he and his sister were finished with high school and out of the house to come out to my wife, get a divorce, and move to Wilton Manors. Jeffrey has come to visit me a bunch of times."

"But you said he's been missing for a while?"

"One day a couple of weeks ago, he dropped off the radar. Closed his email account, shut down all his social media, changed his phone number. Didn't contact his mother or me to let us know where he was going. His mother even called the police, but they said he's a grown man and we couldn't report him as missing unless there was evidence of foul play."

"So you know he's here in Key West now," I said. "You can relax."

"There's more. I've gotten a couple of threatening phone calls on my land line. *You tell Jeff to get his ass back to Gary pronto or things will be really bad for him.*"

"Gary his boyfriend?"

"Jeffrey's straight. He was living in Gary, Indiana before he disappeared." The anguish returned to his voice. "Can you track him down for me? He must be in some kind of trouble and he doesn't want us to know."

"And you don't want to honor his wishes, now that you know he's okay?"

"Jeffrey has always been self-reliant. He doesn't like to accept help. Even when he was a little boy, he hid the fact that he broke his ankle until we noticed he was limping. I'm telling you, there's something wrong, and I can't rest until I know what it is and do whatever I can to help him."

I looked over at Lester. He was going to be busy all night, running a whiskey tasting at a bar. I'd been planning to hang out with him, but I could spend a few minutes looking for a lost drag queen.

"Did this caller say anything else? How he knows Jeffrey, what he wants him for?"

"No. His voice sounded African American, though. Jeffrey taught at an inner city school in Gary this past year. Maybe it was one of the parents? Or a co-worker?"

I pulled out my phone and made a couple of notes. "I'll see what I can do," I said, and Lester and I rode our bikes back to the B&B. After a quick make-out session, Lester left for his demo. I re-buttoned my shirt and sat on the bed with my laptop as I Googled photos of Key West drag queens, looking for the guy who'd photobombed us.

I found him quickly; he was on the bill at a gender-illusion bar on Duval Street, only a few blocks from the B&B. The show was in progress when I got there, and I slipped into a space by the bar and ordered a vodka tonic. The queen on stage, who called himself Iona Trailer, was dressed in a tight-fitting leopard-print mini-dress, with big hair and even bigger hoop earrings. He made a couple of jokes about marrying cousins, and then donned a patchwork bathrobe and lip-synched Dolly Parton's "Coat of Many Colors."

By the time he was done, so was my vodka tonic and I debated ordering another. Then the next performer stepped up to the stage—the queen who'd photobombed my selfie earlier that day.

The hair and makeup were the same, and he wore a pink sweater and matching miniskirt. He was a tall, stocky guy, with no breasts to speak of, though he made up for it by sashaying across the stage. The thing that made me believe he was Merrick Davidson's son was the first song in his set: "You Can't Stop the Beat," from *Hairspray*.

The chatter in the audience subsided as he began, drawing everyone's attention. He was terrific, with the kind of voice made for the Broadway stage, and the moves to match. His was the last act, and after he finished performing, to a big ovation, the lights came up and people clustered around the bar, eager for refills.

I walked to the back of the bar and looked for the dressing room. I found a door labeled ARTISTS ONLY, which seemed a bit pretentious, but whatever. I knocked, and when bidden, walked in.

The man I thought was Davidson's son sat at a long counter, looking at himself in the mirror and using a washcloth to remove makeup. "Jeffrey Davidson?" I asked.

He turned to me, fear in his eyes. "Don't know anybody of that name. You should leave."

I held out my badge. "I'm a special agent with the FBI in Miami," I said. "I'm not here to hurt you or arrest you. My name is Angus Green, and your father asked me to look for you."

"My father? How did he know I was here?"

I held up my phone. "You photobombed a picture I took this afternoon, and your father recognized it on my Facebook page."

He took the phone from me and peered at it. "Shit. I've been so careful. I was in a hurry to get to work and I had no idea you were taking a picture."

"Your father's worried about you. He says you dropped off the face of the earth, and he's been getting threatening phone calls from a guy who wants you back in Gary."

His eyes widened. "Well, you can tell him I'm fine, but I'm going to have to move on now."

"You can't keep running, Jeffrey," I said. "If you're in trouble back in Gary, maybe I can help you."

"Not your business." He handed the phone back. "And like I said, you should go."

Instead, I sat down at the chair beside him. "Have you committed a crime? Are the police after you?"

"Me? No."

His posture stiffened and he put his hand over his mouth. Indications, as I'd learned, that he wasn't telling the truth. "Someone else? Someone you're covering up for?"

"More like hiding from." His shoulders fell. "Look, I can't talk about it. I don't want to get myself killed."

This was getting more complicated by the minute. But I couldn't walk away from someone who was so obviously in trouble. "I see this kind of thing all the time on my job. Let me help you."

"You can't," he said. "I came down here to get as far away from Gary, Indiana as I could. I thought by dressing up in drag and using a different name I could lie low long enough until I didn't have to hide anymore. But you can run all the way to the end of the earth and you can't get away from your problems."

I took a deep breath. "Who are you hiding from?"

"I'm going to need a drink for this conversation," he said. "You mind getting me a piña colada from the bar? Tell the bartender it's for me—he knows the way I like it."

I was about to get up when I noticed the rear door to the dressing room. I was willing to bet that it led directly outside, and that the moment I walked away from Jeffrey Davidson he'd be out that door.

"I don't think so," I said. "You're a straight guy who has the balls to dress up in drag and get up on stage to sing. You can have a conversation sober."

He bit his lip, then in a rush, he said, "I just wanted to be a teacher. Teach for America. Right out of college I got this job in an elementary school in Gary. I loved the kids. It felt like it was the right place for me."

I had no idea where he was going, but I let him talk.

"As you can imagine, the pay is crap for a job like that. So I lived in this run-down apartment complex a few blocks from the school. Some of my kids were in that same complex, so I felt like I was really getting into their lives."

He snorted. "Turns out that was a stupid move, like so many others I've made."

"Stupid how?"

"Because even though some of my neighbors were good people, trying to raise their kids in bad circumstances, some of them weren't. I was determined not to be prejudiced. That's not how I was raised. Just because some guys looked like gangbangers, with backwards ball caps, tattoos everywhere, pants hanging around their asses, didn't mean they were bad people. Right?"

"Absolutely," I said.

"So a couple of months ago I was in my apartment and these two guys were arguing in this kind of sheltered corner below my window. One of them said, 'Don't be a chicken shit, Danny. Nobody's asking you to use a gun or anything. Just drive the car.'"

He crossed his arms over his chest. "The other guy, Danny, said he didn't want no part of no armored car holdup. I realized that I knew who Danny was—his family lived in the same complex and his little brother was one of my students. I thought, good for you, Danny. Don't let anybody rope you into anything stupid."

"And?"

"I thought they were gone. The air conditioner in my apartment had blown a fuse, so I went over to the window and opened it up. The other guy was hanging around out there, smoking a joint. I recognized him, too—he was a friend of Danny's named Rakim. He looked up and saw me, and I pulled my head back in fast."

He took a deep breath. "Then two days later, I read about this armored car robbery in Chicago. One unidentified black male was shot and killed."

I knew where this was going. “Rakim? Or Danny?”

“I didn’t know for a couple of days. Then one day I see Rakim on the street, and he looks at me. Like really stares me down. It freaked me out. I went right home and Googled that robbery, and sure as shit, the guy who got killed was Danny.”

“And you thought Rakim recognized you? Knew you overheard his conversation?”

“I didn’t want to take the risk. They were talking right under my window. The school year had just finished, and I was going to teach summer school. But I called the principal and told her that I quit.”

His shoulders slumped. “I was watching movies on TV, and I saw this one my dad and I had watched when I was a kid, *Some Like it Hot.* About these two guys who see some Mafia guys commit a crime, and I got the idea I could do that, play Edna Turnblad like I did in high school. Nobody could find me if I was all made up and going by a different name, right?”

I nodded.

“I jumped into my car and drove down here.” He shook his head. “I don’t want to end up like Danny.”

He looked at me. “He wasn’t a bad kid. Maybe only eighteen or nineteen.”

“How do you know that Rakim is after you?”

“I don’t know for sure. But this morning I saw a guy who looked like him, hanging around near the bar. It freaked me out so much that I went right back home and put on my makeup there. That’s why I was wearing it when I showed up in your picture.”

“Why don’t you go to the police?”

“And tell them what? That I overheard a conversation? That I saw a guy on the street this afternoon that I thought looked like a guy I knew in Gary? Then get pulled into a criminal investigation that would put me in even more danger? No sirree. I just wanted to be a teacher, for Christ’s sake.”

“Look, I can’t argue with your decision to run,” I said. “But your father is really worried about you. Please, give him a call?”

"I don't want to get him involved. If Rakim comes after him he can't say anything."

I thought that was pretty paranoid, but then, I wasn't the one on the run from a guy involved in an armored car robbery. "Use my phone then," I said. "I spoke to your dad earlier today, so I've got his number in my phone."

"It's late. He's probably asleep."

"Jeffrey."

"Christ. You sound just like him. Fine, give me the phone."

I did my best not to overhear the conversation. Once Jeffrey had called his father, my task was finished. I left him my card, with my cell phone number, in case he changed his mind about talking to the cops about what he had heard, and found Lester at the bar where he was finishing up his demo.

We had a couple of drinks, danced together, then made our way back to the bed and breakfast, where I finally had the chance to feel like I was on vacation with my boyfriend.

The next morning, Lester and I cycled around the back streets. We took the guided tour of the Hemingway House, stopped at the AIDS memorial to read the names of those lost, and ended up eating oysters at the Half Shell Raw Bar.

On our way out, we saw a poster advertising the drag show I'd seen the night before, and I thought again of Jeffrey Davidson. It was a shame that he'd had to run from a job he loved. But one of the things I'd learned in my time at the FBI was that if you were in trouble, you could run —to the end of the country, the southernmost point—but you couldn't outrun your fear. I hoped he'd get lucky, that this Rakim guy would get arrested or killed, and Jeffrey would be able to relax. But often the world doesn't work out that way.

When Lester and I got back to the B&B, I used the free Wi-Fi and initialized the VPN software that let me access the FBI database securely, and looked up armored car robberies in Gary, Indiana.

The robberies I found had actually taken place in Chicago, though the Bureau believed that they'd been carried out by individuals from across the state line in Indiana. The agent from the Chicago office who'd been investigating was named Ina Augenblick, and while Lester went out to the pool, I called her and introduced myself. "Did a guy named Rakim ever come up in your armored car investigation?"

"Rakim Richards?"

"Don't know his last name."

"Richards is a member of the Eighth Avenue Boyz, an African-American street gang that has been tied to organized crime in Chicago," she said. "Often used as enforcers or cannon fodder, if you will. Send them in to dangerous situations and reward them if they come back alive."

"And?"

"And we believe he was involved in an armored car robbery that resulted in a homicide."

"Was the victim named Danny?"

"You're awfully well-informed on this case for a guy in the Miami office," she said. "How do you come by this information?"

"I met a guy down here in Key West who says he overheard a conversation between Rakim and Danny, and it freaked him out, so he ran."

"That is someone I'd very much like to speak with. How can I reach him?"

"His name is Jeffrey Davidson, and he's been performing as a drag queen named Edna Turnblad. But he told me that he's leaving town."

"You can't let him do that."

"It may be out of my hands by now. I spoke to him last night, and he could be miles away. But I'll see if I can track him down."

It was early afternoon by then, and the bar where Jeffrey had performed was already open. I showed the manager my badge, and he gave me the address where Jeffrey had been living, a couple of blocks off US 1 at the entrance to Key West. It was too far to bike, so I had to drive there and park on the street.

The address was a run-down three-story building with a tin roof and a couple of wood-railed balconies. The lock on the front door was broken, and I walked in and up the stairs to the unit number the manager had given me.

I was about to knock when I heard a raised voice. "Just tell me what you know," a man said. "Then I won't have to hurt you."

I quietly checked the door. It was unlocked, and I pulled my gun out and held it in my right hand. Then I kicked the door open and said, "FBI. Freeze!"

Jeffrey was tied to a chair, with blood running down from the side of his mouth. A young black man stood beside him. He looked up at me, then at Jeffrey. "You called the FBI on me?" He smacked Jeffrey once more against his face, hard, the sound like a particularly heavy wave hitting the shore at the Southernmost Point, where Jeffrey and I had first come in contact.

Before I could say or do anything else, Rakim turned and ran for the open French doors that led to the balcony. He put his hands on the balcony railing as if he was going to vault over it, but the rickety wood couldn't support his weight, and it collapsed outward, dragging him over the edge with it.

I rushed forward as Rakim went out into the air, tumbling head over heels the three stories down to the street. As I reached the edge of the balcony, stepping carefully so I wouldn't follow him, I looked down.

His body was sprawled face up on the sidewalk, his eyes and mouth open, and a pool of blood spread outward from his head. A wooden piece of the railing pointed up through his chest.

"Stay right there," I said to Jeffrey as I hurried past him, though of course he couldn't go anywhere. I galloped down the stairs two at a time, only pausing when I reached the foyer to push the door to the street open.

An SUV plastered with diving stickers had stopped on the street, and a hipster with a man bun jumped out. "I'm an EMT," he said, as he knelt by Rakim's body.

I called 911 and reported the incident, and identified myself as an FBI agent. When I hung up the hipster said, "He's gone."

He agreed to stay with Rakim's body until the police arrived, and I ran back upstairs to untie Jeffrey. "I should have left right after work last night but I was too tired," Jeffrey said, after I'd released his bonds and gotten him a glass of water.

"Did he say how he found you?"

"He said he tracked down my dad because he has a land line, but my dad couldn't tell him anything. He hunted down people I worked with, my neighbors."

He shook his head. "I can't go back to Gary after this. Everybody there will think I'm connected to gangbangers."

I steered him back to the question. "If no one knew where you were, how did he find you?"

"In the end, he went after Danny's little brother, the one who was my student, grilling him on everything he knew about me. I had showed the class some pictures of me from high school, singing in *Hairspray*, to celebrate the end of the term. Rakim was starting to get desperate by then, so he grabbed onto that idea and kept hunting for people singing *Hairspray* songs until he stumbled on the bar's website." He shook his head. "I was stupid. I thought by letting them photograph me in drag, I'd be safe."

I hit the redial button for Ina Augenblick, the agent in the Chicago office, and then handed the phone to Jeffrey. When I looked outside I saw flashing red and blue lights and went downstairs to tell the KWPD what I knew.

The officer was only about five-eight but very buff, his uniform tight against his body. I explained the situation to him but he wasn't surprised. "It's like you held up the United States and shook it, and all the nuts fell to the bottom," he said. "You wouldn't believe the weird crimes and criminals we get down here. Midwest gangbanger suicide by balcony railing? That's a normal day here at the end of the rainbow."

I told him that I worked in Miami, so I completely understood what he was saying. When the ambulance crew arrived, they took Jeffrey Davidson in for observation, and I called his father, who was going to fly down to Key West immediately to look after him.

Then I went back to the bed and breakfast, hoping that Lester and I could salvage what was left of our little vacation. No more selfies, though.

QUARTERS FOR THE METER

BY ALEX SEGURA

"I HAD THIS WEIRD DREAM," Pete Fernandez said. "I was in a boat, but there weren't any paddles."

"That is weird," Mike said, sipping his Heineken. The jukebox was playing Waits. The bar—a grungy gastropub located in the heart of Coral Gables—was mostly empty. It was just past six in the evening. They were in a booth a few steps away from the main bar area.

"That's not all of it," Pete said. He took a sip of his drink—a vodka soda—before continuing. "But then my dad showed up. He was standing in front of the boat."

"On the water?"

"Yeah," Pete said. The thought of his dad put a clench in his throat. It'd been only a few months since they had to put the old man in the ground, forcing Pete and his fiancé Emily to return to Miami from their home in New Jersey. "He was just standing there. Looking at me."

"What'd you do?"

The question hung over them for a moment. The bartender, a fit blonde named Lisa, nodded at Pete politely as she walked by.

He'd been back in Miami for less than six months, and he already felt unhinged.

Emily.

She had left a few days ago. He was living in his father's house and he was pretty sure the only reason Mike, his best friend, was tolerating him tonight was because he was worried Pete couldn't last very long alone.

"Nothing," Pete said. He couldn't bring himself to tell Mike he'd woken up to find his pillow wet from tears.

What a mess.

The two men walked in as if nothing, and it took Pete a second to notice they were wearing masks. The cheap, plastic kind you hated as a kid because the elastic band in the back would bury itself in your head. One guy was Sylvester and the other, shorter one, was Tweety. Halloween was months away. *What the fuck was going on?*

The handful of people also in the bar seemed to be having the same reaction.

Sylvester pulled out a gun—a sawed-off—and grabbed the bartender by the hair. Lisa was a bit older than Pete. She was a good bartender—always quick with a refreshed drink or a buyback. Her scream cut through the bar and made the one or two people who were too caught up in their own bullshit turn and take notice.

"Shit," Mike said, turning toward the two visitors. Tweety and Sylvester were facing the bar, their backs to Pete and Mike.

Sylvester had the shaft of the gun resting on Lisa's face. She was sobbing. Tweety had thrown a black garbage bag on the bar in front of him.

He did the talking.

"Put the money in the bag and this'll be over quick," Tweety said. His mask bobbed up and down along with his words, giving the scene the awkward quality of a poorly-dubbed foreign film.

Pete clenched the side of their table.

Mike shot him a glance, as if to say, "Stay where you are."

Sylvester pushed Lisa back, letting go of her hair. The gun was trained on her. He pointed at the bag with his free hand and nodded. She took a few steps to the register and opened it. Even from his seat, Pete could tell there wasn't much in there.

Lisa grabbed the bills and walked over to the bag. She could hold all of the register's contents in one trip.

"You have got to be fucking kidding me," Tweety said, his mask's eyes following the bills into the bag. "That can't be more than a hundred bucks."

He turned to Sylvester.

"What the fuck, man?" Tweety said. "You told me this place was going to be worth something."

Sylvester shrugged. He still had the gun trained on Lisa.

She was shaking, muffling her sobs with her hands.

Pete cleared his throat. He looked around the bar. No one was moving. It was a good place, Pete thought. Right off Miracle Mile. Pete had made it his second home for the last few months. He had little else to do, so why not drink alone?

He glanced at his drink. It was his third—or fourth?—of the night. He wasn't even buzzed yet. Now this. He'd have to find another place to hang out. He rubbed his eyes. He had other things to worry about now, besides where to drink. He had life to worry about.

"Let's get the fuck out of here," Tweety said. He grabbed the garbage bag and stuffed it in his pocket as best he could.

Which is to say, not well. He looked like a guy in a Tweety mask with a garbage bag stuck in his pants.

Pete and Mike's eyes met. His friend was scared. He was sitting up straight, his eyes locked on the two thugs, trying to push them out the door with his vision alone. Pete felt muddy.

He couldn't care less about these guys. About himself. He tried not to think about the tiny voice in his head that wanted something more to happen.

Then it did.

Sylvester started to follow Tweety, but turned around, as if remembering something. He flipped the shotgun in his hands and smashed the handle into Lisa's jaw, knocking her backwards.

She fell behind the bar. The sound of glasses shattering and her body slamming into the wall of bottles was loud and lasted longer than Pete thought it would. She groaned between sobs, making for a long, drawn-out sound no one should ever hear.

Tweety turned around after a few paces—he noticed Sylvester wasn't right behind him anymore.

"What—why, man?" Tweety said. "The fuck did you do that for, yo?"

Sylvester shrugged.

Tweety shook his head and started for the door. They were both still by the bar. The exit was down a ways. Tweety was closer to the door, while Sylvester was still in front of Pete and Mike and hadn't turned around yet to follow his partner.

Sylvester turned to face them for a second. Pete met his eyes.

They were green. His skin was tan—he was probably Cuban, like Pete. Maybe he lived around here. Maybe they'd gone to the same high school or dated the same girl. Where did the road fork off for Sylvester? And were they really that far apart?

"Come on, you stupid shit," Tweety said. He was at the far end of the bar, motioning for his partner to follow. "We gotta get the fuck out."

Sylvester nodded and began to back away from the bar. The shotgun in his hands, the handle wet with Lisa's dark blood. Pete couldn't tell if she was alive. He hadn't heard a sound from her in—he wasn't sure how long.

The taste in his mouth had grown sour and he felt his head begin to throb. He looked at his right hand and noticed his knuckles had gone white from gripping the side of the table.

He wondered if Mike thought he was scared. He wasn't. He didn't really care. If this was the end, it might be better that way.

He turned and moved his legs to the edge of the booth in one smooth motion, as if he were getting ready to get up and head to the bathroom. He unlocked his left knee and slammed his foot into Sylvester's knee. The cracking sound was pleasant to Pete. He'd hit the right spot.

He followed with another kick before Sylvester tumbled to the ground, his scream a mixture of shock and sudden, shooting pain.

Sylvester fell on his back and Pete stood up. He hovered over him and waited. He could hear Mike cursing in the background. Sylvester swung the shotgun toward Pete, but his grip was weak. Another kick sent the gun back toward another table. The two sorority girls and their frat boy buddies all stood up and backed away from the loaded weapon. They seemed too scared to squeal.

Sylvester clutched his leg. It was bent at an odd angle, Pete thought. He still hadn't made a sound.

Pete looked toward the exit. Tweety met his eyes then looked at his partner. No way they'd both get out of this.

That's what he was thinking. Tweety turned and ran out of the bar.

Pete could hear Mike calling the cops from his cell.

Sylvester was rolling around on his back, his hands still clawing at his wounded leg.

Pete sat down. He poured what was left of his vodka soda into his mouth and let the room temperature liquid coat his teeth and tongue. He looked at Sylvester squirming below. What was he thinking? A few moments earlier, he was standing over a bloodied bartender. Now he was lying on the same floor.

"Are you fucking nuts, bro?" Mike said. That's when Pete realized Mike had been talking to him for a while.

"Called the cops?"

"Yeah," Mike said. He got up and walked to the bar. A few of the sorority girls were already tending to Lisa. She was going to be okay. She was alive. Pete rubbed his forehead.

Sylvester wasn't doing much.

Pete got up. He pulled out some change from his pocket and looked it over. He started toward the exit, taking a big step over Sylvester, as if the would-be criminal was a misplaced kid's toy for him to avoid.

"Pete," Mike said. "What the hell, man? Where are you going? Shit is crazy over here and you're just going to leave?"

"Nah," Pete said. "I'll be right back. I just need to put a few quarters in the meter."

BREAKDOWN

BY BRENDAN DuBOIS

IT HAD BEEN A LONG, long time since Ruth Callaghan had suffered a flat tire while driving, so it came as a bit of a surprise when it happened. She wasn't familiar with the Toyota RAV4 she was driving, and so when the tire let loose, instantly there was a heavy vibration in the steering wheel and the car, which had been driving smooth and fair, was now lurching to the right.

She slowed and pulled the Toyota over to the side of the road. She checked her watch, and also checked the RAV's dashboard clock.

Both said the same thing. She had about forty-five minutes to go before she had to make her appointment.

Not forty-four. Not forty-six.

Forty-five.

Ruth got out of the car and went to the rear. The right rear tire certainly was flat.

"Damn." She wiped at the back of her neck. It was hot. It was incredibly hot.

She looked around at her surroundings. She was outside of Miami, in a wooded and flat area that had seen better times, just like the old industrial sections she had earlier driven through. Decades ago those factories had made comfortable livings for hundreds of families. Now, they were broken, shattered, making comfortable homes only for the homeless or rogue animals living out in the wild Florida landscape.

Like one of her instructors had said years back, systems break down if they aren't carefully cherished and maintained.

Breakdown.

Here, there were one-story cinderblock homes on each side of the street, most set back, and most showing years of disuse and neglect. The driveways were cracked, the lawns were scraggly, and there were disabled trucks and cars parked in some of the yards. Down the way a poor dog on a chain barked and barked. Things here looked tough.

But not the home directly in front of her.

This house was two-story, well-built, with tall windows and lots of exposed brickwork and stone and dark wood. There was an attached garage to the left, and two well-washed black SUVs parked in the driveway. Unlike its neighbors, the lawn here was a lush green and there was shrubbery lining the flagstone path leading up to the ornate wooden front door.

She still couldn't get used to the landscape of Florida. So flat, so weirdly green, with odd spikey plants that looked like they belonged on a set from a 1960s science-fiction movie.

And the heat . . . God, the heat.

"Well," she said.

The spare tire for the RAV was mounted on the rear door, covered with a round metal cover. She felt around the edge of the cover and found a latch at the bottom that she unsnapped, and then the cover popped off and struck her in the face.

"Dammit!"

She rubbed at her nose and saw the spare tire was secured by lug nuts, just like the flat tire. Ruth opened the door and thought, well, where's the damn lug wrench and jack? The storage area was flat, but there looked to be a plastic hatch to the left, built right into the car. She popped it open and yep, there it was. Small lug wrench and scissor jack.

She pulled back the glove and checked the watch.

Thirty-nine minutes before her appointment.

Ruth turned and held the wrench in one hand and scissor jack, glanced up the road.

Look at that, she thought.

A police cruiser was coming down the road, and she maneuvered around and sat down on the edge of the open door, her legs stretched out in front of her. The cruiser slowed down and she was pleased the police officer inside didn't switch on the light bar.

A good sign. It meant the cop wasn't too concerned.

He stepped out, a young guy with a short-sleeved blue uniform shirt and black trousers and black boots. He came forward, smiling, his blond hair cut short, about an inch above a crew cut. His forearms were heavily inked with faux Maori tattoos.

He had on a baseball cap.

It was weird to see a cop wearing a baseball cap. Must be a Florida thing.

"Got a problem?" he asked.

Ruth shrugged. "Flat tire. Just my luck."

He peered around. "Know what you hit?"

"Not sure."

"You okay?"

"I'm fine."

"Do you have AAA, or some other auto club?"

Ruth shook her head. "I wish. Can't really afford it."

"Yeah, that's a problem."

She looked at him, and he looked at her, and she was wondering what he was going to do, what he was going to offer.

"Can I see your license and registration?"

"Sure," she said, stepping up. "It's in the RAV, in my purse. All right if I fetch it?"

"Go right ahead."

Ruth went around to the passenger's side of the RAV, opened the door, took out her small leather purse. Her hands were sweating. The young cop was standing at the rear of the RAV, giving himself some cover.

She unzipped the purse, carefully and slowly went in to get the necessary documents and then passed them back to the cop. He gave them a glance, and then passed them back.

"You have any weapons in the car?"

"No, of course not."

"Pistol? Shotgun? Knife?" He smiled. "Tactical nuclear device?"

"Nothing like that," she said. "If you want to take a look, go right ahead."

He seemed to consider that, and then something squawked from the radio at his belt.

"Well," he said. "You look like you got things under control."

Then he did something odd, looking up at the fine house nearby. "You just be . . . careful. Okay? This isn't the best of neighborhoods."

"Really? In what way?"

He said, "Just don't spend too much time here, okay?"

Ruth picked up the wrench and the jack, but stayed put. "Thanks for the . . . advice, officer."

"Good luck."

He went back to the cruiser and got inside, and then put the car in drive, and quickly drove away. Ruth wished him luck, and also wished him a long and safe career in law enforcement, for his traffic stop here was poorly done. Even though he asked for her ID and registration, he hadn't gone back to the cruiser for a records check. And even though he did ask about weapons, he didn't bother to search, just relying on her word.

Not that it mattered, for there were no weapons on her or in the RAV.

But he still should have checked, to make sure.

With the young police officer gone, Ruth went to work, but as she got around to the flat tire, the door to the house opened up, and a large, angry-looking man came out, and came right down the driveway at her.

* * *

"HEY," HE SAID, VOICE LOUD. "What's the problem?"

Ruth knew it didn't make any sense, but she liked having the wrench in her hand, even though it was only about a foot long.

"No problem," she said. "I've got a flat tire."

The man was bulky, with thin hair and a sloping forehead and big hands. He had on a two piece black suit that was well-cut for his big size, black shoes, and a white dress shirt with no necktie. Even though it was blazingly hot under the Florida sun, he looked like a guy who wouldn't allow himself to sweat.

He glared at her.

"There was a cop car, came by and checked you," he said.

"I know," she said. "I was here."

He didn't seem to know he was insulted. "Why did the cop stop? He a friend of yours?"

Ruth shook her head. "I've never been here before . . . whatever this place is." She again gestured to the tire. "I was just passing through, and I got a flat tire. See?"

The man looked down, like he was thinking that Ruth was pulling something over him. He said, "You don't belong here."

"I know."

"You should move along."

"I intend to, right after I change out the tire."

"You don't got the AAA?"

"No," she said. She gestured again with the lug wrench. "Hey, if you gave me a hand, I could get it fixed quickly and get out of here. Feel like helping out?"

He grinned. It wasn't a happy smile.

"You're a liberated woman, right?"

"I suppose so."

"Then you can liberate that tire all on your own," he said. "I'm busy."

And he turned and went back up to the house, moving pretty fast for a big man.

* * *

SHE SPENT A FEW MINUTES puzzling out the lug wrench and scissor jack, and flashed back to a memory of Dad from years back, teaching her how to change out a tire. Dear old Dad was a contractor and auto mechanic, and if he was ever disappointed in having just two daughters, he never showed it. In fact, he made it a point to show them all sorts of skills—tire changing, how to jump a car battery, how to fix a leaking faucet—because, as he said, "I want you girls to be tough and be able to go on your own."

On your own, she thought.

Some made it. Others didn't.

And another thing: always check your surroundings. If you need something, tools are nearby. Sometimes they're hidden, sometimes they're apparent.

A nice piece of advice, especially when she went to college and was recruited by—

Now it came back to her.

First things first, she got the spare tire off the rear of the RAV by using the lug wrench, and made sure each nut was safely placed in the rear storage area, so she wouldn't have to hunt for them later.

The spare tire was put on the grass, and she wondered for a moment if that big moron was going to come out charging again, to accuse her of damaging the lawn, but maybe he was inside drowning kittens or something, because he didn't come out.

Next, Ruth got down on her knees, winced at the heat seeping through the black fabric of her trousers from the hot asphalt of the road. She slipped the scissor jack under the car, and found a gap in the frame that fit a slot in the jack. Using just her fingers, she twisted a knurled length of metal that extended the jack, until it finally touched the frame.

A car drove by.

It didn't stop.

One hell of a friendly neighborhood, she thought.

All right, then.

Time check.

Just a half hour left.

Time to get a move on.

* * *

THE NEXT SEVERAL MINUTES WERE spent cursing, flailing at the lug wrench, the metal tool scraping her knuckles. The way it worked was that one end of the lug wrench went into a hole at the end of the scissor jack, and by rotating the wrench, it extended the jack. Nice in theory, she was sure, but the damn thing either kept on slipping out or getting stuck.

Eventually, though, she got into a rhythm, and the scissor jack extended up until the flat tire was no longer flat. But she recalled Dad's warning, that you had to lift the car up high enough so there was a gap between the flat tire and the ground. "An inflated tire takes up more space," he had said. "You don't want to be caught in a position where the flat tire is off, and you can't fit the spare in."

Good advice, Dad, she thought. *You could have gone far, if you hadn't been burdened by a lousy education and two demanding daughters.*

Once the tire was up high enough, she took the lug wrench and got to work, and one, and then another, and then two more came off.

It left one more.

With her back to the house, she cursed, she moved around, and cursed again, and then threw down the lug wrench in disgust.

* * *

THE WALK ACROSS THE LAWN was a quick but scary trip. She hated the thought of seeing that big guy again; but after she rang the doorbell, another, slimmer and a bit nicer man answered the door. He was dressed the same as the other one, but was younger and didn't seem to be a dick.

"Yeah?" he asked.

She pointed to her car, high up on the scissor jack. Sweat was trickling down her legs and had moistened a big part of her lower back. "I've got a flat tire."

"So? Not my problem."

Ruth carefully said, "I know. It's my problem. And I want to replace the tire and get on my way. But one of my lug nuts won't come off."

"You shouldn't have tried to take the nuts off with the car up like that," he said. "You might push the car off the jack."

"Well, it's too late now," she said.

"So?"

He may have been smaller and a tad friendlier, but he seemed to be stuck on that one word. "Do you have any WD-40 I can use? Something to loosen up the lug nut? That way, I can get the tire changed out and get out of your neighborhood."

He grunted, closed the door.

She waited.

Another car went by, not stopping.

The door flew open. "Here," he said, passing over the familiar blue-and-yellow can.

"Thanks," she said, "Do you think you—"

Her question—*Do you think you could help me?*—was cut off by the closing door.

* * *

BACK AT THE CAR, SHE sprayed the lug nut with the WD-40, recalled Dad's warning to give it a few minutes to soak through, and then it came off with just a few hard tugs. Ruth bent over with a couple of grunts. She got the flat tire off, let it bounce to the ground. Seeing the car without the tire was strange, the lug bolts sticking out of the bare tire hub. It looked . . . unseemly.

Ruth wrestled the spare tire and swore twice more, as she forced the openings through the bolts, and then took the lug nuts and screwed them in by hand, one after another.

There.

She had to take a break.

Checked the time.

Eleven minutes to her appointment.

Damn.

The sky was getting dark in the far horizon, and there was a flash of lightning and a slow rumbling of thunder.

An afternoon thunderstorm in Florida.

Another sweltering day in paradise.

The front door opened and the big guy came out, but he wasn't alone. The second guy was with him, along with an attractive young woman, dressed pretty well, holding hands with two very young girls, as they all went to the near black SUV. The big guy opened up the doors so the woman and her kids could get in, there was a brief talk with the second guy, who then went around and took the driver's seat. The big guy waited until the SUV backed out the driveway and then safely went up the street.

It then started to rain.

The big guy ambled back to the front door and looked to Ruth with a smirk.

"Looks like you're having a hell of a day there, miss."

Ruth just nodded, went back to work, and checked the time.

Just five minutes left.

* * *

She lowered the scissor jack and it got to the point where it wouldn't lower any more, and she kicked it free. There. The damn car was now on four good tires. Her hands hurt, her knees were sopped through, and her back ached. She picked up the flat tire, tossed it in the rear, and then threw in the scissor jack and the lug wrench.

Just one more thing.

The borrowed can of WD-40 was on the ground. She picked it up as the rain really started coming down, and her hair was soaked as she walked up the lawn. Ruth looked up and down the street. Nobody was outside, nobody was driving by.

She didn't bother checking her watch.

At the door, she rang the doorbell, and then knocked on the heavy door.

The rain was heavier, soaking her coat.

Again with the knocking, again with the doorbell.

It flew open.

The big guy was there.

"Yeah?" he demanded.

"I've got the flat fixed," she said. "I'll be leaving shortly."

He just nodded. She held up the can of WD-40.

"I borrowed this earlier," Ruth said. "I just want to return it."

And she brought the can up and sprayed it straight into his eyes.

* * *

THE BIG GUY YELPED AND fell back, both hands up to his face, and Ruth kicked hard at the side of his left knee, and he yelled out again and fell hard to the floor. She moved quickly and pulled aside his jacket, revealing a shoulder leather holster, and from there, she slipped out a black semi-automatic pistol—a Ruger, nice—and then worked the action and shot the big guy twice in the back of his head.

She got up, not bothering to check her watch.

Ruth knew she was right on time.

Moved to the left.

Move, move, move.

Down a long hallway, lined with oil paintings and antique vases and old glassware, she kept to the side of the wall, just as—

A door at the end of the hallway flew open, a man in a black two-piece suit came out, his hand fumbling under his coat, and Ruth shot him in the chest and the throat. He crumpled and again—

Move.

Move.

She stepped around the second dead man and went through the open door. There was an older, larger man sitting behind a wide wooden desk. He was heavyset, wearing a black turtleneck shirt, with a fleshy red face and thin white hair, bushy white eyebrows. His desk was covered with file folders and papers, and there were bookshelves on each side of the wall. Large windows at the rear overlooked a neat and pleasant-looking backyard.

She wondered if alligators or any other carnivores played in that backyard.

His right arm was lowered, like he was reaching for something. But he was frozen in place.

He stared at her.

"Who are you?" he asked.

Ruth said, "Doesn't matter."

"How did you find me?" he asked.

"Raging curiosity on my part."

"I can make a payment."

"Not interested."

"Then why?"

Ruth said, "My sister. Your product killed her. Killed lots of others, but it's my sister I care about."

"She made a choice," the man said.

"And so did I."

She shot him three times, then dropped the pistol on the floor.

* * *

By the open door, she stopped for a moment by the large bodyguard she had just shot. One more check before going out and driving away in her stolen RAV4, with the flat tire that she had earlier slit, ensuring that her car ended up near this drug kingpin's house. Her instructors from long ago would be impressed by her field skills.

Clear.

She looked down at the dead bodyguard.

"Looks like you're having a hell of a day as well," she said.

Ruth stepped over him. "But mine is sure improving."

WINNER

BY MICHAEL WILEY

WHEN MISSY DENNERS WALKED BACK into her house, she left the suitcase of money in her car trunk. Security cameras had recorded her in the Omni Hotel lobby. More cameras recorded her getting off the elevator with Marcel Beauvien at the fifth floor and getting back on without him. She figured she had an hour or so before the police connected her to his death.

Upstairs she found a duffel bag on a closet shelf and put in two changes of clothes. She wrapped a T-shirt around her pistol and put it in too. She dug her passport out of a desk drawer and assembled a kit of toiletries.

National Junior Waterskiing Champion at age sixteen, married at nineteen, widowed at twenty-two when her husband Tom made a dumbass deal with Beauvien and then didn't come through with the cash—Missy knew her ups and her downs, the ecstasy and the agony. She called herself a *Florida Girl* to anyone who asked, though she lived in Jacksonville, which was to Florida what Detroit was to the beaches and northern woods of Michigan. Thing was, she pulled it off. No light seemed to shine brighter than the brilliant spray from her ski as she blasted through the first pair of red gate buoys, whooping like a wild thing, her hair banded in a ponytail, her teeth glinting.

Now, in the bedroom, she lay down on the bed she'd shared for three years with Tom. She felt no regret for shooting Beauvien. She wanted what she lost, that was all. She hated to lose. For a moment she thought of climbing under the bed covers, shutting her eyes, and trying to dream herself back into her former life. Instead, she made a mental list. Clothes, passport, toothbrush. What else might she need? She went downstairs to the garage and found a screwdriver and pliers.

As she zipped the duffel, she felt an impulse to burn the house. She and Tom had made a life there. They'd filled it with themselves. The air smelled of them, their cooking, their lovemaking, their possessions. But now Tom was gone and she was leaving. Burning the house would be easy—there was a can of gasoline in the garage by the workbench.

And Missy had always had a thing for fire. One morning when she was seven years old, she dug a Bic lighter from a kitchen drawer and lit the living room rug. Three weeks later, she hid in her bedroom closet and torched a winter coat. Except for the extinguisher her mom and dad kept in the pantry, the fire would have burned down the house. Hers were minor arsons, but when she burned the hair off one of her dolls in the backyard and left the singed head in the refrigerator, her mom insisted they seek help.

The therapist couldn't get Missy to explain why she was drawn to fire—usually boys, rather than girls, played with matches, he said—and, in truth, Missy didn't understand the impulses herself, so the therapist recommended that her mom and dad distract her with other, healthier thrills and watch her closely.

How best fight fire? they wondered.

With water.

So they bought the seven-year-old girl her first water skis.

Now, she laughed at herself. No, she would let the house stand. She would commit no wild acts. She would find a groove and pull back from the edge.

Then, a fist pounded on the front door. A voice shouted, "Police."

Missy went to a window. Three uniformed officers stood, with their service pistols drawn, between the pots of plumbago on the front porch. Another stood on the lawn.

Missy returned to the garage.

The fist pounded on the door.

Missy brought the gasoline inside, poured it on the living room rug, poured more in the dining room, and said, "It isn't my fault."

The fist pounded.

Missy went to the kitchen and fished through a drawer for the lighter she and Tom used when the spark system on their barbeque grill didn't work.

"Police," the voice shouted.

"Be right there," Missy said, and she lit the gasoline.

As she stepped from the kitchen into the backyard, the officers yelled. They smelled smoke and saw flames through the front window. She knew they would either break the front door and rush inside or retreat to their cruisers. If they retreated to the cruisers, Missy might as well walk into the front yard with her hands in the air. If they came inside, she had a chance.

The officers kicked in the front door, and Missy ran to the driveway and got into her car.

It wasn't her fault. Marcel Beauvien killed Tom first. He threatened to kill her when she went to the hotel to get back Tom's partial payment. *Her* money, as much as Tom's. "I hate to lose," she said, as she drove to the end of her street.

Forty minutes later, she pulled into long-term parking at the airport and steered through the aisles until she found an open spot next to a dusty Toyota Avalon. Using her screwdriver and pliers, she exchanged license plates. The effort seemed as silly as putting on a funny hat for a disguise. But one sometimes heard of a gunshot passing through a hat brim and missing skin and bone.

She drove out along the airport service road until she reached a Red Roof Inn, flanked by stands of palm trees. She paid for the room and carried in her duffel bag, leaving the suitcase of money in the trunk. The room, on the second story at the rear of the motel, faced scrub pines and loblolly bays at the edge of an expanse of wetland forest. The bright afternoon sun silvered the loblolly leaves.

Missy locked the door and pushed the desk chair against it, then put the duffel in the closet, and sat on the stiff bed. Closing her eyes, she breathed the stale motel air deep into her lungs and tried to focus her thoughts.

She'd spent many nights in places like this when competing on the waterskiing circuit, usually with three or four other girls crammed into the room, along with skis, wetsuits, and luggage, the cords of their hairdryers tangling in the bathroom, their swimsuits drying in the shower, the television on too loud, empty soda bottles on the floor. Back then, she would leave the chaos of the room and ride in the van to a competition. The moment she dropped into the water her mind would clear and she would focus only on speed and more speed. When she raced, the whole world shrank to the few square inches where fiberglass touched water.

Now, she fought for such clarity. She'd killed a man. The police were looking for her. Tom was gone. What should she do next?

She opened her eyes, grabbed her phone—and looked at the pictures.

The oldest ones showed Tom when they first met—hanging out at a lakeside cabin, drinking beer, tubing behind a motorboat, sitting at a campfire. In almost all of them, he looked drunk and happy.

She skipped several years to the photos from their wedding. Missy and Tom stood under a wire arch decorated with flowers as they told a minister they would hold and honor and all the rest. Missy fed Tom a first bite of wedding cake. Missy stood on a dock in her wedding dress and water skis, grinning at the camera. The groomsmen threw Tom in his tuxedo off the dock into the Intracoastal.

The pictures made Missy feel cold.

She looked at recent shots. She and Tom stood outside their house on the day they signed the contract. Tom stood in front of the submarine sandwich shop he opened before getting involved with Marcel Beauvien. The signs in the window said—

Real Cuban Rolls

Do it with a Cuban.

Eat a Cuban.

The sandwich shop was a bad idea. She knew it when Tom first said he wanted to open it. She saw it now. She had to reassure herself the past couple of years had been happy.

Missy went to the motel window and stared at the wetland forest on the other side of the parking lot. A large bird soared high above the trees. She watched its wings. If they tilted side-to-side, it would be a turkey vulture. If they stayed flat, it would be a hawk or osprey, maybe an eagle. The bird carved a broad turn to the west. Missy couldn't tell if its wings tilted. Tears pushed against the corners of her eyes. Ever since she was a young girl, she was fiercely independent, relying on no one else to build her strength or take care of her injuries. When she met Tom, though, she gave herself to him—slowly at first, then with a blind love that surprised her and everyone who knew her.

But Tom lied to her. She didn't know what *all* he'd done, but she knew he lied. And now he was gone.

The forest on the other side of the parking lot seemed to call to her. If she walked into the wetlands and kept walking, she would leave the world behind. She would climb over roots and rotting leaves and tree trunks. When she tired and could go no farther, she would lie on the ground until the woods took her.

For the second time that day, she laughed at herself. No, she wouldn't commit suicide by opening herself to the wild. She would turn herself in to the police. A slower suicide?

Maybe—what would they do with a girl who'd killed a man? But where else could she turn?

She called Tom's friend Peter Frankel.

"Hey," she said when he answered.

"Jesus, Missy—you're on the news."

"I'm not surprised."

"You *shot* a man?"

"I had to. Listen, I—"

"Jesus, Missy—"

"Listen, I need a lawyer. I'm turning myself in. Can you help?"

He was quiet for a moment. "Let me make a couple calls."

"Thank you, Peter."

"Why'd you do it?" he asked.

"Not for any reason I'm ashamed of."

When they hung up, Missy walked outside to the swimming pool. A man in a red tracksuit sat on a lounger. Two kids, a girl and a boy, swam in the pool. The kids laughed and splashed and raced across the water to the deep end. Missy felt a pang for all she and Tom would never have. She sat on a deck chair across the pool from the man and said, "They're beautiful."

Her phone rang.

"Peter?"

He said, "I talked to a lawyer named Stuart Wainwright. He says, if you turn yourself in at night, it'll look like the police caught you. If you walk in on your own in the morning, with him by your side, news cameras flashing, you'll look innocent or at least like you're in charge."

"What does that mean?" Missy asked.

"Wainwright will call the sheriff's office and tell them he's bringing you in tomorrow, doing it your way, not theirs. You meet him in the morning at eight. Tonight you're on your own. Can you handle that?"

The girl in the pool yanked a foam kickboard away from her brother.

"Tell me where to meet Stuart Wainwright."

* * *

THAT EVENING, SHE ATE AT a Denny's on the airport service road and returned to her room early. As the sun set, she lay on top of the bed covers with the lights out and the window open. Every few minutes, a jet roared over the motel. In the silence between, cars passed on the service road and night birds cried in the wetlands.

She slept, startled awake in the blue of the night, closed the window, slept once more, and woke again in the dark as the clock ticked past four a.m.

She got up, showered, and stepped out to the walkway, carrying her duffel bag. "I hate to lose," she said, and she climbed into her car. She drove out from the Red Roof Inn, away from the airport, and onto the highway to the beach. The sun would rise in a couple hours. A little later, she would turn herself in to the lawyer. This was her last morning of freedom—unless a judge let her out on bail. But what would she do then? She would work, she supposed, if the judge let her. Maybe one of the waterskiing shows in central Florida would hire her as a freak act. *Missy Denners—murderess—does flips on skis.* Or maybe she would sit in jail, while lawyers and judges debated her life like she was a broken-legged dog.

She drove to the Sixteenth Avenue beach access and parked facing a concrete barrier that divided the street from the sand. She reclined her seat and closed her eyes. She knew she should rest, but adrenaline coursed through her veins. She opened her eyes and waited for sunrise. When it came—orange, huge, the ocean waves rolling in under it, slow, as if the Atlantic itself had been sleeping—she got out of the car, took off her shoes, and walked onto the sand, which was still cool from the moisture of the night.

She walked into the surf, the receding waves tugging at her ankles, and went in further until the water eddied around her knees. When she got waist deep, the pull of the ocean stopped, and she lowered herself until the salt waves splashed at her mouth and stung her eyes. She went deeper and her feet touched the sandy bottom only in the wave troughs, and the swells lifted her toward the sky. She matched her breathing to the rise and fall of the ocean, and she watched the rising sun transform from an enormous orange sphere into a hard yellow disk.

She waded to the shore and sat on the sand. When a man and a woman with a small boy walked onto the beach, she got up and went to her car, her clothes still damp. She would eat breakfast, she decided, and then see the lawyer.

* * *

SHIVERING IN THE AIR CONDITIONING at the diner, she ordered coffee, fried eggs, and toast, wondering when and what she would eat again—what she should tell the police—whether the police would believe her when she told them she shot Beauvien because she feared for her life—whether she believed that entirely herself—and, if not, then what?—and whether anyone's belief mattered now. Beauvien killed Tom. She killed Beauvien. That was that. Everything was done. Everything was gone.

The waitress eyed Missy as if she saw something wrong and wanted to help—or at least wanted to stop her from shivering—and so she refilled Missy's cup with hot coffee and refilled it again, then leaned in as if to share a secret and said, "They're all bastards."

Which made no sense to Missy—except it *did* make sense—and she smiled up at the waitress and said, "Who?"

"You've got to take care of yourself," the waitress said. "You've got to protect what's yours." When Missy looked at her, puzzled, the waitress added, "We've all been there. God knows, *I* have. Don't give up, honey—that's all I'm saying."

For a moment after the waitress left the table, Missy felt dizzy. She thought she might get sick. She stood and rushed to the bathroom. She steadied herself at the counter and stared at her reflection in the mirror. Then she felt the itch to light another fire.

When she felt the itch during the years when she was winning trophies and sponsorships, she would imagine herself flying over the wake from a motorboat, her ski raising a rooster tail as bright and powerful in the afternoon sun as the red-hot flame of a flare. Sometimes that worked. Other times, she would light a match and let it burn until it scorched her fingers, drop it, and rub the crumbling black charcoal into the floor until all evidence of the flame had disappeared. Now, as she stood at the sink in the diner restroom, the itch stayed with her even as she splashed water on her wrists and face.

She stared at the mirror and said, "I hate to."

So she went back to her table, left a twenty for the waitress, and walked out of the diner. She got in her car, drove the highway toward downtown, squinted at the glint of high rises, and hooked west, as if carving a broad turn.

* * *

I-10 STRETCHES FROM JACKSONVILLE ACROSS the United States to Los Angeles. If you strap on your seatbelt and hit the gas, thirty-eight hours later you can climb out of your car and step into the cold Pacific Ocean.

Missy drove out of the city at eight in the morning. She'd watched the sun rise over the Atlantic, and if she avoided long stops she would watch it set between New Orleans and Baton Rouge. As she drove into the pine forest outside the Jacksonville city limits, she saw a bird the same size as the one she saw from her window at the Red Roof Inn. This one dipped its wings side to side as if it were balancing on a high wire. A turkey vulture. It circled and, seeing something dead or dying, lowered through the tree branches.

Missy's phone rang, and she looked at caller ID. Peter Frankel.

When she answered, Peter said, "Stuart Wainwright's waiting for you at his office."

"Tell him I won't be coming. Tell the police too."

"Huh?"

"You've been a good friend, Peter," she said and hung up, then rolled down her window and tossed her phone out.

* * *

SHE CRUISED THROUGH THE MIDDLE of the state and, in the afternoon, drove across the Panhandle. She passed slash pine plantations and longleaf pine forests and rode embankments through swamps grown thick with red maples and black gum trees. She loved this place, and who could blame her? But now she was leaving.

With tears in her eyes, she didn't notice when, fifteen miles east of Pensacola, two cream-colored Dodge Chargers entered the highway and fell in behind her.

Unmarked highway patrol cars, maybe.

Maybe Beauvien's men.

Only after Missy wiped her eyes with the back of her hand several minutes later did she start to watch them in her rearview mirror. The men in the Chargers looked relaxed, easing through the afternoon. Missy's car, with unidentifiable plates, should have been invisible to them—no more remarkable than the semis, SUVs, and other cars on the road.

But the Chargers stayed with her, accelerating when she accelerated, slowing when she slowed.

They trailed her onto the causeway over the slate green water of Escambia Bay, twenty miles from the Florida border. They trailed her through the little West Florida towns of Ferry Pass and Ensley.

Almost visible a mile further west on I-10, Alabama felt like a finish line. But the fiery itch dug into Missy's skin—so deep no fingernails could ever scratch it.

One of the Chargers sped up, pulling alongside Missy. The driver glanced over. He looked enough like Tom that a shock of recognition, matching the driver's own, flashed across Missy's face. The man gave her a sad smile and raised a pistol to the window. She gave him a smile that looked like his own.

Then, for a third time that day, she laughed. Her laughing eyes and laughing mouth made the man in the Charger think of sparks of light. Missy tilted her head, her ponytail falling down toward the small of her back. "Not my fault," she said, and she whooped like a wild thing and mashed the gas pedal to the floor.

Hours later, when the wreckers pulled the remains of the Chargers from woods at the side of the highway, Missy was long gone.

FRONTIER JUSTICE
BY JOHN M. FLOYD

THE CAR WAS WAITING IN the alley, with Eddie Stark at the wheel and half a dozen cigarette butts littering the pavement below the driver's side door. Eddie had flipped a seventh out the open window and exhaled a lungful of smoke when he saw Charlotte Baxter stroll around the corner and head in his direction. Even from a distance, Baxter's face looked as calm as always. Eddie Stark's was sweating.

Baxter climbed in, set a thick brown attaché case on the seat between them, and peeled off her honey-colored wig. She also took off a pair of glasses and removed two wads of cotton from inside her cheeks. Eddie hefted the case up and over into the back seat. It didn't feel as heavy as it had been, twenty minutes ago, and he knew why: half its contents had been left in the building across the street.

With trembling hands Eddie started the engine and steered the big Lincoln out of the alley and into the downtown Tallahassee traffic. Finally he turned to look at Baxter.

"How'd it go?"

"Fine." Baxter leaned back and closed her eyes. "Mission accomplished, package delivered."

"Sure nobody recognized you?"

"Would *you* have recognized me? What they saw was a blond with a chubby face."

So it's done, Eddie thought. "Good." He stopped at a red light, and without looking down he thumbed the AC up to max. He was a Florida native, born and raised, but the heat and humidity still ran him crazy. As he cooled off and his heart rate slowed he felt himself adrift in memories. "You said you never knew Kincaid, right? Never met him?"

Baxter opened her eyes and stared at the windshield. The early-afternoon sun struck diamonds off the chrome and glass of the cars ahead.

"No," she said. "I've only heard about him. Mostly from Jake. And all that was years ago."

Eddie Stark nodded to himself. He wished *he*'d never met Tom Kincaid. As for Jake Baxter . . . well, that was a memory that still tormented Eddie, even after all this time.

"How's Jake doing?" Eddie heard himself say. "He's in Canada, right?"

"He was. He's down here now, at County General. He's dying." Baxter's tone of voice was no different. She might have been discussing politics, or the weather, or what she planned to have for dinner tonight. "I talked to him last week."

All of a sudden it was quiet in the car.

"He say anything about me?" Eddie asked. His heart was thudding again now, making it hard to speak. His throat had gone dry.

"Jake? No. Should he have?"

Eddie hesitated. He could feel new perspiration on his forehead, his neck. Finally he took a breath and said, "Your uncle Jake and I were friends, Charlotte. You know that, right? I was still doing time when I heard about what happened to your dad."

Eddie stared at Baxter's profile while Baxter stared at the street ahead.

"The light's green, Eddie," she said.

* * *

THEY FOUND GEORGE MARTELLO WAITING for them in a huge, expensively furnished office on the second floor of his home. He made no effort to rise from his chair as they entered. The reason was evident: like his office, Martello was larger than life. He weighed almost four hundred pounds.

Eddie and Baxter stood there facing him across his desk. They probably looked, Eddie thought, like counsel approaching the bench.

"Well?" Martello asked.

"It's done," Eddie said. "Set for two sharp." He looked up at the wall clock. One forty-six. It was plain and round and ugly, like the one in his old high-school hallway. *Who puts a clock like that on the wall of his home office?* he thought.

"No problems?"

Eddie swallowed. *God, I hope not.* "No. No problems."

Charlotte Baxter cleared her throat. "I'm sorry to be rude," she said, not looking sorry at all, "but when am I supposed to get paid?"

Martello studied her. "You'll get your money, Ms. Baxter. At two o'clock."

She shrugged, crossed the room, tossed the briefcase onto a couch, and sat down beside it. She leaned back and propped both feet, still in dress shoes, on a coffee table.

Martello eyed her a moment more, then said to Eddie, "Let's hear it."

Eddie perched on the edge of a leather chair and blew out a sigh. He was still shaken, mostly from Baxter's mention of Jake, in the car.

"Not much to tell," Eddie said. "Joe Gallegos did the work. I told him it had to be small enough to fit in a briefcase alongside a book, large enough to level an office, and plain enough not to attract attention out in the open." He paused. "Gallegos suggested a clock radio—a big one, battery-powered and old-fashioned enough to be what he called 'quaint.' He set the timer this morning, before we put it in Baxter's briefcase." Eddie jerked a thumb over his shoulder, toward the couch.

"You're sure it's enough?"

"No question. Where it's placed, it should knock out most of the fourth—"

"All I care about," Martello said, "is the D.A.'s office."

"It's enough," Eddie said.

"And the bomb's in position right now?"

"Twenty minutes ago Baxter put the clock radio on an assistant's desk just outside the door to Kincaid's office. We knew the assistant was scheduled to be out today—her desk was vacant."

Eddie turned to glance at Baxter, but knew she wasn't listening. Her job was done.

Watching her sitting there, Eddie felt another stab of unease. All the Baxters were deadly, no one knew that better than he did. It was the reason he'd contacted her for this job. Eddie wondered what Charlotte Baxter would do if she knew that Martello had personally ordered her father's murder—Warren Baxter and his brother Jake had run a rival drug ring—and that Eddie himself had arranged the hit, from the inmate side of the visitor's grid at Raiford Prison, about one hundred miles east of here.

He also wondered if Jake had known. It was unlikely, but possible. So many years, so many connections. Anything was possible.

Eddie's thoughts were interrupted by Martello's voice.

"So she just marched up to the fourth floor like she owned the place? What if she'd been stopped and questioned?"

"The clock wasn't the only thing in the briefcase," Eddie said. "There was also an electronics catalog labeled with an address and phone number. The number goes to a throwaway cell phone in Paulie Wahlberg's pocket, in a coffee shop just down the street—remember Paulie? Anybody called to check, Paulie would answer the call and vouch for Baxter as one of the sales reps."

Eddie did a palms-up. "Turned out Baxter wasn't challenged, so the book wasn't needed. It stayed in the briefcase."

Martello seemed to ponder that. "What if somebody happens to fiddle with the radio, or the clock?"

"Wouldn't matter. There's no radio parts inside the housing anymore, and the clock has its own timer." Eddie smiled. "It's foolproof, boss."

Martello checked the time. So did Eddie. One fifty-two. The D.A.'s Monday staff meeting should already be underway, in his office.

George Martello leaned back, his swivel chair groaning under the weight, and studied the ceiling. Eddie was reminded of a giant walrus he'd once seen sunning himself on a rock at the Jacksonville zoo.

Finally the big man nodded. "Good work, Edward." He righted his chair and lit a long cigar. "I'll sleep better once this is finished. Tommy Kincaid took five years of my life." He squinted at Eddie through a cloud of blue smoke. "And yours."

Eddie remembered. His conviction had closely followed Martello's, and his feelings for Kincaid were just as strong. But today's mission was more than revenge. The truth was, the district attorney and his group were close to uncovering a statewide heroin ring that grossed a hundred million a year. When that case was solved, Martello and Eddie and a dozen others would find themselves in quicksand too deep to escape. In short, the investigation had to be stopped, and Joe Gallegos's little care-package would make sure that happened.

Martello was staring down at his desktop, the knot in his tie hidden under half a dozen chins. "It's set for two, you said?"

"On the dot." Eddie pulled out a gold pocket watch. "Five minutes to go."

Martello swiveled his chair to face the window. Four miles away, the skyline—if you could call it that, in a city like Tallahassee—looked to Eddie like a cluster of children's blocks stacked on a green carpet. Martello gazed at them awhile, then put down his cigar, reached into a drawer of a credenza underneath the window, and took out a pair of binoculars. To Eddie he said, "Time?"

"One fifty-seven." Eddie handed the gold watch across the desk to his boss. "Gallegos gave me this—it's synchronized to the timer inside the radio."

The big man took it and raised the binoculars. Eddie knew he was looking at the windows on the fourth floor of the John K. Sullivan office building.

Martello checked the watch. "Less than three minutes. By God, I'm going to enjoy this," he said, smiling. "It's frontier justice, that's what it is, Edward. As swift and final as the hangman's noose."

The sound of slow applause came from behind them, and both men turned in their seats.

Baxter stopped clapping but kept her shoes propped on the coffee table. "Marshal Earp would be proud," she said. She put her feet on the floor, gave her employers a long look, and rose from the couch. "Could one of you vigilantes point me to a bathroom?"

Martello glared at her, then turned away. "Down the hallway, second right." When Baxter had left, the big man lowered the glasses and looked at Eddie, then glanced over his shoulder at the door and back again. "When this is over . . . "

Eddie nodded. "I'll take care of it."

The telephone on the desk rang. Martello, watching the window again, ignored it. Eddie picked up the receiver and said, "Martello Investments."

"Eddie? Paulie Wahlberg. I'm in the coffeeshop across from—"

"I remember. What is it, Paulie?"

"One minute till two," Eddie heard Martello say.

Paulie's voice sounded odd. "Rico Simms just sat down beside me and said the job was done. Said he saw the Baxter woman come out of the building half an hour ago."

"That's right. In all the excitement, I forgot to call you off. Go on home and—"

"No, no, that's not what I mean." The voice paused, then said, "You won't believe this, but somebody just called me from there."

"From where?"

"From the Sullivan Building. Asked about the prices on Blu-ray players."

Eddie blinked. "What?"

"Yeah. He got the number off the catalog, the one Baxter had in her briefcase, and called me just as I was about to take off. Said the catalog was on the D.A.'s assistant's desk." Another pause. "What's going *on*, Eddie?"

"Fifteen seconds," Martello said, from another world.

Eddie's mind was racing. He looked at the door, but Baxter was still gone to the john.

Think, Eddie told himself. He was certain he'd felt the weight of the catalog when he'd lifted the briefcase over the seatback after Baxter's return to the car. He'd even heard it sliding around inside—

Suddenly he knew, and in the same instant he pictured Charlotte Baxter a hundred yards away, sprinting barefoot down the sidewalk with her shoes in her hand.

Eddie dropped the phone and turned to look at the couch where she'd been sitting. And at the brown leather briefcase.

"Three seconds," Martello said.

WHEN AGNES LEFT HER HOUSE

BY PATRICIA ABBOTT

WHEN AGNES LEFT HER HOUSE, she picked her moment carefully. Only the greenhorn oil trucker battling the steep road coiling around her house might have caught a flash of red gingham in his mirror. He did not.

As she crossed the fields lying between the house and Haycock, her resolve hardened. A walk turned into a trot, and then into a sprint, as she moved as fast as she could toting Henry's old track bag. She wasn't sure where she was headed, having seldom been south of Lancaster and never east of Smoketown.

The boys would be home from school in a few hours and find the kitchen table scrubbed clean but no snacks laid out. Had there been a day in the last eighteen years when she hadn't baked cookies or brownies, made popcorn, or cored apples? And dinner was usually half-made by one o'clock, the smell of soup or a stew welcoming their return. Today not a single pot sat on the stove and the oven was cold. The only sign of tonight's dinner was the chicken in the fridge, lemon and thyme sprigs resting inside and garlic tucked under the skin. She'd prepared it before the idea of escape overtook her.

Tim and George would come home first. The only thought in their heads would be grabbing their fishing poles and heading for the creek. At sixteen and seventeen, they were crazy about fishing, even if it turned out to be sunnies and catfish in their pail. They might not even notice her absence. If she'd just thought to leave snacks on the table, she'd have given herself an extra hour or two. Her boys would have to fend for themselves today. The words "her boys" made her go funny in the stomach.

Eddie came home next. His bus from Zinzendorf Junior High dropped him half a mile down the road. He was a daydreamer though and might not get home before his younger brothers. Her middle boy was the one most likely to follow some animal's tracks into the woods, checking to also see which birds were nesting. Sometimes Tim or George had to be sent after him with a scout whistle. On days when she couldn't stop him, Henry went out himself, stripping his trousers of the belt on the way.

Kyle and Jamie came home on the K-5 school bus and would see something was wrong as soon as their eyes lit on the empty table. Most days they'd lost their lunches to bigger, smarter kids in the lunch room or on the playground, trading for a Twizzler or a coveted baseball card. So they came home starving. She spoke to their teacher about this only last week.

"They really need to learn how to fend for themselves, Mrs. Frick."

"My boys see it as a good day if they come home with empty stomachs but a Mike Schmidt card," Agnes told her.

She was leaving behind five boys and a husband,. Not for a man as people might guess. She'd had her fill of the male sex. Married at seventeen, five children by twenty-eight. At thirty-six now, taking to the road seemed her only choice. Better than getting beaten again or cut off without a penny. Threats Henry made last night. As if she could support six people on her part-time salary from the fabric store.

"We'll see how you do on your own," he sniped. "Maybe Jo-Ann Fabric will give you more hours. What is it they pay you?"

"Should I show you where the stove is? Or the school?" Her threats seemed feeble and unimportant compared to his.

"You're crazy, girl," her mother said when Agnes married Henry Frick, then said it again when she kept having his babies. "What do you want all those boys for? Bet not one of 'em ever wipes a plate dry."

Her mother's vicious tongue was what had pushed her toward Henry to begin with.

Twenty minutes after passing the oil rig, Agnes trotted up to the bus station in town but hung back when she saw a few familiar faces. She wasn't ready to explain the gym bag or to say where she was going. The town only had a bus station because a paper factory and a flour mill sat upstream and the necessary workers were scattered. As more people got laid off, the station became a place to socialize rather than buy tickets. The vending machine's burnt coffee served as their Starbucks.

She plopped her bag down by the road, waiting to see what happened. Waiting often worked best although Henry mocked it.

"Make up your mind what you're gonna do and do it," he said.

But a quick decision was often the wrong one. She had no idea of where she wanted to go or what she would do when she got there. The money inside her purse would get her somewhere, but where? Maybe the New Jersey shore? She'd only seen the ocean twice and both times she was playing in a high school basketball tournament and saw the Atlantic Ocean from her school bus window.

"I thought it would be bluer," she had said turning toward Alfreda Disch, who was sitting next to her.

"Don't look at me," Alfreda said. "I just wipe the sweat off balls."

Alfreda was prone to say things like that and it took Agnes a minute to get her meaning.

"Hey, lady, need a ride?" It was a young, dark-haired guy in a black truck, hardly older than George. The bumper was covered with stickers giving advice like IF YOU CAN READ THIS, I COULD SLAM ON MY BRAKES AND SUE YOU. OR KEEP HONKING, I'M RELOADING.

"Where you headed?" she asked, shading her eyes.

"Haven't decided," he said, tossing his head like a horse. "Want to come along?"

"Why would you want to take an old lady?"

"I fall asleep when I drive alone. It's called narcolepsy."

"Narcolepsy? That sounds like a disease." Agnes was rising however, picking her bag up. "Not catching is it?"

"Nope." He reached over and pushed open the door with his foot. "Name's Jason."

"My Jamie has four Jasons in his fifth grade class and Kyle has two in his third. Must have been a sale on the name ten years ago." He snorted.

They rode together for about two hours, barely saying a word. On some back road in New Jersey or Delaware, she was pretty sure he robbed a gas station. Or maybe she dreamed him running out the door of a CITGO, tucking a brown bag into his fatigue shirt pocket. She watched half-asleep as he crawled into his side of the truck, starting it up before his backside was on the seat. Then she truly did doze off, dreamily hoping his narcolepsy didn't kick in. Maybe it was catching.

"We're in Glasgow, Delaware," he said, shoving her awake half an hour later. "You can hitch a ride on 301. I'm guessing you're headed south." He was counting the money in his bag. So it hadn't been a dream. It was the kind of bag Henry usually brought his whiskey home in.

"Did you stick up that gas station back in Jersey? Sure came flying out the door."

"What if I did?" he said, still counting, but he tossed her a few bills. "That oughta ease your conscience." He looked out the window. "Of course, taking money makes you an accessory." When she didn't say anything, he added, "You need to get out of the truck now. Unless you want to head west, that is."

"I'm thinking Florida," she said, looking at the bills. It was only thirty-five dollars, but how much was an accessory worth? She wasn't sure how much money was in the envelope she took from Henry's bureau drawer and hadn't had the nerve to count it. Not knowing what she took seemed less calculating. The idea of Florida seemed to have come to her in a dream but it felt right.

"Then you want 301." He pointed to the road crossing this one.

"Does it go all the way to Florida?" She put the bills away and zipped up the bag.

"Far as I know, but I've never been south of Maryland." He looked at her carefully. "Maybe you should take a bus, lady. Things can happen to a woman alone on the road. Didn't nobody ever tell you that?"

Like becoming an accessory, she thought, climbing down. Jason was probably right about buses being safer, but before she could find a bus stop, a car with a man and woman pulled up. A couple seemed harmless enough.

"If you can drive and are willing, you have yourself a lift." His words sounded oddly formal and rhythmic. Like Wimpy in the Popeye cartoons pleading for his hamburger. The man wiped his forehead with a blue-patterned bandana. "That's what you're after, right? A ride? I am pretty much done in. And Cookie doesn't drive," he added, nodding toward his wife.

"Are you headed to Florida?" Agnes asked.

"South Carolina," Cookie said, poking her head out. "But that'll get you closer." She whipped her sunglasses off and looked hard at Agnes's blank face. "You know, closer to Florida, Sweetie. You'd just have Georgia in between." She turned to her husband. "I don't know about her driving, dear."

"She'll be just fine," he said. "Got a license, right?"

Nodding, Agnes got into the car while the man changed places, and the woman climbed into the backseat and stretched out. Both promptly fell asleep. Seemed like being on the road made everybody tired. The clock on the dashboard said seven-thirty. It was dark now. She wondered whether Henry had fed the kids. He'd have no idea how to cook a chicken but putting it in the oven and turning it on would surely occur to one of them. Six men and all helpless. The boys had never once fried up the fish they caught. Maybe Henry would call his girlfriend, Judy Bushkill, and have her come over and cook that bird. But he wouldn't want the boys to know about her.

Agnes was struggling to stay awake herself when she felt a hand cupping her breast.

"Shhhh." The man gave her a little pinch. "It'll all be over before you know it." He continued to poke around, making it hard for her to drive. Soon his other hand was climbing up her leg.

Crossing her legs, she captured the errant hand and squeezed. "That's just about enough of that mischief. Why do you think I left home?"

"Beats me." He was still poking around with his free hand. His fingers were thin and pointy like sharpened pencils.

"Ouch! I'll get out right here, thank you."

His hand froze. "We're in the middle of nowhere."

"I've always been in the middle of nowhere."

She brought the car to a stop, grabbed her bag, and climbed out, slamming the door behind her. After a moment, the car took off, leaving her in the middle of the darkest night she'd ever known. She walked for as long as her feet could bear it, finding no houses, no towns, no lights. But she found a place to lie down. Good thing it was May and not December, though the ground was damp beneath her and she thought she was sharing the spot with some sort of keening animal. As each hour passed it became clearer that leaving her home and boys, if not her husband, was a dreadful mistake. And perhaps not one easily undone.

In the morning, damp and starving, she made her way to a town with a bus station. She debated throwing in the towel and heading back to Haycock, but couldn't bear to face the six faces waiting for her. She wondered if they'd called the police. Probably not. If it wasn't for the need of a dinner and now a breakfast, she'd probably not have been thought about at all.

"What's the cheapest ticket you have to Florida?" she asked the man at the counter. She was in Bowling Green, Virginia according to the sign above his head.

"Where in Florida?"

"Wherever's cheapest."

The man consulted his tables. "Guess that would be Jacksonville."

"Is it warm there?"

He massaged his chin. "Not as warm as Miami."

She stood for a minute, thinking.

He pushed his glasses up on his forehead. "Look, lady, you'd better step out of line until you decide where you want to go. See that kiosk over there?" He pointed to a circular booth with brochures tucked into metal pockets. "See the big map of Florida wrapped around it? Why don't you figure it out and then come back. The farther south, the more money. Pretty much anyway."

She browsed the brochures and thought she liked the look of Pensacola.

* * *

"KIDS CALLED ME AT WORK," Henry Frick told a police officer the next day. "It was George, my oldest. Said his mom wasn't at home, but I figured she'd been called into the store. Agnes works at Jo-Ann Fabric when they need an extra hand." He paused. "She's mostly home though—especially when the boys come in. They can run kinda wild . . . "

"Wouldn't she have left a note or called you?"

"Yes, she would've done that. Maybe the note's on the floor somewhere. Cat's been known to jump on the table, looking for food."

The cop looked at the man in front of him and thought it was fifty-fifty the guy had put her out of commission. He had the look of a wife-beater: red-faced, sweating, his arms bulging in his faded knit shirt, belly draping his belt. Domestic disturbances were the second most common problem in Haycock. DUI was number one. Despite the large Amish population, alcohol fueled most of their problems. What else was there to do for recreation in small town Pennsylvania?

"So I went home," the guy continued. "The boys were all standing in the driveway, like something bad was going on inside. But I went in anyway, and there wasn't anything out of place. Everything was right where it was supposed to be." He scratched his head. "Beds made, sinks clean, floor swept. Except there was no food on the table. Oven wasn't turned on. And it was past six o'clock. I work late sometimes—do the late shift at the mill if need be—but she usually just puts my plate in the oven and feeds the boys. So I called 911 and the cop said, "Wait until morning. See if she turns up. So we did." He paused. "She didn't turn up. So here I am."

"Does she have a history of this? Taking off, I mean?"

Henry shook his head. "There's no way she'd ever leave those kids. Freely, I mean. Ask anyone." He pounded his fist on the counter, adding fuel to the idea Agnes had come to harm through him. "She was devoted to 'em."

"Boys like her? Get along, I mean." Maybe the kids were worth looking at.

"Well, of course, they like her. She's their mother."

The officer didn't bother to tell him how often kids hated their mother. With five boys, she was either a drill sergeant or a push-over.

* * *

SHE HATED SPENDING ANY OF her money on a motel so Agnes found a bridge to sleep under in St. Pete's. Seemed like a town named after a saint had to be lucky and St. Pete's was okay, especially after the manufactured housing communities of Pensacola. She took most of her food from restaurant waste bins. Denny's was her favorite. Her boys were fond of Olive Garden, but pasta didn't survive dumpsters well.

A few days later, a man with a camper invited her in.

"Not for sex," she warned. "I'm done with that."

"Don't flatter yourself, honey."

She'd have to admit she probably didn't look so great by now. Spending money on haircuts or makeup or even new clothes was impossible. The few mirrors she'd come upon in gas station restrooms were cracked or blackened enough to be kind.

"But you cook, right?"

It turned out Len had lost his wife to MS and was looking for some help. Her money was dwindling and so was she. She could remove her skirt without unzipping it.

It was a good gig for a while, but life in the camper was too much like life back home in Pennsylvania, especially when his two adult sons started showing up for dinner.

"Hey, I said I would cook and clean for you," she reminded. "It wasn't a group offer."

"I'm buying, ain't I? How much trouble is it to throw on two more chops?"

Too much. When all three fell asleep watching a Gator's game one night, she lightened their wallets and moved on, wondering how she'd become a woman who robbed sleeping men. She didn't recognize herself anymore and doubted anyone back home would either. She didn't deserve the life she had had. But maybe she didn't deserve this one either.

She hitched a ride from a guy who cleaned boats and spent nearly a year in Fort Myers helping him. They were paid in cash and weren't asked for any ID. The money wasn't bad, but it was backbreaking work. Being in the sun so much got on her nerves. So did the guy. They spent hours arguing over the best techniques for cleaning boats and even what to call their business.

"Rub a Dub Tub?" she offered.

"Detail Your Sail," he countered.

"All Decked Out."

"Spongebob Squaresails."

After a while, the bilge cleaner they used on the boats made her skin redden, blister, and peel off. There was a different cleanser for every part of the boat. The startup costs were substantial with the vacuums, steamers and wash-down kit. Mostly they rented what they needed, hoping to get ahead enough to buy the equipment eventually.

"It's all different surfaces," Doug explained to her. "You can't use vinyl cleaner for the plastic parts or bilge cleaner when only Amazing Roll Off works for the fiberglass or deck."

She sat in the ocean for an hour every day after they were done, letting the salt water heal her. So far, that was the only thing she liked about Florida: the ocean. Even the sand seemed to redden her legs with an itchy rash. Florida was for rich folks, she decided. The ones who lived in the condos that lined the shore. It bugged her that thousands of those condos sat vacant while she sometimes slept under the boardwalks. The insects deviled her wherever she went. Insects, rodents, and reptiles too.

"A good frost would take care of this little toad." She pushed at it with her sneaker.

"Ain't you ever seen the commercial?" Doug said. "That's a gecko."

Occasionally she'd take a chance and lift something she found on a boat. Money left carelessly around. A piece of jewelry that seemed to be forgotten under a bed. That sort of thing. When Doug caught her tucking the odd ten spot into her bra, he sent her packing.

Life in Pennsylvania hadn't been so bad she thought again. Maybe it wasn't too late to head back. She could make up a story about being kidnapped by a white slaver. She decided to stand near the entrance ramps of I-75 and if the driver who stopped for her was going north so would she. If he drove south, she'd keep heading south too. That was how she ended up in Key Largo.

"Doesn't look a thing like the movie," she said to Luis.

"What does?" he said, stopping at a place called the Caribbean Club. It was a diver bar.

"You mean dive bar, right?" she said.

"Nope, diver," he said, nodding at the wetsuits coming out of the water and onto the deck.

"Geez, what a place," she said. "It's like they're creatures from the black lagoon."

He looked at her for a moment, then started to laugh. "Hey, I had an uncle in that movie."

"What movie?"

"*Creature from the Black Lagoon.* His name was Henry Escalante. Whole family is in show biz, in fact. Ever hear of the Escalante Circus?"

She shook her head, wondering why Luis was telling her this. She had found though that people on the road shared strange information. Irrelevant information if the word had been known to her. But not Agnes. She never shared a story. Not a soul knew where she was from or what she had left behind. It was too embarrassing.

* * *

HENRY FRICK WAS A SUSPECT in the early days. The police asked if he wanted an attorney present when they questioned him (in excess of a dozen times), but he declined, saying, "I've got nothing to hide."

He gave them total access to his home, his computer, even his kids. The cops dug up Judy's existence fairly quickly. After that, the backyard and the fields near the house were dug up too. But over time, official interest in Henry waned. It was a rural police force and their resources were limited. There were those kids to think of. They'd already lost a mother.

"When you don't solve the biggest case you ever had, pretty soon you sneak off with your tail between your legs," one officer admitted. "We were all positive she'd been murdered the day she disappeared or why had no one ever spotted her? This is a small town. There's not many places to hide."

Off and on, Agnes was homeless, but more often than not she was resourceful enough to land a place to stay. She cleaned motel rooms up and down the west coast of Florida, a job that was always available if you'd work for the salary the motels paid illegals. She supplemented her salary again with the occasional theft. For a year or two she had a female friend, Valeria, and they worked motel rooms in tandem. But eventually Valeria took off with a fruit picker from Guatemala.

Next Agnes was in Key West, waitressing at a Cuban place.

"Do you speak Spanish?" the female manager asked.

"I've picked some up." And this was true. Somehow over her years in Florida, with the jobs she had had, the people she had lived with, she'd become fluent. Sometimes she didn't even realize she was speaking in a foreign language. In Pennsylvania, the only foreign language spoken was an odd dialect of German.

The tips were good in Key West, but now and then she thought again of going home. By her calculation, which had become a little sketchy, she'd been gone almost seven years. George and Tim would be in their mid-twenties by now, possibly even married. Even the youngest two would be in high school. She hadn't meant to stay away this long, but each day problems arose that needed solving and she pushed thoughts of her family in Pennsylvania out of her head. Henry had probably declared her dead and remarried. What was that woman's name? Judy Fishkill?

Throughout Agnes' seven years in Florida, she'd expected to be discovered for one transgression or another countless times but nothing ever happened. As far as she knew, no one had once looked for her. She was truly a Floridian now, with the weathered skin, muscular arms and legs, and thinning hat hair to prove it.

One day she was counting the money in her purse on a bench near a Publix when someone knocked her over the head and grabbed the purse. Knocked was too mild a word. They practically smashed her head in, probably believing that no one would continually remove, count, and replace cash that wasn't a substantial amount. No one will ever know how much she had in that purse because the purse and its contents were gone when some early morning Tai Chi practitioners found her. She wasn't dead but remained in a coma for ten days. When she finally awoke, she remembered nothing. Not her name, her age, she even had to be coached in how to hold a fork.

"Retrograde amnesia," the doctor said. A minute later, Agnes had forgotten that term too. And when she finally began to speak, a few weeks later, she spoke in Spanish only.

"Do you remember anything about yourself? Do you have any family? *Una familia*?" the therapist asked again and again in Spanish. "¿Siempre has vivido en Florida?"

The therapist thought that perhaps her patient had drifted north from Cuba or somewhere else. Her accent was an unusual one and she didn't seem to know a word of English. How had she survived her life in Florida without knowing how to say hello? She was probably an illegal. Perhaps pretending not to know anyone or anything about herself. Maybe there was stuff she didn't want to remember.

"*Si, si,*" Agnes said eventually. "*Soy un Floridano.*"

* * *

AGNES FRICK'S MISSING PERSON FLYER, yellowing but intact, remained posted on the Haycock police department wall for years. Every once in a while, someone came in and swore they saw a woman looking just like Agnes in New Jersey or Arizona or Florida.

Various members of her family had an assortment of ideas on what her fate was. Most remained convinced she would have never left her family unless forced.

THE ENDING
BY REED FARREL COLEMAN

EVERYTHING ENDS. HE COULDN'T ARGUE that. But what he had tried to say to her all those years ago was it wasn't always about the end coming, but how the end came. How mattered. It mattered a lot. It mattered to him then and it mattered more to him now as he stepped off the Southwest flight and walked to the rental car bus at Palm Beach International. When she had ended it, there was more to his life than there was now. There was a family and a career. There was still a family of sorts, but his wife was dead and the kids were moved away. His career had morphed into golf, sad memories, and revenge fantasies. Currently, how she had ended it mattered more than anything had ever mattered.

At the counter, the pretty young blond with impatient blue eyes asked if he wanted a free upgrade to a midsize car. It hit him, hit him hard so that the wind almost emptied from his papery old man lungs. Except for what he and Marlene had done for those ten years, he had always operated in a very narrow bandwidth. His life had been a midsize car.

"You got a Corvette convertible?" he asked, barely believing the voice he heard was his own. "Red or yellow, something fast and sleek that makes a statement?"

The blond, her long silver-painted nails clicking on the keyboard, smiled at him in a way that made his blood run cold. *Another old man looking for excitement on his way to the grave.* But he hadn't come here for her. Their ending would come as soon as she handed him the little paper binder and the keys.

"Yes, we have a red Corvette convertible. It's in spot A12," she said.

He didn't pay much attention after that, wasn't sure what insurance coverages he had agreed or not agreed to, wasn't sure which gas option he'd taken. All that mattered was the red car in spot A12. The rest of his life, no matter how short, would no longer be easy to measure in bandwidth nor would he ever think of his life again as a midsize car.

As he strode to collect his car, he thought about Marlene and how beautiful she had been. Thought about how being with her was like being with no other woman. Thought about how he had known the end was coming, supposed he had played games with himself to convince himself otherwise. He knew, though. In his bones, he knew. Over the long course of their affair, they had met two or three times a month at one of three motels—the two out by Republic Airport or their fallback, the one on Route 109. They had always preferred the dingiest of the three because it had the baddest porn and because it suited them the way they suited each other. But over the last year of their affair, two corrosive elements—embarrassment and guilt—had crept into their motel beds with them and had put a stink on their illicit perfection.

He knew the end was at hand because three times a month became once a month became once every other month, supplemented with an awkward deep kiss or a stolen feel of her breast or his crotch, a quickie in the back of the car. Even when they managed the motel, there were excuses. For nine years they had used every minute of their two hours together to screw themselves sore and make sure that when they closed the motel door behind them that they walked back to their cars on weak, wobbly legs. Then, in that last year, there were always reasons for her to have to leave. *Bob's getting home early. The kids have something at school tonight. There's a sale I can't miss.* There'd be a feverish round of sex, a hasty shower, a kiss, an apology, and the sight of her back as the door closed behind her. It had taken him a while to figure out why the loving had been so feverish. The fever chased away the guilt and embarrassment. Then it would come rushing back in as soon as they were done.

Phone calls that had once been ignored and left to the vagaries of voicemail were answered and answered no matter when the calls came. Even in the wake of an intense orgasm, she would scramble to grab her bag and get the phone. It was almost as if the calls were a lifeline, a means to rescue herself from herself. Sometimes it felt to him as though she was hoping the call were anything but a lifeline, but rather a call from her husband or a detective to say, "I know. I know what you've been doing." It was in her nature to avoid confrontation and if she could be caught, it would save her from having to take responsibility for ending it on her own. But he supposed he knew the end was near when the ground rules started.

Suddenly, there were dos and don'ts. There had never been dos and don'ts. Never, not even from the first day. And the funny thing is, that's how they knew. From the initial moment they spotted each other at a PTA-sponsored gathering at a local bookstore, their communication had been almost telepathic. They caught each other's eyes and the intensity of that single stare felt like it was full of enough energy to burn out the sun. They knew they were going to be together without having to say one word. Two people in loving but boring marriages, they were like tuning forks that had never before been able to find resonance. Then, with a glance across a bookstore, they hummed together in perfect harmony. That night she had followed him to the bathroom, snuck into the men's room with him, and they had coupled in a stall without even knowing the other's name.

As he drove out of the rental facility, he felt both exhilarated and ridiculous in the red Corvette. The sun burned the top of his bald head because he hadn't thought to bring a hat. What did a man in a midsize sedan need a hat for? He pulled to the side of the airport road and put the roof up. By the time he'd pulled off Interstate 95 and turned west into Boyton Beach, his head had cooled down. Not his heart. It still burned with all the anger and resentment he'd felt for the past twenty-five years.

The man from whom he had agreed to purchase the Colt Python lived on Jog Road, south of Indian Spring Country Club. Just as at the rental counter, he felt disembodied, almost as if he were observing someone else making the deal and getting instructions on how to properly store the weapon. The seller wanted to discuss other collectibles and the history of the Python. He listened as patiently as he could to the man because he didn't want to give away the fact that the pistol wasn't actually a gift for an old friend, but the intended instrument of revenge against an old friend. The joke was that he actually knew almost nothing about firearms, but purchased the Python because he'd read about it in a mystery novel called *Gun Church* written by some no-name hack author. He had to admit, it was a terrible and beautiful thing to behold. And as he held the blue steel and wooden-gripped pistol in his white-gloved hand, its ventilated rib barrel throwing an odd shadow on the wall, he remembered how bitterly the end had come.

Marlene had come over to the house after work. His wife was away on business. Her husband and kids were down in Texas visiting relatives. He had been looking forward to her visit all day, thinking that there would be no rushing away, no excuses, no phone calls, no dos and don'ts, no hasty showers or pecks goodbye. But after he let her in and began making his way to the bedroom, she stopped him.

"I can't do this anymore," was all she'd said.

There it was, the truth.

Before he could recover, she continued, "I want us to still be friends, but we just can't be together anymore. I feel choked by the guilt. You must've seen this coming," she said as if that made it all right.

He had to admit that he had seen it coming. He guessed that in some ways, he was relieved as well. He'd thought that there would be this one last time together and then they would get on with their lives. He wasn't pleased about it. His tuning fork still hummed for her.

"No," she said. "I can't. No more."

And those were the words that had eaten away inside him for the past twenty-five years. They'd hollowed him out until there was nothing left of him, not even a soul. Those were the words that had gone round and round in his head so many times that it felt like they were the only words that mattered any longer, the only words in his vocabulary. She had refused him a goodbye.

Driving down to Boca Raton, with the Python in the case beside him, he thought he might even have been able to live with her refusing him that one last time together. He had ended relationships before, ones where the woman on the other end had been crushed. Unlike Marlene, he had always been open to a goodbye fuck. Something for the both of them to either remember fondly or not, but something to hold onto just the same. Still, he would have lived with it. He was living with it . . . until he caught her.

It had been six months since she'd ended it and they were friends, as difficult as that was for him. He had tried several times to engage her in a conversation about how things had ended. He'd even gotten down on his knees and begged her for that one last time together. But she said she just couldn't. So on a rainy raw day in February, he drove by their old favorite motel. He wasn't sure why he did it. Maybe it was because he hoped to recapture a little something of what they had once shared or maybe he just wanted to torture himself. It was difficult for him to distinguish between the two.

Stupidly, masochistically, he stopped by the desk to say hello to the clerk who, for ten years, had accepted his John Smith registration cards with a smile and slid a room key across the counter to him. They didn't know each other, not really, except in context. The smells of curry and hot gee filling up the little registration office. At first the elderly Indian man with the wizened face smiled at him, but that expression changed and the clerk excused himself, heading hurriedly through the door behind the desk. This man, too, had denied him a proper ending, so he got back into his car and drove around to the back of the motel.

When he got there, he was sick, getting out of his car and throwing up in the snow. He was sick because Marlene's car was parked there in front of Room 122. One twenty-two had been their favorite room. And then he understood the desk clerk's hurry. Worse, parked next to Marlene's car was Greg Walton's BMW.

He had always despised Greg, a blowhard lawyer still stuck in the '80s, a man who believed greed was good and that he who died with the most toys wins. The thought of Greg Walton kissing Marlene, the thought of his tongue in her mouth, of his hands on her breasts, of him in her mouth, of him inside her . . . He parked in a corner of the motel lot, waiting as darkness fell to camouflage him and his car. At six, they emerged from the room, kissing, before getting into their cars and heading off. It was a familiar scene, only this time he was watching it and not part of it.

Murdering Marlene wouldn't be nearly as hard for him as it had been to murder Greg Walton. Firsts are always hardest. Back then, Walton was fit and took a lot of killing. He'd had to hit him at least five times with the sap to make sure he'd crushed the prick's skull. He was proud to have done it in such a way as to convince the cops it had been a robbery gone wrong. He'd tossed Walton's empty wallet in a dumpster, but still had the asshole's

Rolex at home as a souvenir. He had only two regrets: he couldn't make Greg's pain last long enough and he couldn't let Marlene know what he'd done. Well, he could now.

He pulled up to the gate at the Raton Harbor Club, gave the guard his name, and said he was expected. The guard gave him a day pass to keep in his windshield and directions to Marlene's condo. His heart pounded, the blood rushing in his ears so loudly he could barely hear anything of the outside world. Paradoxically, his breathing sounded like a symphony. He parked in the designated spot, loaded the big Colt and slid it under his jacket in the small of his back.

He went to the door, but the guard had already called ahead and Marlene was pulling the door open. Although now seventy-five, she was still beautiful, and her blue eyes were as bright as ever. She smiled broadly at him and came out of the house to hug him. He had a moment of panic, worried she might hug him low and feel the handle of the Python beneath his sport jacket. He needn't have worried. She hugged him as she always had since the day she said no more, high around the shoulders. She kissed his cheek and showed him in.

They made awkward small talk for a few minutes, asking about the other's kids and grandkids. They had once been more familiar with the intimate details of each other's lives and secrets than their spouses, but after the affair ended, they drifted apart. And once her husband Bob retired and their kids moved south, they moved to Boca. For the last ten years, they barely communicated. A holiday card, the occasional call, messages passed between mutual friends going for a visit to Florida or coming up to New York for a visit. He hadn't even gone to Bob's funeral.

As Marlene went into the kitchen to make them coffee, he stayed and looked around the house. The photos of their old gang—Bob, his wife, their friends at parties with all the kids—made him cry. He wiped his eyes dry. Being here, smelling her, touching her, brought it all back to him. He had never felt more alive than when he was next to her in bed. They didn't even have to be doing anything. That sense had never gone away. Nothing, not the distance between them nor the years had changed that. It was that tuning fork thing.

When Marlene returned with the coffee, the gun was already in his hand. He held it down by his thigh. She didn't seem to notice it. Finally, he raised it up and pointed it at her. And as had always been the case between them, there was no need to explain. She understood or thought she did.

"I should have told you I was thinking of ending things between us and I should have stayed that afternoon, but I was so guilty." Her voice was calm and she seemed confident she could talk the gun out of his hand. She seemed that way until he uttered three syllables.

"Greg Walton."

Her hands, which had remained steady even as she stared down the barrel of the Python, began shaking. The silverware and cups on the tray rattled and clinked. He smirked, laughed a cruel barking laugh.

"You felt guilty about me, but not about Greg. Explain that to me, Marlene. For how many months were you doing the both of us and hiding the one from the other?"

She didn't answer, panic robbing her of her voice. Her eyes darted about the room, looking for a way to escape, but she knew the only way out for her now would be in a liquid proof vinyl bag in the arms of men from the medical examiner's office.

"You shouldn't have taken him to our room, Marlene. Of all the things you did, that was the worst. Our room. You robbed me of everything when you did that."

"Please," she said, her voice cracking and feeble.

"Please. Please what, Marlene? Please don't kill me? Please tell me you're not the person who killed Greg Walton?" He smiled at her after he said that.

She dropped the tray and fell to the floor.

"That's right, Marlene. His blood is on your hands. Six months after you gave me your edict and your bullshit about guilt, I went to our motel for old time's sake and guess whose cars I found parked in front of Room 122? I sat and watched you come out together and kiss just the way we used to. I think maybe if you hadn't kissed him like that, I wouldn't have crushed his skull. Now you really do have something to feel guilty about."

She was sobbing, but he couldn't tell if it was for her dead lover or herself. Eventually, she sat up, the tears dried.

"Do you want that last goodbye fuck now?" she said, as if the last twenty-five years had never happened. She began taking off her clothes.

When he saw her bare breasts again for the first time in all those years, he pointed the gun away from her and said, "This time, the ending is up to me. Remember, it isn't always about the end coming, but how it comes."

And with that, he stuck the barrel of the Colt under his chin and pulled the trigger.

ABOUT THE CONTRIBUTORS

Patricia Abbott is the author of the Edgar, Anthony, and Macavity-nominated books *Concrete Angel* and *Shot in Detroit. I Bring Sorrow and Other Stories Of Transgression* debuted in March 2018. Author of more than 125 short stories, "My Hero" won a Derringer in 2009. You can find her at www.pattinase.blogspot.com.

J. D. Allen's Sin City Investigations series launched with *19 Souls* earlier this year. She is a Mystery Writers of America Freddie Award-winner. She has short stories in the Anthony Award-winning anthology, *Murder under the Oaks* as well as *Carolina Crimes: 20 Tales of Need, Greed, and Dirty Deeds.* She's the chair of the Bouchercon National Board, a member of MWA, PI Writer's of America, and president of her local Sisters in Crime chapter. She's an Ohio State University alum with a degree in forensic anthropology and a creative writing minor.

Jack Bates writes some pretty good crime fiction. His stories have appeared all around the web, in various anthologies, and in a few magazines. Three have been finalists for the Derringer Award from the Short Mystery Fiction Society. He's also written award-winning scripts for stage and screen, including a short-lived web series. An incomplete list of his works can be found on his blog flashjab.blogspot.com. When not writing, he plots or travels or runs errands or chats it up with other old movie buffs on Twitter.

Lawrence Block has been writing crime, mystery, and suspense fiction for more than half a century. He has published in excess (oh, wretched excess!) of 100 books, and no end of short stories. He is best known for his series characters, including cop-turned-private investigator Matthew Scudder, gentleman burglar Bernie Rhodenbarr, globe-trotting insomniac Evan Tanner, and introspective assassin Keller. He is a Grand Master of Mystery Writers of America, a past president of MWA, and the Private Eye Writers of America. He has won the Edgar and Shamus awards four times each, and the Japanese Maltese Falcon award twice, as well as the Nero Wolfe and Philip Marlowe awards, a Lifetime Achievement Award from the Private Eye Writers of America, and the Diamond Dagger for Life Achievement from the Crime Writers Association (UK). He's also been honored with the Gumshoe Lifetime Achievement Award from *Mystery Ink* magazine and the Edward D. Hoch Memorial Golden Derringer for Lifetime Achievement in the short story. In France, he has been proclaimed a Grand Maitre du Roman Noir and has twice been awarded the Societe 813 trophy. He has been a guest of honor at Bouchercon and at book fairs and mystery festivals in France, Germany, Australia, Italy, New Zealand, Spain and Taiwan. As if that were not enough, he was also presented with the key to the city of Muncie, Indiana. (But as soon as he left, they changed the locks.)

Susanna Calkins, born and raised in Philadelphia, lives outside Chicago with her husband and two sons. Holding a Ph.D. in history, Susanna writes the Lucy Campion historical mysteries set in plague-ridden 17th century London (back when people used to write murder ballads as a form of news!). Her books have been nominated for several awards, including the Agatha, the Mary Higgins Clark award, and the Lefty. Her third novel was honored with the Sue Feder Historical Mystery (Macavity) Award. She is currently working on a new series for Minotaur, set in Prohibition-era Chicago. Check out her website at www.susannacalkins.com.

Reed Farrel Coleman's love of storytelling originated on the streets of Brooklyn and was nurtured by his teachers, friends, and family. A *New York Times* bestseller called "a hard-boiled poet" by NPR's Maureen Corrigan, and the "noir poet laureate" in the *Huffington Post*, Reed is the author of novels, including Robert B. Parker's Jesse Stone series, the Gus Murphy series, the acclaimed Moe Prager series, short stories, and poetry. Reed is a four-time Edgar Award nominee in three different categories—Best Novel, Best Paperback Original, Best Short Story—and a four-time recipient of the Shamus Award for Best PI Novel of the Year. He has also won the Audie, Macavity, Barry, and Anthony Awards. A former executive vice president of Mystery Writers of America, Reed is an adjunct instructor of English at Hofstra University and a founding member of MWA University. Brooklyn born and raised, he now lives with his family—including cats Cleo and Knish—in Suffolk County on Long Island.

Angel Luis Colón is the Anthony and Derringer Award-nominated author of *No Happy Endings*, the Blacky Jaguar series of novellas, the collection *Meat City on Fire (And Other Assorted Debacles)*, and *Pull & Pray* (July 2018). His fiction has appeared in multiple web and print publications including *Thuglit*, *Literary Orphans*, and *Great Jones Street*. Keep up with him on Twitter via @GoshDarnMyLife

Hilary Davidson has won the Anthony Award as well as the Derringer, Spinetingler, and Crimespree awards. She is the author of the Lily Moore series—which includes *The Damage Done, The Next One to Fall,* and *Evil in All Its Disguises*—the standalone thriller *Blood Always Tells,* and the short-story collection *The Black Widow Club.* Her next novel, *One Small Sacrifice,* will be published in spring 2019 by Thomas & Mercer. A Toronto-born journalist and the author of 18 nonfiction books, she has lived in New York City since October 2001. www.hilarydavidson.com

TIM DORSEY graduated from Auburn University in 1983. While at Auburn, he was editor of the student newspaper, *The Plainsman.* From 1983 to 1987, he was a police and courts reporter for *The Alabama Journal,* the now-defunct evening newspaper in Montgomery. He joined *The Tampa Tribune* in 1987 as a general assignment reporter. He also worked as a political reporter in the Tribune's Tallahassee bureau and a copy desk editor. From 1994 to 1999, he was the Tribune's night metro editor. He left the paper in August 1999 to write full time. Tim has since published nineteen novels in several languages: *Florida Roadkill, Hammerhead Ranch Motel, Orange Crush, Triggerfish Twist, The Stingray Shuffle, Cadillac Beach, Torpedo Juice, The Big Bamboo, Hurricane Punch, Atomic Lobster, Nuclear Jellyfish, Gator A-Go-Go, Electric Barracuda, When Elves Attack, Pineapple Grenade, The Riptide Ultra-Glide, Tiger Shrimp Tango, Shark Skin Suite, Coconut Cowboy* and *Clownfish Blues.* He lives in Tampa.

BRENDAN DUBOIS is the award-winning author of twenty novels and more than 160 short stories. He's currently working on a series of novels with bestselling author James Patterson. His short fiction has appeared in *Playboy, Ellery Queen's Mystery Magazine, Alfred Hitchcock's Mystery Magazine,* and numerous anthologies including *Best American Mystery Stories of the Century,* published in 2000, as well as *Best American Noir of the Century.* His stories have thrice won him the Shamus Award from the Private Eye Writers of America, and have also earned him three MWA Edgar Allan

Poe Award nominations. He is also a "Jeopardy!" game show champion. Visit his website: www.BrendanDuBois.com

John M. Floyd's work has appeared in more than 250 different publications, including *AHMM, EQMM, The Strand Magazine, Mississippi Noir,* and *The Saturday Evening Post.* A former Air Force captain and IBM systems engineer, John is also an Edgar Award nominee, a three-time Derringer Award winner, and a three-time Pushcart Prize nominee. Two of his mysteries have been selected for inclusion in the annual *Best American Mystery Stories* anthology and his seventh collection of short fiction, *The Barrens,* is upcoming in late 2018. Visit him at www.johnmfloyd.com.

Barb Goffman has no idea how to cook pot roast, but it sure was fun to write about. She's won the Agatha, Macavity, and Silver Falchion awards for her short stories, and she's been a finalist for national mystery short-story awards twenty-two times. Her book *Don't Get Mad, Get Even* won the Silver Falchion for the best collection of 2013. Barb works as an independent editor and proofreader and is a coeditor of the Chesapeake Crimes series. She lives with her dog in Winchester, Virginia, and blogs at www.SleuthSayers.org and www.PensPawsandClaws.com. Learn more at www.barbgoffman.com.

Greg Herren is the award-winning author of over thirty novels, fifty short stories, and has edited over twenty anthologies. He has won two Lambda Literary Awards (out of fourteen nominations), two Moonbeam medals for excellence in young adult fiction, and an Anthony Award. He has been shortlisted for the Shirley Jackson and Macavity awards. His short stories have been published everywhere from *Ellery Queen's Mystery Magazine* to *Mystery Weekly* to *New Orleans Noir.*

Eleanor Cawood Jones began writing in elementary school, using #2 pencils to craft crime stories starring her stuffed animals. She is author of *A Baker's Dozen: 13 Tales of Murder and More* and *Death is Coming to Town: Four Murderous Holiday Tales.* Recent stories include "Killing Kippers" (Malice Domestic 11: *Murder Most Conventional*); "Salad Days, Halloween Nights" (*Midnight Mysteries*); "A Snowball's Chance" (*Chesapeake Crimes: Fur, Feathers, & Felonies*); and "Keep Calm and Love Moai" (Malice Domestic 13: *Mystery Most Geographical*). A former newspaper reporter and reformed marketing director, Eleanor lives in Northern Virginia and travels frequently.

John D. MacDonald was a prolific author of crime and suspense novels, many of them set in his adopted home of Florida. One of the most successful American novelists of his time, MacDonald sold an estimated 70 million books in his career. His best-known works include the popular and critically acclaimed Travis McGee series, and his novel *The Executioners,* which was filmed as *Cape Fear* (1962) and remade in 1991. During 1972, MacDonald was named a grandmaster of the Mystery Writers of America and he won a 1980 U.S. National Book Award.

Paul D. Marks is the author of the Shamus Award-Winning mystery-thriller *White Heat. Publishers Weekly* calls *White Heat* a "taut crime yarn." His story *Ghosts of Bunker Hill* was voted #1 in the 2016 *Ellery Queen Readers Poll. Howling at the Moon* (EQMM 11/14) was short-listed for both the *2015* Anthony and Macavity Awards. *Midwest Review* calls his novella *Vortex* " . . . a nonstop staccato action noir." Marks' story *Windward,* from the *Coast to Coast: Private Eyes from Sea to Shining Sea* anthology, has been selected for the 2018 *Best American Mystery Stories* (Fall 2018), edited by Louise Penny & Otto Penzler. www.PaulDMarks.com

CRAIG PITTMAN is a native Floridian. Born in Pensacola, he graduated from Troy State University in Alabama, where his muckraking work for the student paper prompted an agitated dean to label him "the most destructive force on campus." Since then he has covered a variety of newspaper beats and quite a few natural disasters, including hurricanes, wildfires and the Florida Legislature. Since 1998, he has covered environmental issues for Florida's largest newspaper, the *Tampa Bay Times,* winning state and national awards. He is the author of four non-fiction books: *Paving Paradise; Manatee Insanity; The Scent of Scandal;* and *Oh, Florida! How America's Weirdest State Influences the Rest of the Country,* which won a gold medal from the Florida Book Awards. He lives in St. Petersburg with his wife and children.

NEIL S. PLAKCY is the award-winning author of *The Next One Will Kill You, Nobody Rides for Free* and *Survival is a Dying Art* (Diversion Books, 2018). *Publishers Weekly* wrote of *The Next One Will Kill You,* "readers will look forward to seeing a lot more of Angus [Green], the affable hero of this brisk series launch set in South Florida." A graduate of both the FIU MFA program and the FBI Citizen's Academy, Neil writes mystery and romance novels about gay men in love and danger. He lives in South Florida with his partner and two rambunctious golden retrievers.

ALEX SEGURA is a novelist and comic book writer. He is the author of the Pete Fernandez Miami Mystery novels, which include *Silent City, Down the Darkest Street, Dangerous Ends,* and *Blackout,* all via Polis Books. He has also written a number of comic books, including the best-selling and critically acclaimed ARCHIE MEETS KISS storyline, the "Occupy Riverdale" story, and the ARCHIE MEETS RAMONES and THE ARCHIES one-shots. His work has appeared in the anthologies *Protectors 2, Waiting to Be Forgotten: Stories of Crime and Heartbreak Inspired by the Replacements, Unloaded 2,* and *Apollo's Daughters,* and in publications including *The Daily Beast, The Los*

Angeles Review of Books, Literary Hub, The Strand, Mental Floss, LitReactor, and more. A Miami native, he lives in New York with his wife and son.

Debra Lattanzi Shutika is a writer and folklorist. She is author of *Beyond the Borderlands* (2011, University of California Press), winner of the 2012 Chicago Folklore Prize. Her fiction has appeared in *Abundant Grace* (2016, Paycock Press). She is a professor of English at George Mason University and lives in Northern Virginia. She escapes to her native West Virginia as often as possible.

Holly West is the author of the Mistress of Fortune historical mystery series. Her short crime fiction has been honored with two Anthony Award nominations and her stories appear online and numerous anthologies. She's currently editing *Murder-a-Go-Go's,* a crime fiction collection featuring short stories inspired by the music of the Go-Go's for Down & Out Books, with net proceeds benefitting Planned Parenthood. Holly lives in Northern California with her husband and two dogs.

Michael Wiley is the Shamus Award-winning writer of seven crime novels, including, most recently, *Monument Road,* about an exonerated convict investigating the crime that sent him to prison and the cop who seemed obsessed with sending him there. Michael also writes the Joe Kozmarski PI mysteries and the Homicide Detective Daniel Turn thrillers. He is a frequent short story writer and book reviewer. He lives in Northeast Florida and sets most of his books there.

RECENT AND FORTHCOMING BOOKS FROM THREE ROOMS PRESS

FICTION

Meagan Brothers
Weird Girl and What's His Name

Ron Dakron
Hello Devilfish!

Michael T. Fournier
Hidden Wheel
Swing State

William Least Heat-Moon
Celestial Mechanics

Aimee Herman
Everything Grows

Eamon Loingsigh
Light of the Diddicoy
Exile on Bridge Street

John Marshall
The Greenfather

Aram Saroyan
Still Night in L.A.

Richard Vetere
The Writers Afterlife
Champagne and Cocaine

Julia Watts
Quiver

MEMOIR & BIOGRAPHY

Nassrine Azimi and
Michel Wasserman
Last Boat to Yokohama: The Life and Legacy of Beate Sirota Gordon

William S. Burroughs & Allen Ginsberg
Don't Hide the Madness: William S. Burroughs in Conversation with Allen Ginsberg
edited by Steven Taylor

James Carr
BAD: The Autobiography of James Carr

Richard Katrovas
Raising Girls in Bohemia: Meditations of an American Father; A Memoir in Essays

Judith Malina
Full Moon Stages: Personal Notes from 50 Years of The Living Theatre

Phil Marcade
Punk Avenue: Inside the New York City Underground, 1972-1982

Stephen Spotte
My Watery Self: Memoirs of a Marine Scientist

PHOTOGRAPHY-MEMOIR

Mike Watt
On & Off Bass

SHORT STORY ANTHOLOGIES

SINGLE AUTHOR

First-Person Singularities: Stories
by Robert Silverberg
with an introduction by John Scalzi

Tales from the Eternal Café: Stories
by Janet Hamill, with an introduction by Patti Smith

Time and Time Again: Sixteen Trips in Time
by Robert Silverberg

MULTI-AUTHOR

Crime + Music: Twenty Stories of Music-Themed Noir
edited by Jim Fusilli

Dark City Lights: New York Stories
edited by Lawrence Block

Florida Happens: Tales of Murder, Mayhem, and Suspense from The Sunshine State (Bouchercon 2018 Anthology)
edited by Greg Herren

Have a NYC I, II & III: New York Short Stories;
edited by Peter Carlaftes & Kat Georges

Songs of My Selfie: An Anthology of Millennial Stories
edited by Constance Renfrow

The Obama Inheritance: 15 Stories of Conspiracy Noir
edited by Gary Phillips

This Way to the End Times: Classic and New Stories of the Apocalypse
edited by Robert Silverberg

MIXED MEDIA

John S. Paul
Sign Language: A Painter's Notebook (photography, poetry and prose)

FILM & PLAYS

Israel Horovitz
My Old Lady: Complete Stage Play and Screenplay with an Essay on Adaptation

Peter Carlaftes
Triumph For Rent (3 Plays)
Teatrophy (3 More Plays)

Kat Georges
Three Somebodies: Plays about Notorious Dissidents

DADA

Maintenant: A Journal of Contemporary Dada Writing & Art (Annual, since 2008)

TRANSLATIONS

Thomas Bernhard
On Earth and in Hell
(poems of Thomas Bernhard with English translations by Peter Waugh)

Patrizia Gattaceca
Isula d'Anima / Soul Island
(poems by the author in Corsican with English translations)

César Vallejo | Gerard Malanga
Malanga Chasing Vallejo
(selected poems of César Vallejo with English translations and additional notes by Gerard Malanga)

George Wallace
EOS: Abductor of Men
(selected poems in Greek & English)

HUMOR

Peter Carlaftes
A Year on Facebook

POETRY COLLECTIONS

Hala Alyan
Atrium

Peter Carlaftes
DrunkYard Dog
I Fold with the Hand I Was Dealt

Thomas Fucaloro
It Starts from the Belly and Blooms

Inheriting Craziness is Like a Soft Halo of Light

Kat Georges
Our Lady of the Hunger

Robert Gibbons
Close to the Tree

Israel Horovitz
Heaven and Other Poems

David Lawton
Sharp Blue Stream

Jane LeCroy
Signature Play

Philip Meersman
This is Belgian Chocolate

Jane Ormerod
Recreational Vehicles on Fire
Welcome to the Museum of Cattle

Lisa Panepinto
On This Borrowed Bike

George Wallace
Poppin' Johnny

Three Rooms Press | New York, NY | Current Catalog: www.threeroomspress.com
Three Rooms Press books are distributed by PGW/Ingram: www.pgw.com